Kayla singled out a strapping woman. "You there! Get together a group of the largest and strongest, and follow me."

"Yes," Cristobal cried. "Who'll follow us to the bridge? Who'll come and take the ship with us?"

The prisoners voted with their feet, massing behind the two of them, a new and obedient army. As they moved from level to level, ever more prisoners joined them. They fought through crowded hallways, stepping over the bodies of guards. By the time they reached the bridge, it seemed that every prisoner on the ship was pressing in behind Kayla and Cristobal.

The bridge was swarming with chaotic activity. The captain swung around angrily to face them. "What are you doing here? Get off my bridge!"

Before Kayla could stop him, Cristobal had pulled out a disruptor.

"Wait, Cristobal!" she shouted. "That's set for kill, not stun."

Cristobal fired once, and the captain of the *Lovejoy* gasped and fell backward over his control console.

The first officer lunged at him and again Cristobal fired. The man sprawled across the deck, unmoving, dead.

Cristobal faced the rest of the bridge crew. "Join us," he said. "You've got one chance. If you don't, you'll be spaced. . . ."

Be sure to read all the books in this action-packed
DAW science fiction series from
KAREN HABER

WOMAN WITHOUT A SHADOW
(Book One)

THE WAR MINSTRELS
(Book Two)

THE WAR MINSTRELS

KAREN HABER

D A W   B O O K S ,   I N C .
DONALD   A.   WOLLHEIM,   FOUNDER
375 Hudson Street, New York, NY 10014

ELIZABETH R. WOLLHEIM
SHEILA E. GILBERT
PUBLISHERS

Copyright © 1995 by Karen Haber.

All Rights Reserved.

Cover art by Romas Kukalis.

DAW Book Collectors No. 1005.

All characters and events in this book are fictitious.
Any resemblance to persons living or dead is strictly coincidental.

If you purchase this book without a cover you should be aware
that this book may have been stolen property and reported as
"unsold and destroyed" to the publisher. In such case neither the
author nor the publisher has received any payment for this
"stripped book."

First Printing, November 1995
1 2 3 4 5 6 7 8 9

DAW TRADEMARK REGISTERED
U.S. PAT. OFF. AND FOREIGN COUNTRIES
—MARCA REGISTRADA.
HECHO EN U.S.A.

PRINTED IN THE U.S.A.

In memory of my father,
DAVID HABER
With all my love,
always

"All things are changing:
and thou thyself art in continuous mutation
and in a manner in continuous destruction,
and the whole universe too."

—MARCUS AURELIUS

Chapter One

Explosions in the dark vacuum of space are soundless but no less destructive for their lack of percussive accompaniment. Kayla John Reed stood poised by the air lock of the light cruiser *Falstaff,* a sleek silver disrupter rifle resting easily in her arms, waiting to board the freighter *Megan II* and, if necessary, cause several silent explosions.

She glanced back at her companion hovering just behind her, tall, blond, and blue-eyed, his arms full of lethal plasteel. He nodded his readiness. Good, steady Iger, her companion in danger, in play, and in love.

"On my signal." The voice, a rich deep contralto, belonged to Salome, captain of the *Falstaff*. She was two floors below them, in ops, leaning above the winking orange lights of the com board, offering the captain of the *Megan II* several uncomfortable choices, the least violent of which was to prepare to be boarded and looted.

"Go."

Kayla hit the air lock switch and the space doors parted instantly.

A black tunnel led from their ship to the dark gray air lock of the freighter, a long, rubbery tube snaking through the void between the ships. Would those doors at the far end open or would she have to risk a shot to force them and maybe puncture the tube? Kayla punched the wall com and said, "Salome, they're still locked up tighter than the Arguillean treasury."

"They'll crack in a moment. Stay ready."

Kayla sighted down the narrow barrel of the disruptor. She sensed Iger beside her, similarly poised.

The *Megan II*'s doors slid open.

"Let's go!"

Running within the air lock umbilicus was impossible. Kayla and Iger took broad, crouching steps, clinging to the webbed handholds as the walls of the tube quivered.

"I hate this part," Iger said.

"Me, too." Kayla leaped through the freighter's air lock onto blessedly solid floor plate and took a lungful of brackish recycled air. The corridor was deserted; scarred walls led to the massive doors of the lift. A faded blue numeral by the doors indicated that this was deck five.

Kayla's green eyes took on a glassy, distracted cast as she sent out a tendril of farsense, searching for active minds nearby. Aside from a faint murmur coming from several levels above, she sensed nothing.

Brushing a strand of dark red hair out of her face, she keyed her belt com to her own ship's bridge. "Salome, there's no welcoming party here. And I don't sense anyone around for at least two levels."

"I don't like it," came the reply. "They're probably bracing for a fight. I'm sending Rab over. Wait for him."

But Kayla was in no mood to wait. She and Iger were easy targets out in the open air lock. They could wait in the lock tube, but it wasn't a choice she liked much. Moving, they were much harder to hit. "C'mon," she said. "Let's go see if we can soften this place up a bit."

"Salome said to wait."

She cocked an eyebrow in Iger's direction. "Since when are you such a good little soldier?"

"She's the captain."

"And if we get our rears shot to hell, she'll still be the captain, but we'll be the ones who won't be able to sit down, won't we?"

"Point taken." Iger gave her a crooked smile, white teeth in a tanned face. "Lead on."

The lift controls were old-fashioned, but Kayla managed to get them working with a little effort. The doors squealed open on their rollers. "I wish Rab would get here," she muttered. The bridge was on the fourth level. Kayla cast her farsense ahead of them, reaching out until she sensed the five-member crew poised at their stations.

They were waiting, and, yes, they had guns.

"So how do things look?" Iger said. "Y'know, farsense-wise? Anybody home?"

"Not good at all." Kayla reversed the lift. "I think I want to withdraw my previous suggestion. Let's lock this thing down and go get Rab."

"... for a breath I tarry ..."

She turned on Iger, stared. "What did you say?"

"Nothing."

"I could swear that you were reciting a line of poetry just now."

"Are you going space batty on me?"

"... that once seemed a burning cloud ..."

"I don't think so." She was dizzy, suddenly assaulted by lines of poetry that streamed past her, purple words dancing upon the brackish air. "Goddamn it, not again!"

"What is it? What's going on?" Iger's grip on his disruptor tightened.

"Some kind of weird mind thing," she told him. "Third time this week. Never mind." Kayla shoved the unwelcome words and images out of her mind. *Concentrate on what's happening here,* she ordered herself. Rab. Cargo. The money that was needed to keep the *Falstaff* out of the hands of its creditors.

They were met at the lift entrance by the *Falstaff*'s burly first mate, bearded, towering Barabbas, Salome's lover.

"About time you got here, Rab."

He gave Kayla a sour look. Rab hated the air lock tube even more than she did. "What's the story here? You got a fix on these clowns?"

"There's a bunch of them sitting on the bridge sharpening their knives," Kayla said. "I suggest we go elsewhere."

"How about the cargo bay?" said Iger. "We could jam the lift doors at the bridge, lock 'em in, and take the cargo."

"Take too much time," Rab said.

"Watch out!"

A beam of light sizzled past their ears and vaporized part of a wall panel.

Rab ducked as Kayla and Iger dived onto the floor plates. Above their heads damaged circuitry spilled out of the wound, sparking and hissing.

"Where are they?" Iger said. "How did those bastards get down here? A maintenance chute?"

Footsteps clattered in the hallway, growing louder.

"Katie," Rab said, sounding annoyed. "I thought your damned mindpowers were supposed to warn us before anything like this happened."

"Let's talk about that later, okay?" she yelled. "Here they come again!" She and Iger rolled across the floor as lasers crisscrossed the corridor, raking the spot where they had been just a moment before. Bright sizzling drops of molten metal splattered onto the floor.

"They've got us pinned down," Iger said.

"Not quite yet." Rab lifted his massive disruptor, held it steady, and got off a solid round of fire.

They heard a scream and the sounds of someone thrashing in pain.

"All we want is your cargo," Rab yelled. "Nobody else has to get hurt."

In answer came more gunfire.

"Okay, you asked for it." Rab aimed his disruptor, indicating that Kayla and Iger should do likewise. "Now!"

The combined firepower bent the floor plates, raddling them into a humped mess that walled off the *Megan II*'s crew.

"The lift," Kayla said. "Let's grab that cargo and get the hell out of here."

The echoing hold was dark and half-empty. Rab cursed in disgust as he surveyed its contents. "God's bloody eyes! Broken screenbrains. A lot of good this'll do us."

"Someone will want them," Kayla said. "Come on. Let's get them loaded."

It was hot and heavy work shifting the crates into the lift and dragging them back along the air lock tube. Seven crates. Seven lung-bursting, leg-wobbling trips.

"I'm glad that job's done," Kayla said. They stood grouped at the *Falstaff*'s air lock as Iger deflated the tube and sealed the doors. Rab punched his belt com. "Honey, can you hear me down here?"

Salome answered at once. "Loud and clear, Rab.

"Give 'em a little goose with our light cannons. Slow 'em down a bit, just leave them sublight capacity."

"Firing."

As they watched, the *Falstaff*'s light armory took out the *Megan II*'s directionals in a silent hail of laser bolts. The freighter grew smaller and smaller in the viewport as the *Falstaff*'s engines drew her away toward safe harbor.

"Lousy job," Rab said. "Lousy goddamn screenbrains. Let's get 'em below."

* * *

An unhappy crew brought the *Falstaff* in for landfall at the Bitter End on Kemel.

The Bitter End was not the choicest of establishments, which was what attracted the rougher edges of the intergalactic merchant trade to its bar and gaming tables.

It was dark and claustrophobic, the air thick with smoke and the smell of stale beer. Glowfloats drifted through the air, half of them guttering like spent candles. The floor was usually sticky, and patrons were loath to pick up any object they might happen to drop.

Salome leaned back in her battered chair and took a swig from the self-heating cider container in her hand. Her dark, pretty face was contorted with disgust. "I never thought I'd see the day when we raided other ships for scrap metal," she said. "It's worse than embarrassing. It's stupid."

"I don't know which is worse," Arsobades said.

"I'd settle for embarrassing," Kayla replied morosely. She quickly downed a Red Jack and signaled Chloe, the barkeep, for another. Her few remaining credits jangled tinnily in her pocket. Times *were* tough, and getting tougher. The ever-tightening grip of Pelleas Karlson's trade restrictions forced honest smugglers into piracy, and worse. Kayla knew that it must be eating at her captain, and whatever ate at Salome took a bite out of Rab, too. Sooner or later it would have the whole jolly lot of them for dinner.

"Damn Karlson," she said. "This whole damn mess is all his fault."

Down the bar and back, twice around the room, smugglers forced onto hard times held up their glasses, slapped their palms against tables, and roared, "Damn Karlson! Damn 'im!"

"And don't forget his lieutenant in hell, Yates Keller!" cried a lone voice.

"Damn 'em both!" came the general response.

Yates Keller. The name brought a flood of unwelcome memories. The man had been responsible for the deaths of Kayla's parents and the loss of her family's holdings on Styx. Because of Yates Keller, she had lost every single thing, every person whom she had once held dear.

Kayla shifted edgily on her seat. She had thought Keller dead, mortally wounded and left on the paving stones of the grand plaza outside Vardalia's Crystal Palace years ago. But no such luck. He had survived, the bastard—flourished even—to become the right hand of Prime Minister Pelleas Karlson and a power feared throughout the Trade Alliance.

"Damn them both," Kayla said. "And while you're at it, double-damn 'em."

"Snappy phrase," said Arsobades, passing behind her. "It'd make a good song title."

Rab gave him a dark look. "If anybody happens to feel like singing. Which we *don't,* thank you. Chloe, give me another just like the one before."

Tall, thin Chloe, the Bitter End's bartender, eyed Rab's empty glass and said loudly, "Salome, I'm sorry, but I don't run tabs for anybody these days. Can't afford it. When we call time, we'll be calling for payment as well. Nothing personal. Just want you to know."

The frown on the *Falstaff* captain's lovely face could have been carved from ebon stone. "Things have gotten that bad around here?"

"If you have to ask, then I guess you haven't been paying attention."

"Hey, Salome," a grizzled captain shouted down the bar. "If you're not good for your bar bill, I'll front you the cash. Just sell me the *Falstaff*. I've always fancied that bird."

Everybody in the Bitter End laughed. Everybody but the crew of the *Falstaff*.

"Why shouldn't you fancy her, Franco?" Salome

said. "Considering the rusting tub you've got. Your ship's not even good for scrap."

"You should know scrap," Franco said, his smile turning mean. "That's all I hear you're running these days."

"Hey, you," Rab said, getting unsteadily to his feet. "Shut your ugly face."

Disgusted, Kayla jumped up as well. "Stop it!" she shouted. "We're all of us being squeezed to death by Karlson and dying by inches."

Traders all around her slapped their tables in hearty agreement.

"We'll be at each other's throats soon. Which is just what Karlson wants."

The room grew quiet.

Kayla felt the drink coursing like a hot river through her veins, loosening her tongue. "So go ahead. Play into his hands. Show Karlson that he's got us figured right: We're just a bunch of drunken fools."

"Says who?" somebody yelled.

"Of course, it doesn't have to be that way." Kayla smiled craftily. "Why should so many suffer while a few rich politicians live well?"

"That's right."

"Tell it, sister."

"I say we demand justice!" Kayla's voice rose. "Let's kick back at Karlson, disrupt the next Trade Congress! Fill that pretty hall with so many Free Traders—so many of us—that even Pelleas

Karlson's police will be overwhelmed. Let's lean on him, hard, until he begs for mercy."

A few cheers came from the back of the room.

"The hell with Karlson," someone yelled. "And that bastard, Yates Keller."

More cheers and table slapping. Chloe began to look alarmed as glasses crashed against one another.

Heart pounding, Kayla pressed them. "Why not now? What are we waiting for?"

Again, everybody cheered.

"Kick Karlson! Kick Karlson!"

Suddenly a woman's voice cut through the din: "Hell, who can afford the fuel?"

"Yeah," someone else said. "With St. Ilban a bloody two jumps away."

"Drink's cheaper."

"And less dangerous!"

"Chloe, fill 'em."

And the talk turned to mundane matters, traders shrugging and returning to their private conversations. Kayla watched in mounting frustration. She told herself that someday, somehow, she would have her revenge.

Someday, Karlson, she thought, *I'll teach you a hard lesson for ruining the mindstone trade, for setting Keller loose where he could kill my parents and enslave my friends. Someday there'll be a reckoning. We'll come for you and we'll pull your grip off our necks if we have to break every one of your fingers to do it. I swear it on my parents' graves!*

Beside her, old Hiller Guillen muttered thickly into his cup, something about mindstones.

"What'd you say, Hiller?" Kayla peered at him, grateful for any distraction.

Hiller Guillen, whose green, tombstone-shaped teeth leaned one against the other in his rotting mouth. An ancient wreck of a man and merchant, he was. Guillen had seen the back end of too many deals gone sour and nowadays spent most of his time stationside drinking on somebody else's credit.

"I'm telling you," Guillen said, his voice rising steeply and cracking. "It's bigger than a man's fist and brighter than a star."

"A mindstone?" Kayla said. "Don't talk to me about those damned stones, Hiller. They bring nobody any good."

Guillen fixed his rheumy eyes on her. "*Stone*. One you've never seen the likes of, girlie. The Mindstar. Best ever. Purple of the sky just past sunset, and a golden light deep within. A man would gladly kill for a stone like that. And believe you me, men have died for it already. Died for the Mindstar. Men and women, both."

"Mindstar?" Kayla found herself getting interested. "What in the Three Systems are you talking about?"

A wily smile split Guillen's seamed face. "Did I ever say it was in the Three Systems? Not me. Outside. Way outside. But worth the trip."

"And?"

He held up his cup and tapped it. Empty. "Hard to talk on a dry throat."

Kayla counted her credits. She had just enough left to buy another Red Jack. She could almost taste that beer. But Hiler's words had intrigued her. And she could probably borrow the price of another drink later from Arsobades. Sighing, she signaled to Chloe to fill his cup once more.

The whipcord-thin woman squinted tired eyes at her. "Hasn't he had enough? Most nights he's falling-over drunk even before he gets here. We have to carry him out."

Kayla gave the bartender a sharp look. "Fill it. Or do I have to pay extra for the advice?"

Chloe glared back at her, but she filled Guillen's cup to the brim. Then, without a word, she turned and walked to the far end of the bar.

"Okay, Hiller," Kayla said. "Drink up. You just cost me my last credits and maybe Chloe's friendship. So drink your damned drink. This had better be good."

Guillen gave her a conspiratorial smile and took a long, slow sip. Nodded. "The Mindstar, it's Cyrilite."

"Like every other mindstone."

"But this one's a super mindstone," he whispered. "Big as my fist. Gives incredible powers to whoever owns it. Problem is, no one can ride it. Too powerful. Many've tried."

"What happened?"

"Some burned out their minds, others died.

Folks call it cursed. But even cursed, it's worth all of Karlson's treasury, and then some."

"Is that right? And just where is this fabulous Mindstar?" Kayla kept her tone casual. No use letting Guillen see that he had really hooked her: he'd expect another drink.

"Yep, worth Karlson's own treasure house. And doesn't he know it? Karlson wants it, does our prime minister. He's got scouts out all over the place. But nobody knows where it is. Nobody." He smiled a green smile.

"Except you."

"Maybe." His look grew frankly lecherous. "Maybe I do, maybe I don't. But you'll have to do more than just fill my cup once to get that secret, darlin'. Much more, I should say." He reached out a shaking hand and grabbed hold of her shoulder, massaging it.

Kayla controlled her temper and smiled sweetly. "I already spent my last credits on you, Hiller. But come give me a hug." She leaned close, wound her arms around his neck, and bored into him with a mind probe, searching for what he knew about the Mindstar's whereabouts.

Guillen shuddered, shut his eyes, and sagged helplessly against her under the mental onslaught. Kayla sorted impatiently through the jumble of his mind. Drink had roughened the outlines of his thoughts, and she had a hard time separating fantasies from reality. But she could make out, just barely, a bit of information concerning mindstones, and she saw the glowing image of a huge round purple stone, perfect, with a golden star glowing in its midnight depths. A small female hand stroked the stone as though it were a living thing. Then the slender fingers closed over it and it was gone.

The name of that hand's owner burned briefly in the space where the stone had been: *Shotay*. As the name faded, a prison ship appeared, awkward in its gray bulk, ponderously making its way between planets. The *Admiral Lovejoy*.

The image faded.

Kayla pulled out of Guillen's mind and released him. The old drunk tottered forward until his head came to rest on the bar. Kayla gave him one last mental command.

—*Sleep*.

Guillen began snoring gently.

Chloe walked over and picked up Guillen's empty glass. "Told you." Her nose wrinkled in disgust.

Kayla smiled. "Here's the credits for the drink, Chloe. Keep the change."

"Thanks. I can use it."

"Can't we all?"

She found Salome, caught her eye, and gave her the high sign: a raised eyebrow and nod. The captain of the *Falstaff* nodded back, excused herself from her drinking companions, and joined Kayla at the door.

"What's up?"

"I think I've discovered the way to get the *Falstaff* out of hock."

The expression on Salome's lovely face shifted from cautious curiosity to annoyed disbelief. "Katie, just how much have you had to drink?"

"I'm serious. You interested?"

Salome tossed a strand of fine golden hair over her shoulder. "After your little rabble-rousing speech back there? I'm not so sure that your judgment is exactly what I would call trustworthy this evening."

"Fine. Then I'll sell what I know to the highest bidder. There's bound to be one here."

"All right, all right." Salome held up her hands in surrender. "What did you have in mind?"

Kayla smiled. "Well, first of all, I've got to get myself arrested.

* * *

The lights burned late into the night in the *Falstaff's* mess. Eyelids were drooping around the table—Arsobades frequently jerked awake from the beginning of a full-blown snore—but Kayla and Salome were sharp-eyed and intent on their conversation even as their crewmates wilted in exhaustion.

"You understand?" Kayla said. "We've got to be clear about this."

Salome nodded. "And you? You're certain that

you can find this so-called Mindstar by locating the owner of it on this prison ship?

"Absolutely. Once I find out where it is, I'll signal you directly to come and get me. And you'll be shadowing the ship the whole time."

"Right."

Rab looked up from the cup of choba tea he was nursing and said, "This is all easier said than done, Katie. What are you going to do, march up to the bridge, introduce yourself to the captain, and say, "Excuse me, I'd like to make a long-distance call?"

"Don't you worry about how I'll do it, Rab. I'll manage it. You can bet on it."

"Use a code name," Arsobades said, rousing slightly. "I like code names."

"Cute," said Rab. "Madame X calling? Please come and get me. And so we just come cruising in, knock on that floating armory's air lock, and say, "Excuse us, warden, one of your prisoners has a prior engagement, thanks awfully." He shook his head, obviously giving them all up for hopeless cases. "We'll get our asses shot into space dust."

"I agree with Rab," Iger said. "Katie, you've gone space-batty. Completely." Beside him on the wallseat the dalkoi Third Child uttered a faint squeak in her sleep and turned onto her back, toes twitching.

The resolute expression on Salome's face wavered. "What if something goes wrong?"

Kayla shook her head fiercely. "Nothing will go wrong. I won't let it."

"It's a huge risk for you, Katie." Amber eyes bored into her. "What if we can't get you back?"

"I have faith in you. Besides, people escape from prison all the time."

"If we weren't right up against the edge, I wouldn't listen to you."

"But we are."

"And this scheme is just bizarre and crazy enough that it might work. Might."

Arsobades yawned, stretched, reached for his mechlute, and began plucking out random chords. Slowly a tune emerged, a faintly martial air.

"When will you do it?" Salome asked.

"Tomorrow."

"And what's your code name?"

Kayla tilted her head and listened to the song Arsobades was playing. Her lips curved in a faint smile. "War Minstrel," she said. "I'll be the War Minstrel."

Chapter Two

"It's cold," Greer said. "Katieeee, it's cold. How did you get here? What are you doing here?"

Kayla stared up at her former crewmate in amazement. "You of all people should know why I'm here. For the cause. Yours, ours: free trade."

"Whose cause?" Greer's smile flickered, gone almost before it had registered.

"I told you. Free trade."

"So you say. If you ask me, you've just taken on a pile of kark." She grabbed hold of Kayla's shoulder and began shaking her, hard. "Wake up, Katie. Do you think you can really handle all of this? Really?"

"Of course." Kayla wanted to tell her much more, to say that she was sorry for what had happened back in Vardalia, that it was good to see Greer. But it *was* cold, so cold that her teeth clamped shut in her mouth, so cold that Greer's face was freezing and blurring, changing before Kayla's eyes to a strange face, a woman's face but an older, thinner one than Greer's, with pale eyes and jagged scars running across the bridge of the nose and over the right cheek.

"Wake up." The stranger's voice was a broken chord. "You've been talkin' in your sleep. Like to have drove me crazy. Thank the elder gods, it's morning." The woman released her grip on Kayla's arm.

Kayla sat up, shivering, and took a lungful of sour, recycled air. Her thin gray stretchsuit was little protection against the chill. Distant clanks and strange murmuring voices made ghostly echoes above her head.

Bad air. Bad dreams. She remembered where she was now, and why.

Greer was years dead, shot down during the riot in front of Karlson's Crystal Palace, and Kayla was aboard the *Admiral Lovejoy*, a prison ship bound for an orbital factory in the Demetria System.

She had been arrested for elaborately incompetent pickpocketing, arraigned by a mechjudge, and sentenced to five years' hard labor. After the *Falstaff*'s sensors had tapped prison records to locate the prisoner Shotay, owner of the Mindstar, currently aboard the *Admiral Lovejoy*, a touch of Kayla's farsense convinced the records clerk to assign her to the same vessel.

Stained walls enclosed her. Her bunk was hard, the air frigid, and the look on her roommate's scarred face distinctly unfriendly. Gerdred, the old woman's name was Gerdred, Kayla recalled hazily.

Keys jangled and the sound of approaching feet

was suddenly loud in the corridor. Breakfast. The morning of her third day as a convict aboard the good ship *Admiral Lovejoy.*

The wide, opaque door clicked. Small plasteel trays slid through slots in the door, each holding flat bread, coffee, a tired sausage, and a small pile of pink and green pills.

"Palm the pink ones," said Gerdred *sotto voce.* "They'll knock you right on your ass."

"And do what with them?"

"Flush 'em down the john during shower."

"Thanks."

"And if you don't stop talking in your sleep, I'm going to save some and toss 'em in your open mouth all night long, pain in the ass."

Kayla ignored the old woman's tone. "What do the green ones do?"

Her only answer was a shrug.

The lukewarm coffee had a thin layer of grease floating on its surface. Kayla gulped it down fast. The food, colorless and cold, had little taste. It sat on her stomach, cold and heavy, like a stone.

Click.

A key in the door. "Showers," said a simian-faced guard. "Move it!"

The slam of metal, and the murmur of voices. A slow shuffle with numbed feet along crowded corridors, left, right, left, into a large, cheerless room lined with gray tile. Water, when it came, was like liquid ice on her skin.

Wham!

The blow knocked Kayla into the wall near a showerhead.

"Where'd you get that tattoo, bitch?" The woman was large, with broad shoulders, short dark hair, and a wide face in which two small dark eyes shone with rabid ferocity. "That black starburst on your back. Free Trader! I hate the Free Traders! What good did they ever do me except get me an interview with Karlson's mind spies and a reservation here?" She punched Kayla again, slamming her back once more against the slippery tile.

By instinct alone Kayla lashed out, using her Free Trader training to pivot quickly and hook her antagonist just above the ankle with a backward kick, knocking her to the floor of the shower. "Next one is in the face," Kayla warned her. "If you're looking for a flatter nose, keep asking questions."

Their eyes met in hatred. The woman let out a snarled curse and started to get up, moving toward her.

Kayla pulled her concentration together—how reliable were her already shaky emphatic powers under the influence of these prison drugs?—and grabbed at the woman's mind.

Nothing happened.

Freezing water rained down upon them.

—*Come on, damnit!*

She tried again, pouring all the energy she could muster into the effort.

The woman reached for her.

Nearsense kicked in and Kayla caught her opponent in a punishing mindgrip, bearing down until the woman gasped and sagged to the wet floor.

Kayla kneed her in the head. "My tattoos are none of your business, understand? They're nobody's business." Glancing up angrily at the handful of wet and shivering women grouped around her, she said, "Well? Anybody else here have any questions she wants to ask?"

They backed away. She had won that point.

Kayla dried herself silently, shivering from the cold. The others gave her plenty of room as she dressed.

The gray-green stretchsuit she pulled on was worn at the knees and bottom. *Might as well be naked,* she thought, *for all the good this miserable rag does me.* Her skin puckered with chickenflesh and her spirits sank even deeper into a black pit of despair. Was she ever going to be warm again? Would she see any light and any color other than the yellow lamps in the prison corridors and the gray metal of the walls? No wonder so many of the convicts fought to the death, or killed themselves.

She shuffled along the grey hallways with the other prisoners and longed for a viewport, for something other than this eternal sameness, these worn beige walls and dirty floors. Even the cold light of the stars would be preferable to the windowless tunnels within the ship. Even the caves of Styx, her home world, would be more hospitable.

* * *

Make-work and routine, a dreary prison day: Shower, laundry, lunch, then back to the laundry. It was a high-ceilinged, steamy room filled with whirring machinery. Despite the mechs, the process needed human hands to sort the soiled gray prison garb, to move and stack the cleaned stretchsuits. Kayla moved like an automaton, part of the throbbing metal, as subdued and insubstantial as the other silent convicts.

I feel dead as a mech, she thought. *This is no good at all. Got to be sharper, get with it.* She gathered herself, trying for a farsense scan of the Lovejoy's bridge, and managed a weak probe. But nothing registered save the distant mutter of a hundred minds. *Damn! What's wrong? Even on bad days I'm stronger than this. I palmed those meds, but I still feel drugged. Is it the food? Maybe there're additional doses of the tranquilizers in the food they give us so we'll all stay nice and docile, nice and dead. Last thing I need. It looks like this is one prisoner who just started a diet.*

She pretended to eat dinner that night, watching hungrily as the others around her polished off their portions. Well, what did they care if they all went through their days and nights like zombies?

"Hey," Gerdred said. "You gonna finish that stuff?" Greedily she eyed Kayla's plate with its cold ragged cutlet sitting in congealed yellow gravy.

"Here. Have it."

Her cellmate didn't hesitate, reaching over to grab the food, tray and all.

A thin, sweet-faced girl with short pale hair and a scar over her left eye glanced at Kayla and said quietly, "You should eat. You'll need it, where we're headed."

"You look like you could use it more."

At Kayla's words Gerdred glared and clutched the extra tray closer to her sagging bosom.

The girl smiled slightly. "Don't worry, Gerdred. I'm not going to take your food from you. I may not look it, but I'm strong enough."

"Oh, sure, you're strong." This from a big, muscular, androgynous-looking inmate with long silvery hair pulled back into a braid.

The girl made a face. "Evlin, don't start."

Heavy footsteps sounded behind their bench. The trusty Mogul was surveying the flocks. He was a short, heavy-featured man, brutal in his actions, and Kayla had taken an instant dislike to him. He stopped now, breathing down heavily upon her exposed neck.

"Number 172," he said. "Come with me."

"Why?"

She felt a sharp prod and a sudden shock in the small of her back from a flashstick. "No questions. Come along."

A knowing look spread over Gerdred's face. Kayla didn't like it, but she had no chance to attempt a probe. As she followed the man from the hall, she saw her cellmate snatch up the remains of her coffee and down that, too. Gerdred the opportunist, wasting no time.

Mogul led her along the grimy hall and into the trusty's office, closing the door behind them. It was a moderately well-appointed room with a few worn orange wallseats and a low table upon which sat a battered vid cube player and screenpad.

Kayla stared once into the trusty's small, malevolent eyes, saw hunger there, saw madness, and looked away.

"You're new," Mogul said. "And you don't know the rules yet, so I thought I would explain them to you."

"Very kind."

A sharp poke in the gut made Kayla gasp.

"I don't like smart-asses. You'll get along with me if you don't play games. And you'll get along even better if you give me what I want."

"Which is?"

"Help."

"Help you? How?"

"I like to know what's going on in the cell blocks. What's going through the prisoners' heads."

I could help you there more than you know.

"Something funny?"

"No, I just felt a gas pain. Must be from the wonderful food we eat here. You ever get any of those? Or maybe you eat better food."

Mogul's hand shot out, grabbed the front of her suit, and roughly pulled her close. "Shut up and listen. I can be a good friend. And a good friend can help you do easy time, understand?" His hand was straying now, moving down the front of her stretchsuit. "Are you interested?"

He's a damned spy for the government, and he wants me to be his eyes. Bastard. Kayla dug her nails into his thumb, hard. The trusty hissed in anger and pain.

"Sorry," she said. "Guess I really need a manicure. But you know, Mogul, you ought to be careful. Where you touch me, I mean. I've got Hendrick's Syndrome. You wouldn't want to catch that, would you? Oozing sores on your dick, under your eyelids and toenails. . . ."

Mogul scowled and took a step back from her. "You've got to be joking."

"Check the medical records. I'm sure you can get hold of those." Kayla shrugged cheerfully. "Just wanted to warn you. As a friend."

The trusty swore softly. "Get the hell out of here, and don't talk to me unless I talk to you first."

"I thought you wanted to talk."

Mogul pulled away until his squat bulk was practically crammed into a corner. "Out! Out! And keep quiet about this or I'll make sure your time here is twice as hard."

Kayla stepped out into the hall where two guards were waiting and let the door come between her and Mogul. Docilely, she followed them back to the prisoners' mess.

But the universe seemed to lurch and the corridor bent away from her, stretched long and thin, and she went rolling along it like a marble, like a glass bead whizzing along a string in the middle of space. She was a fleck of space dust, mere gossamer shreds of thought. . . .

Gods, it's happening again. What is it?

She had the sickening sense of falling through low-g, plunging through one mind and then another, enduring a torrent of assaulting images and emotions. Buzzing, relentless shredding filled her head.

Pink lights and then the rats come, the teeth, the claws . . .

Crawling back into the cave of my skull, finding the bones of old thoughts . . .

Kayla tried to halt her fall, to find some purchase, some character trait of which she could grab hold, but there was no texture, no specific memory, no distinct identity behind any of these images.

Whose minds are these?

She couldn't even tell if the thoughts belonged to anyone aboard the *Admiral Lovejoy.*

And just as suddenly, it stopped.

She was in the prison corridor again, walking between blank-eyed guards back into the communal mess hall.

Kayla was convinced now that something was wrong, really wrong. It was as if the barriers between minds were dissolving, as though her mind were being flooded by a torrent of random thoughts, subconscious babble. She wished briefly that there were someone, some other empath, to whom she could tell this. But no. No. She had to stick to her plan, ignore all distractions, find this Shotay and, through her, the Mindstar. Anything and everything else would have to wait.

* * *

On her ninth day in prison Kayla began to think that she would die there, expire in that dim, gray place, that her entire plan had been some foolish suicidal gesture. Just five days more and they would be in the Demetria System, docking at Bryce Station, the orbital factory where the convicts would serve out their sentences—and their lives. Bryce Station, bristling with defenses and sensors. The *Falstaff* would never be able to get in under Bryce's sensors, never be able to find her and bring her out. She had just five days left before she was trapped for good in her own plan. If only she could think straight. But hunger gnawed at her gut and fogged her mind.

"You're not eating, are you?" It was the thin, sweet-faced girl sitting beside her who spoke, the sweet-faced girl with a scar that made a deep jagged line from above her left eye to the edge of her earlobe.

All along the communal table the convicts were bolting down their gray and tasteless food as if they found some pleasure in it. Kayla's stomach rumbled.

The girl gave her a wise look. "Trying to avoid the meds? They're not in everything, y'know. The bread is okay." She shifted a biscuit from her tray onto Kayla's plate. "Here. Have mine. I'm not really hungry."

Kayla roused herself, made an effort, and was suddenly wolfing down the stale bread. Belatedly, she looked at the girl and felt shame for taking her food. "But you're skin and bones. You should've eaten it."

"I don't seem to have much appetite these days." A shadow crept into the girl's eyes, tarried for a moment, fled. "Not that you could with this food, especially tonight."

"Come on, Shotay," a midnight-skinned inmate called down the table. "It's no worse than last night's."

Shotay.

A chill went down Kayla's neck, down her spine, and all the way to her feet. Shotay. The name of the person who owned the Mindstar. Her? This thin-ribbed slip of a girl? Was it possible? Kayla stared in amazement.

"Maybe your mouth has died, Toran. Not mine. Not yet." Shotay smiled briefly, nodded at Kayla, and picked up her tray. "See ya. Remember about that bread."

Kayla turned to watch her go, and saw Mogul come up behind Shotay and put his hand possessively on her shoulder. There was a quick exchange of words. The girl nodded sullenly, put down her tray, and followed him out of the room. The bitter, defeated look on her face made Kayla's innards roil with anger.

What does that bastard want with Shotay? He forced her to go with him! I know it. What does he have on her? What does he know about her?

Kayla felt a sudden frantic need to protect her, to protect the frail source of the Mindstar's location. A mind probe would let her know what was happening. She sent one whizzing after them and hooked onto Shotay.

They were in the trusty's office. Mogul was handing the girl a cup. Frothy pink liquid. But there was something in the drink, something added. Shotay protested, Mogul insisted. She shook her head. He slapped her.

—*No, Shotay! Don't drink it, it's mindsalt.*

She drank.

Tied to Shotay on the nearsense probe, Kayla felt the first giddy exultant surge, the early flickerings of embryonic glee, and tried too late to escape. She was caught, mired in Shotay's mind, saw what Shotay saw, felt what she felt, thought what she thought. Kayla and Shotay, two minds melded into one.

Their heart beat in heavy percussive waves. Blood flowed through their veins, burning like lava. They were brilliant, invincible, burning with incandescent powers. Anything and everything was possible to them. All doors were open. They could read the mind of a flea, see subatomic particles, swoop through the air with the ease of a feathered creature. They laughed, and musical notes fell out of their mouth to break melodiously upon the floor. They danced along gaily in midair with the thoughts of hundreds of open minds below them, mere paving stones far beneath their feet.

But the path shifted, turned inward, downward, and there were bodies strewn along the path, eyes open but staring sightlessly. They all had the same familiar, beloved, awful face. Golias, Shotay's—their—brother.

Bones by the side of the road, bones underneath them, crackling as they walked. The bones of life.

Out out out! Get out, hurry.

Clutching what little separate awareness she still possessed, Kayla battered her way up and out of Shotay's mind, cutting off the nearsense probe, fleeing to the safety of her own separate head.

Mindsalt. Shotay had been a mindsalt addict. *Had been,* and had recovered. But Mogul was cold-bloodedly hooking her back onto it again. She didn't have to ask his purpose. It was obvious that Shotay, once drugged, was an easy mark and would willingly climb between the sheets when asked, regardless of who was doing the asking. Even if it was Mogul.

That one needs killing, Kayla thought. *Badly.*

By the end of the hour Shotay was back in the communal meal hall. Pale-faced, withdrawn, she spoke to no one, kept her head down, and filed out with the rest of the prisoners for the walk back to the commons between the cells. It was the free hour, between dinner and lights out.

Kayla pushed into line behind her. "Shotay," she said. "Hey, kid."

"Who're you calling kid?" came a voice from the side, a mellow alto, half-amused in tone.

Kayla turned to see Evlin, the tall, androgynous convict standing just behind her, staring down at her from pale gray eyes framed by painted silver-pink cartouches.

A woman? No, a man. Kayla noted the prominent Adam's apple. the faint stubble of beard. But such delicate pale hands. Such a soft voice.

"I'm her friend," he said. "You, too?"

Kayla nodded. "Name's Kate. I don't like what that bastard is doing to her. She needs protection."

Their eyes met in understanding.

"Don't worry. I'll take care of her, Kate." Evlin draped a graceful arm around Shotay's shoulder. "She used to be like this all the time. I know how to deal with it."

The girl gave no evidence of hearing anything at all. She seemed lost in her own little world, the world of mindsalt hallucinations, walking through her own bad dreams, oblivious to the hands trying to help her.

"Damnit, look at her," Kayla said. "A zombie. Can't we report Mogul for dosing her?"

"To whom?" The voice this time was deeper, more overtly masculine. The speaker was a black-haired, golden-skinned man with piercing dark eyes shaded by epicanthic lids. "What good would it do? If you want to survive here, you would do well to avoid Mogul's attention."

Kayla stared at him, held by his rich, resonant voice.

He noticed her gaze and smiled. "I'm Cristobal," he said, and it was beautiful music in a terrible place. "You're the new one. I've heard about you."

"Kate. Kate N. Shadow." What, she wondered, was a man like this doing here?

"You're a Free Trader, yes? I heard about the tattoo." He smiled at her surprise. "Very little is private here."

"A friend gave me the tattoo. And I guess she gave me the cause as well."

"Is that why you're on the *Lovejoy?*"

"I'm here because I got caught picking a pocket."

"You don't look like a common thief."

"Did I say I was?" Even in the crowd of convicts she was aware of his nearness, too aware. She pretended to listen to the buzz of conversation around them and realized, to her surprise, that the inmates were discussing mindstones and the Mindstar in particular.

"I'd buy my way out of here with it."

"You'd just buy enough drink to drown in."

"Wouldn't need it if I had the 'star."

"Might just as well talk about owning Karlson's treasury."

"The Mindstar, imagine it. Just holding it in your hands. I'll bet it's warm."

"Fiery hot!"

"Has a pulse like a living thing."

"Holds enough souls to be alive!"

Kayla grew impatient with such foolish talk. "That's just bull," she said. "It's impossible. No mindstone could do that. It's just a stone, not magic."

Cristobal gave her a knowing look. "Speaking from firsthand experience, are you?"

"So what would you do with it?" asked Evlin. Shotay rested, eyes closed, in the crook of his arm. He pointed a long, graceful finger at Kayla. "Buy a thousand beautiful gowns?"

"Maybe *you* would," she countered. "I'd destroy it. I hate those damned things." She expected him to be horrified, but Evlin merely shook his head in obvious disbelief.

"No, you wouldn't either," he said. "You'd keep it and use it, same as the rest of us." Beside him Shotay smiled emptily. But her lips formed and re-formed the words "destroy it."

Kayla couldn't bear to watch her. She turned back to Cristobal. His dark glance was warming. "What about you? What would you do with it?"

He smiled a wolf's smile. "That's easy. I'd re-

claim my power, get back my land, clear my name.
I was a senator at the Trade Congress. Repre-
sented Teco, in the Salabrian System. I'd buy my
way back into Karlson's good favor, and then stran-
gle him." His tone was light and teasing, but Kayla
had no doubt that he meant what he said. A powerful rage flickered beneath the smooth surface of
this man. Heat and lightning. "With or without
that stone, I'd like to bring that bastard down."

"And maybe I'd like to help you," she said.

Their eyes met again. Kayla felt herself caught
by his magnetism. She could not look away.

"I'd enjoy that." His voice was silky, his breath
warm on her ear.

"Lockdown!" came the announcement. "Five
minutes."

Damn it, she thought. *Just when it was getting
interesting.*

Reluctantly, Kayla pulled her gaze away from
Cristobal. He gave her a look of regret and
squeezed her hand briefly before moving past to
join the queue for the men's cells.

* * *

At night in the ship all sounds seemed to travel
farther, with fewer solid obstacles between them
and the receptive ear. The rumble of distant machinery. Click of transfer switches. The hiss and
whisper of breath.

Kayla lay awake on her hard cot, listening. She

heard Gerdred's faint snoring but, even fainter and yet more piercing, came the sound of sobbing nearby.

Go ahead and weep, wherever you are, she thought. It surely wouldn't be the first time someone has cried the night away in a place like this.

But some instinct told her that it was Shotay crying in the dark. Kayla sent out a tiny tendril of nearsense and found the girl. Sure enough, she was curled up on her cot, weeping herself to sleep. She cried as though she would never stop. The sound bored a burning path right into Kayla's soul.

—*Shhh,* she thought at her. —*Calm, shhh.* She crept through the girl's mind, binding her panicked and turbulent thoughts with shadowsense.

The sobbing faltered, ceased.

—*Sleep.*

As the girl drifted off, Kayla tried to probe deeper, searching for the essential information she wanted—the location of the Mindstar. But the mindsalt had so jumbled Shotay's brain that all Kayla could read were hazy fragmentary images, elusive and maddening. Something about them was familiar, so familiar, and yet so mysterious.

She thought suddenly of the strange hallucinations she had experienced earlier—the buzzing, the static, the thought fragments. Could it be the mindsalt that was responsible for them? Was the addiction so pervasive, so widespread that it was affecting the boundaries between minds, dissolving them so that breaching took place?

Unshielded thoughts from thousands of addicted minds, flooding the minds of any empath who listened.

The idea made Kayla shiver in fear.

To divert herself she began thinking of the man she had met at the end of the dinner—Cristobal. How striking he was! Such fine glossy black hair. Golden-skinned and charismatic, sure of himself. A senator, once. Powerful, accustomed to attention, accustomed to command. But something had gone wrong there, something named Pelleas Karlson.

She fell asleep and dreamed that she and Cristobal were running, hand in hand. Fleeing, with the brutal guard Mogul in hot pursuit. And Shotay danced gaily before them, casting twinkling stone flowers to the ground. They crushed them to powder beneath their feet.

Chapter Three

Only four days remained before the *Lovejoy* made rendezvous with Bryce Station, and Kayla had not yet managed to get the secret of the Mindstar from Shotay. It was maddening. How could she persuade the girl to confide in her? In desperation she cast about with her mindpowers, found the guard in charge of the women's cells, a blank-eyed, slack-jawed woman, and made her switch cell assignments so that she could become Shotay's cellmate. Gerdred scarcely looked up when Kayla moved out.

But even sharing a cell, Kayla found it difficult to get time alone with Shotay. Mogul's interest in the girl was accelerating. She returned to the cell hours past lockdown, weaving on her feet, too delirious from mindsalt to even notice there was another person there.

Three days left.

Two.

Morning.

Kayla awoke suddenly. Someone was touching

her arm. She threw off her covers, ready to defend herself. Seconds before her hands closed around her attacker's throat, her head cleared and she saw that it was Shotay who clung to her. The girl was struggling to remain upright.

"Sit down," Kayla said, pulling Shotay down onto the narrow bunk beside her. "You don't look good."

"Mogul." Despite her obvious weakness, Shotay whispered the name with enough vehemence to make it sound like the worst curse she knew. "He found out I kicked the mindsalt. Been making me drink it. He won't leave me alone." Her voice cracked and tears began to leak down her face.

"We'll report him."

"No use. It's not going to matter soon." Shotay's eyes seemed to focus directly on Kayla for the first time. "Katie, it's you. Good. Got to tell you about something. Something important." But before she could say more she began to wobble, her eyes rolled up, and she pitched forward.

Kayla caught her. "Hey, you're in bad shape. Maybe you should lie down."

"No." The grip on Kayla's wrist was desperate, punishing. How could there be so much strength in that small hand? "Got to tell you, tell somebody. You, Katie, because you said you would destroy it."

Kayla froze, scarcely daring to breathe for fear of distracting the girl.

"Everybody wanted it, didn't they? Asked and asked. Threatened. Drugged me, even. Stupid.

Nothing that anybody can do to me now that hasn't already been done before, and worse. I'm stronger than I look and I'm not afraid of pain. But what I've got to say I'll only tell once. To you, Katie. Only to you." Shotay nodded determinedly.

"Go on. Tell me, Shotay."

"Go to the Argentum Cluster. It's just beyond Corday's Star. There's a binary asteroid in the Cluster, doesn't have a name, you'll have to use your sensors. Find it. Land on the smaller twin. It's got a little gravity, not very much. There's a magnetic casket about the size of a cot. Scan for it and you'll see it. Reverse the magnetism on it to open the lock."

"Find what?" Kayla's heart beat so loudly she was afraid that the entire ship could hear it.

A wan smile lit Shotay's face. "The Mindstar, of course. That's what's in it. We put it there, Golias and I, before he died. Poor Golias. He was the one who really wanted it, and it killed him. Get it, Katie. Go get it."

"I will."

"But be careful. It eats souls."

"Don't be silly."

"Does. Got my brother's, and everybody's before us who tried to use it. 'S magic."

"Who's everybody?"

"Well, maybe not all of them. The first owner, rich lady, ran skeining satellites off Xenobe. She could handle it all right, but then she died, and it got stolen, and restolen, and everybody who's ever tried to own it and use it since then has gone crazy, killed themselves, or burned out their minds." Shotay shook her head. "It's so beautiful. You really can't believe it's evil." Her eyes glittered with tears. "Promise me you'll kill it, Katie. For me, for Golias. Promise." She was panting. Her skin was far too pale. She clutched feebly at Kayla. "Damn you, promise me! I'm dying!"

Kayla made soft reassuring noises while she probed the girl, trying to comfort her. What she found chilled her.

Gods, she's right.

Shotay *was* dying. Her vital forces were ebbing away, moment by moment. Before Kayla could say another word, Shotay fell back, motionless, in her arms, a faint smile on her face.

"Shotay? Girl, can you hear me?"

No response. Kayla felt for a pulse and found none. Leaned closer and searched for any sign of respiration. Nothing. Dead, really dead. Gently, she closed the staring eyes. "Sorry," she whispered. "I'm sorry." For what, she didn't know. Perhaps for all the ugliness that she had earlier glimpsed in Shotay's mind. Such a short lifetime in which to accumulate so much pain, so many tears.

She thought of Mogul and sorrow turned to rage. *You bastard. She died because of you. The mindsalt doses you gave her were too strong.*

For a moment the urge to avenge the girl's death burned in Kayla's mind. But no. She told herself that she had found out what she had come for.

There was little sense in fighting a dead girl's battle. It was time to leave while she still could. She sent a farsense probe winging up three levels to the bridge of the ship, casting for the mind of the communications officer. There. A touch of shadowsense, a signal sent, a pause, another received. That done, she withdrew.

All night she sat sleepless beside Shotay's body. At dawn she listened for the step in the hall, the keys in the door. Breakfast. Mind-numbing routine. She covered Shotay's body, ate, and joined the queue for the showers, all the while imagining the *Falstaff,* a tiny light getting closer, getting larger. In a few hours she would steal away, wait by an air lock, and . . .

"You. Where's your cellmate?" It was Mogul, his breath foul upon her.

"She's where you put her," Kayla said. "In hell."

His small dark eyes glinted, piglike, at her. "What are you talking about?"

"Look in our cell if you're so curious."

Mogul brandished his flashstick warningly. "Don't play games with me."

Kayla thought of Shotay's pitiful body, cold and still on her cot, and her control snapped. "Pig," she said. "She's dead. You killed her. Killed her with your damned drugs, you walking slimebag!"

Mogul backhanded her across the mouth.

She had expected the stick and the blow caught her by surprise, rocking her head back before she could catch herself. She licked her lips and tasted coppery blood. Her hands balled into fists.

"Bastard."

As Mogul drew back to hit her again, she grabbed at him with her mind. *—Die,* she thought. *—I'll crush your mind like a stale biscuit.* For once her mindpowers were steady, and she increased the pressure, clamping down hard on the trusty's mind. He gasped, turned pale. She squeezed tighter.

Mogul slumped slowly to the floor. His eyes were open, but they focused on no particular thing, no particular place. The flashstick rolled out of his nerveless hand and rattled across the aisle.

Kayla smiled.

All work in the laundry had ceased. The convicts were staring, round-eyed. Only Cristobal moved. He nudged Mogul with his foot and, when there was no response, shook his head. He turned to Kayla, took her arm, and said, "What happened? Katie, what did you do?" His eyes bored into her.

Kayla stared back and felt a sudden insane urge to tell him the truth.

A grinding noise drowned out her attempt to answer. It sounded as if the ship's engines were attempting to reverse, and failing. The floor beneath their feet seemed to shudder, and then the walls. Again, the grinding noise. Lights flickered and went out. Emergency beacons, yellow and harsh, lit the room. The inmates exchanged uneasy glances. "What's happening?" someone asked. "What's going on?"

Alarms set up a thin, high piercing wail. Kayla heard the sound of running feet, of shouting, and, somewhere far away, of screaming.

"An attack?" Cristobal said.

Evlin shook his head. "Some kind of systems failure, I think."

Kayla tried to probe the upper decks for information, but all she received was a confusing tumult. "I don't know either. Maybe the ship's been holed. Could be decompression, but I'm guessing. Whatever it is, it sounds bad."

A loudspeaker blared: "Secure quarters! Hull perforation! Secure quarters!"

Cristobal swore. "I thought these ships were all screened to avoid anything like this."

"Maybe they were all asleep on the bridge," Kayla said. She heard a steady crashing sound. "What's that?"

"Section doors, locking. To maintain pressure. We're stuck here."

"No!" Kayla cried. She had to get to an air lock. *The Falstaff* was coming.

"Standard procedure."

"I need to get out of here. You don't understand."

Cristobal bent down and pulled something off Mogul's belt. "The only thing I know right now is that we've got a ticket to freedom here and I intend to use it."

Kayla stared in wonder at the section key ring. "You mean a general jailbreak?"

"Absolutely. Are you with me?" Not pausing for her answer, Cristobal jumped atop a wash mech and held up his hands, jingling metal, shouting above the din. "Look, everybody! Look! Mogul's keys. This is our chance! We can take the bridge and get the hell out of here. Who's coming with me? Who wants their lives back?"

The inmates, every man and woman, gathered around him, their upturned faces drawn like moths to his light and heat, and shouted their approval.

"Me."

"I will."

"Screw the bastards, Cristobal. Let's get 'em!"

"Yeah!"

Cristobal turned to Kayla. "Well? Coming?"

"Do I have a choice?" She knelt and pulled Mogul's disruptor pistol from its holster. "Let's go."

The corridor outside the laundry was filled with noise and movement. It was pandemonium, prisoners fighting with guards, vid eyes being smashed. Everyone, it seemed, had had the same idea at once: Escape. But prisoners were turning on one another as well, fighting like crazed animals.

Kayla and Cristobal were swept up in surging bodies, pummeled, elbowed, slammed against one wall, shoved into another. Kayla heard Cristobal cry out, but there was no way to reach him. She ducked a ferocious blow from a wild-eyed old man, spun, kicked her way between two guards and darted toward a doorway. But someone had gotten there before her.

Two men had dragged a red-haired woman—officer? prisoner? it was impossible to tell—into the door's alcove and were pulling off what was left of her clothing.

Without thinking, Kayla fired a bolt from Mogul's disruptor over their heads.

They let go of the woman and fell back, the one on the left scrambling out of range. The woman crawled away, moaning. But the man on the right pulled a knife and, with a feral grimace, went for Kayla.

She fired at him point-blank.

He was airborne, flying up and away from her to crash noisily against the far wall and slide slowly down to the floor. Blood trickled from his mouth. He didn't move.

A blow landed squarely on Kayla's arm, knocking the disruptor to the floor. A guard, his eyes crazed with fear, raised his flashstick and started to swing it at her. Kayla ducked, brought her head up hard, and butted him in the chin. He sagged and went down.

Cristobal was just to her left, struggling with two men at once. "No, let go," he yelled at them. "You don't understand! We're on the same side in this."

Kayla swung around and kicked one of them in

the jaw. He fell to the floor and stayed there. The other punched wildly at Cristobal, who stepped easily aside and gave him a punishing blow to the gut.

"Stop it," Kayla shouted. "Stop the fighting!"

No one listened to her. Why should they? But she had to gain control, somehow, get some order. The *Falstaff* was coming. She could die in this melee unless she found a way to stop it. But her mindpowers alone weren't up to taking control of an entire ship.

Just take over this section.

Yes, that was it. A bit at a time. Breathing deeply, she summoned her internal resources—*come on!*—and wove a coercive nearsense field. Strand by strand, tiring work, but she dared not falter. *The* Falstaff, she thought. *Salome. Rab. Arsobades. Got to be ready.*

Kayla energized the field, and dropped it over the rioting inmates like an invisible net.

—*STOP!* she thought.

"Stop!" she cried.

The combatants fell back, bloody but quiet, the nearsense field dampening their aggression.

"If we're going to take the ship, let's do it together," Kayla shouted. "You, there!" She singled out a strapping woman. "Get together a group of the largest and strongest, fast, and follow me."

Cristobal gave her a swift look of approval. "Yes," he cried. "Who'll follow us to the bridge? Who'll come and take the ship with us?"

The prisoners voted with their feet, massing behind the two of them, a new and obedient army.

"Let's go!"

As they moved from level to level, ever more prisoners joined them. They fought through crowded hallways, stepped over the bodies of guards. By the time they reached the bridge, it seemed that every prisoner on the ship was pressing in behind Kayla and Cristobal, eager to follow.

The bridge, half-lit, was swarming with chaotic activity. An authoritative-looking, gray-haired man in a blue and gold uniform, obviously the captain, swung around angrily to face them. "What are you doing here? Get off my bridge!"

Before Kayla could stop him, Cristobal had pulled out a disruptor.

"Wait, Cristobal!" she shouted. "That's set for kill, not stun."

Cristobal fired once. The captain of the *Lovejoy* gasped and fell backward over his control console.

The first officer lunged at him and again Cristobal fired. The man sprawled across the deck, unmoving, dead.

Cristobal faced the rest of the bridge crew. "Join us," he said. "You've got one chance. If you don't, you'll be spaced in an escape pod."

A dark-haired woman gripped the com board, staring at her dead companions through widened eyes. "You're crazy," she said. "Murderer! You'll be caught."

Wild-eyed, Cristobal raised the disruptor and pointed it at her.

Kayla grabbed his arm. "Stop it. If you kill them all, we won't have anybody left who knows how to run this ship. We'll just hang here in space, helpless, and wait for the police to come get us. Is that what you really want?"

Cristobal stared at her. He started to say something, then slowly lowered the gun.

"Okay," Kayla said. She selected three intelligent-looking inmates. "You, you, and you. Here." She handed them disruptors, all set on stun. "Get over to those boards and watch everything that goes on. Any incoming messages, I want to know about them right away. Look sharp! And nothing, absolutely nothing gets sent out without my approval. We'll maintain com silence until I say otherwise."

The prisoners scurried to follow her orders.

"Well done," Cristobal said. "We're a great team."

"As long as I do most of the thinking," Kayla said. She turned to the com officer. "Get me an open channel to the rest of the ship."

The woman hesitated.

Kayla gave her a fiery look. "Do it."

The officer leaned over her board, pressed a button, and nodded. "You're on."

Kayla took a deep breath. "Attention," she said. "Everyone who can hear my voice. This is Kate Shadow. We've taken control of the ship. Repeat, the *Admiral Lovejoy* is in the hands of its inmates. Secure your sections, select a representative, and make your report to the bridge. I want a head count from each section, alive, dead, wounded." She paused as a thought occurred to her, and signaled to have the com board shut down. "What's the status of the clinic? We're bound to have casualties. Let's get some people down there to help out those medics."

Cristobal nodded and dispatched five inmates toward the lift at a run.

Kayla indicated with a gesture that she wanted the com officer to reestablish the open channel. "I want everybody to cooperate with the medics," she continued. "We have wounded people, and they'll need assistance. Get them to the clinic. And wait your turn. I want things orderly!"

"What about the corpses?" It was graceful Evlin, his face pale, his voice unusually deep. A smear of silver facepaint bisected his left cheek. "The dead. What do you want us to do with them?"

"Jettison the bodies," Cristobal said.

Evlin stared at him and his color began to rise. "And should we bother to even log their deaths or just shovel them out into the dark?"

Kayla cut in. "Log 'em."

Evlin's face softened. He gave her a grateful look and smiled slightly. "Then I'll do it."

"You?"

His eyes flashed. "Somebody's got to, yeah? So

I'll be your undertaker, Madame Shadow. I promised Shotay as much, anyway."

Kayla watched the wiry body move off and thought that she never would have credited silver-haired Evlin with having the guts for such a task.

The com board chimed to announce an incoming message. The com officer reached for her board, hesitated, and looked uncertainly at Kayla.

"Where's it coming from?" Kayla said.

"Internal."

"Answer it."

The woman tapped the keypad and leaned closer, adjusting her headset. "It's a casualty report from deck three, section five." Another light, another chime. "And one from deck two." The board began to light up, ringing constantly.

Kayla turned to a stocky man crowding her on the left, peering in obvious fascination at the board's blinking lights. "You. If you're so interested, you can help log those calls. Get over there and give me an hourly report." He blinked, then shuffled over next to the com officer.

A dark, heavyset man in a blue uniform strode toward Kayla, shouting as he came. "I don't care how many guns or men you have. You're still going to have to get that hull patched if you expect to survive."

Cristobal grabbed him by the shoulder. "Who the hell are you?"

"Meakins. Security."

"Can you do it?"

The man gave him a surly look. "Me? Not my line."

"I was a vacuum welder," a small woman volunteered. "Grew up on a low-g world. I think I can do it."

"Good. Take him along as an assistant." Cristobal shoved Meakins toward her. "He can show you where the equipment is. And take a couple of people as backup."

After the repairs, scenes of carnage had to be cleansed and bodies disposed of, so cleanup crews were assigned. Meals needed to be prepared and the surviving kitchen staff set to the task. Kayla knew that security was going to be a problem. Some of the more violent former prisoners might erupt at any time. She probed several inmates until she found people who seemed steady enough to assign the job of enforcing control.

Each task took another precious piece of her energy. Soon she was merely coping with whatever came at her. Planning was a luxury for sometime in the future. The *Falstaff* was a faint whisper in the back of her head, and sleep a barely remembered delight.

By evening she and Cristobal were in the captain's lounge with guards posted outside. She had never been so tired.

"Sit before you fall," Cristobal said. He pulled her down beside him on a wallseat. "Have you eaten anything? Here." He divided a portion of choba rolls and forced one into her mouth. "Chew this."

It tasted like the finest meal she had ever eaten. Kayla chewed greedily and reached for another roll. "What about the hull?" she said. Is it finished?"

"An hour ago. While you were checking the casualty list with Evlin."

"And the com board?"

"All quiet." He pulled her back against the cushions. "We can take five minutes. Relax."

She sighed, closed her eyes. When she opened them again, it was dark. There was another body against hers. Confused, she leaned over the face and tried to see. Who was it? Iger? Where was she? On the *Falstaff*?

No. No, the cloth of his tunic was thick, scratchy, and smelled of disinfectant. Iger had never worn anything like this. Now she remembered. Cristobal.

He stirred and pulled her closer. His lips, soft, warm, were on her cheek, her neck. A long-submerged part of her awoke, stretched, said yes, and Kayla moved deeper into Cristobal's embrace. Their tunics slid to the floor and time slowed around them as they explored the universe of touch. There was no need to think, no need or time for anything but sensation, the lovely feel of skin against skin, and the growing warmth at the center of her being that crested, exploded, and crested again. She didn't even know if she liked this man but right now she needed him, needed the scent of his skin, the strength of his hands, his lips upon her, and that was all that mattered. She would sort out the rest tomorrow.

* * *

When Kayla awoke, she was alone and a light was beeping on the wall console. The intercom.

She sat up, pressed the keypad. "What is it?"

"There's a message coming in, ship to ship." The voice belonged to the com officer. "I don't recognize the ID, it's not in any of our records. Looks like a light cruiser."

Kayla's spirits leaped. "I'll be right there." She smoothed back her hair, pulled on her tunic, and hurried out to the bridge. Leaning over the com officer's shoulder, she saw a familiar pattern on the board, the *Falstaff*'s com code.

"Acknowledge," she said eagerly. "And send this: Greetings from War Minstrel. Prepare to rendezvous."

Cristobal came up behind her, smiling, but the smile faded as he overheard her message. "What's this?" he said. "Do you know that ship?"

"Yes."

"Why are they here?"

"They've been following me," she said. "They're my friends. They've come to get me."

"What?" He stared at her with wounded eyes. "You can't just leave me with all of this."

"Cris, you'll do very well."

"No, no, no. It's all wrong. We have to continue, to get to the factory. You've got to stay with us at least until then. I can't hold it all together without you." His grip on her arm was firm, his look ferocious. "Katie!"

Kayla wanted desperately to get away from the claims he was making on her. The *Falstaff* was here. She had what she needed. Let Cristobal cope with this mutiny, these people. "No, Cris. I have to go."

"You can't."

"You can't stop me."

"No? Watch me." He released her, strode to the weapons board, and grabbed the shoulder of the officer sitting there. "Train all guns on any incoming craft. Fire as soon as they get into range."

"No!" Kayla cried.

Cristobal looked her squarely in the eye. "Then promise me that you'll stay," Cristobal said. "That you won't desert me, desert us."

Everyone on the bridge was watching them.

Kayla stared back at him and felt her blood lust rising. How dare he try to manipulate her like this! What if he was bluffing? She might be able to face him down. But if not, she would have to kill him.

And if she was forced to kill Cristobal, she might have an even bigger mess on her hands. Those rebels loyal to him would come after her, no mistake. During the melee, the officers on the

Lovejoy's bridge might be able to send out a distress call, alert authorities, call back the police squadrons. And the *Falstaff* might be fired on, her friends hurt. She was in trouble up to her neck.

"All right," she said, teeth gritted. "I'll stay, but only until the factory." She could already imagine the look on Salome's face as she explained to her that there'd been a slight change in their plans, a tiny prison revolt.

"Take those guns off them now."

Cristobal nodded. The weapons officer leaned forward and erased the code.

"Signal them that we're ready for docking and wait for their signal." *I'll settle with you later, Cristobal.* "What's our estimated time of arrival at Bryce Station?"

"Eighteen hours, forty minutes."

Evlin came up behind them. A gaudy silver cross was painted upon his face. "Repent, sinners," he said "Repent, while there's still time."

Cristobal frowned at him. "What's the new makeup about, Evlin?"

"I am become death," he intoned mysteriously. "Or is it death's bookkeeper? I get so confused." He grimaced, all teeth. "Care to make a little wager, Cris-old-man? Tell you a secret, though. The game's rigged. It's death's house, and the house always wins."

"You've gone around the bend, dancer. Counting bodies must have sent you over."

All trace of mockery and wildness drained from

Evlin's face and he gazed coldly at Cristobal. "You should know," he said. "Your Highness. I pray fervently to be delivered from this evil. *Your* evil."

'Stop it," Kayla said. "Both of you. Evlin, go get some sleep. Cristobal, find somebody to relieve him."

Cristobal's face darkened. "I don't take orders from you, Katie."

"And I don't have time to waste on your ego. Start using your head." She glared at him. "If you want my cooperation—without holding a gun to my head—then you'd better start thinking straight."

For a moment Cristobal returned her stare. His lips moved silently. Then he turned and stomped out of the room.

"Watch him, boss lady," Evlin said softly. "His Majesty wants to think, but with your head. Soon he might try to make speeches with your mouth."

"Shut up, Evlin. Get some bunk time. I mean it."

He gave her a lavish mocking salute with many flourishes and left.

The *Falstaff* was a miniature sun in the viewscreen, growing steadily larger and larger until it was well within docking range. Kayla watched as a shuttle pod detached from the ship and, with maddening slowness, moved across the space between the two vessels.

The sight of Rab and Salome, of Iger and Arsobades on the *Lovejoy*'s bridge, brought a lump to Kayla's throat. But it was evident that her former shipmates didn't completely share her emotion.

Salome gazed sourly around the bridge for a moment and then said, voice sharp, "Katie, just what in nine hells is going on here?"

Several inmates frowned at the tone of her voice and moved closer menacingly. Rab bristled, but Salome could recognize a threat when she saw one. Amber eyes wide, she took a step back and said, "Can we talk somewhere? Alone?"

"Follow me." Kayla led them into a small meeting room off the main room and locked the door. "Sit down. I am VERY glad to see you. All of you." She nodded in Iger's direction but avoided his glance although she could see that he was eager for a reunion. *Not yet,* she thought. *I've got too much to deal with here right now.*

"What is all this?" Rab said. "Why are you in charge of this ship, Katie? How'd you get free? Where's the captain?"

"Dead."

"Dead? How did he get dead?" Rab sat back against the cushions, obviously baffled.

"It's a long story."

"So start telling."

In terse sentences Kayla explained the situation aboard the *Lovejoy*—the meteorites, the riot, the killings, and the mutiny. "All I want to do is get out of here, but I can't. Not yet. Not until we reach Bryce Station."

"The orbital factory?"

"Yeah. That was our destination before, and Cristobal wants to land there. We can leave the *Lovejoy* once we're there. But if I try to leave before that, there'll be a riot and we might all get killed."

"I see. What happens after Bryce Station?" Salome said.

Kayla took a deep breath and smiled.

"Simple. We'll go after the Mindstar."

Chapter Four

Bryce Station loomed, a central domed multilevel satellite with sixteen dependent pods cantilevered around it on vanes, circling the parent structure like tiny moons. Yellow and blue lights blinked along the vanes. A small fleet of ships was grouped like pups along the curve of one pod. Behind the station Kayla glimpsed the misty star-laden petals of a far-off galaxy.

She watched the station grow larger as they neared it, and her sense of anticipation grew with it.

Her old friends had agreed to play along until they reached the orbital factory, and the *Falstaff* was keeping pace with the *Lovejoy*, an odd minuet of massive cruiser and tiny light ship moving in tandem.

Cristobal came up beside her and peered down at the screen. "Do we know which of those vanes is the station's main communications center?"

The com officer pointed. "Lowest on the starboard, number three, just coming into view."

"Knock it out with our laser cannon."

The officer in charge of armaments turned, startled, to stare at him.

"Cris," Kayla said. "What are you doing?"

"We don't want them warning anybody. Hit that vane, hit it now!"

The officer shrugged and pressed his hand against the keypad. "Armed and ready. Target has been sited."

"Fire!"

"But—"

"I said fire!"

"Firing."

White flowers blossomed all along the length of the station's com vane. They spread, mingled, dispersed, and the vane was gone. The pod itself had gone dark. But apparently Cristobal wasn't finished yet.

"Have you got a fix on their defenses?" he said.

"Affirmative."

"Fire when ready."

Again flowers bloomed in space.

"Now give them a ship-to-station message," Cristobal said. "We demand immediate surrender."

The com officer leaned over her board, listened closely, and said, "They refuse."

"Put it on repeat. If they haven't capitulated in fifteen minutes, destroy the rest of the outer pods."

"No!" Kayla grabbed his arm. "You've already gone too far. What good is crippling the factory and killing half the people on it? They're mostly prisoners and debt laborers."

"If the survivors join us, then it's worth it."

"Join us? What are you saying?"

"It's war, Katie. War against Pelleas Karlson. And we're building an army."

His words hit her with the force of physical blows. *War against Pelleas Karlson.*

An army to throw against Karlson, and his lieutenant, Yates Keller. Against *her* enemies. It made a crazy kind of sense, the longer she thought about it. Yes, take three hundred prisoners, add a space station's worth of forced laborers. Free them, arm them, and point them in any direction that you desire. Take that, Karlson. And that, Keller!

Yes. They could do it, really do it. What did it matter what Cristobal's motives were? He needed her help. And under her direction the army could march on Vardalia and bring Karlson to his knees. Later, the Mindstar would consolidate her control. She could take her revenge in spades.

Kayla threw her arms around Cristobal's neck. "You know what you are?" she said. "A genius. Pure genius."

She ignored a strange, throbbing pressure building up between her shoulder blades, moving up her spine.

Cristobal pulled her closer into the embrace. "Haven't I been trying to tell you that?"

Someone cleared his throat noisily behind them.

Kayla spun to see Iger standing, staring at

her. His eyes were hard and glittering, his hands balled into fists. Third Child stood beside him.

"Iger!"

A steady, pounding force was pressing against Kayla's eyeballs, but she fought it back, tried desperately to clear her head, to think. Static was forcing its way behind her eyes. Fragments of words were buzzing, pulsing in her mind.

"Why haven't you come back to the *Falstaff*?" Iger said quietly. "Why haven't you talked to me? What's happening to you?"

Kayla started to answer, to try to explain. But a wall of fog was flowing between her and Iger, between her and everybody. Dense, impenetrable, composed of tiny thoughts, a web of them, enfolding and trapping her.

—*Blood, wash our hands in blood, never enough blood.*

—*Make it stop, Mommy.*

—*Ginso took my knife. I'll kill him for it, later.*

—*I'm so hungry. I'm so hungry and frightened.*

—*Mommy, make it stop, please.*

—*When the roaring ends, I'll wake up, wake up, wake up . . .*

—*Going home to do it right this time. No more mistakes.*

—*MAKE IT STOP, MOMMY! GODDAMN STUPID BITCH! STOP!*

Some of them prayed, some screamed, some were mindlessly cheerful, others sobbed incoherently. And behind them all was darkness.

* * *

"Katie! Katie, can you hear me?"

Someone was calling her, long syllables trolling for her, wiggling in the air above her head.

"Leave me 'lone," Kayla muttered, swimming deeper. Why wouldn't they let her be?

"Katie, sit up."

An arm went around her back and the pressure of a hand forced her head up. She opened her eyes to a tanned face, blue eyes. Iger. Good, strong, dependable Iger, who wouldn't know the first thing about prison and darkness and dying girls crying in the night.

"Hi," she said.

"What happened? You collapsed like somebody hit you from behind. And another thing, who's that son of a bitch you were hugging?"

Kayla's eyes closed. She struggled in vain to remain conscious. But she was going under again.

Sleep. Take another deep breath and go back under the surface where no one can find you. . . .

Someone was shaking her. "Katie, come out of it! I know you can hear me."

"Yes," said another voice, a soft contralto. At the sound of it, Kayla came awake.

Salome. Kayla looked up as the *Falstaff*'s beautiful dark-skinned captain leaned over her, golden hair cascading.

"Katie," Salome said. "This thing has taken its

toll on you. It's time for you to wake up and give up this ship, this rebellion, all this scheming. Let's get out of here before the police arrive, or you collapse for good."

"I can't," Kayla said. She was still a little foggy. "I promised I'd stay."

"What?"

"You're sick," Iger said. "This whole crazy scheme has sent you bonkers. Prison ships. Mindstars. Rebellions."

"No." Katie shrugged him off, ignoring his hurt look. "I'm all right. You're the one who's wrong, Iger. Don't you see? We've got an entire army here."

Rab loomed behind Salome, frowning. "An army? What do we need one for? What the hell do we need any of this for?"

Oh, why were they so blind? "It's exactly what we need. Rab, we can't keep sneaking around hiding and picking at Karlson's leavings. We'll starve. We *are* starving. This is the only way. To confront that bastard and finish him."

"You've been spending too much time listening to your friend Cristobal."

"Cristobal," Iger said. "Who is he, anyway."

Salome nodded. "Yes, and can we trust him?"

Kayla hesitated only a moment before replying. "I think we can trust him. He was once a senator. Karlson finished him, sent him to jail. He lost everything and now he wants revenge."

"So let him take it," Iger said. "Why does he need your company?"

"Yeah," Rab said. "I still don't see what it's got to do with any of us."

Kayla wanted to shake him, shake each of them. Why wouldn't they listen? Fuming, she got to her feet. "His cause helps ours. Wake up! People all over the galaxy are sick to death of Karlson and his rules and regulations. He's strangling trade, killing all of us. Let's stop him now. We've got the means and the momentum."

"No," Arsobades said. "This isn't our fight, Katie. Salome let you go out on this crazy scheme, and you got what you wanted. Okay, fine. That's the end of it, then, and consider yourself lucky to still have your skin intact. I say we leave now. You've delivered the ship to the factory. That's the end of it. Nobody owes anybody anything any more."

"That's where you're wrong," said a loud voice from the doorway.

Cristobal stood there holding a disruptor rifle. Five burly men flanked him, armed in the same way. "I knew you were all in here plotting against me. Good thing I was smart enough to eavesdrop." He gestured with the rifle. His men moved forward to encircle the crew of the *Falstaff*. "Nobody is going anywhere. Katie stays here on the *Lovejoy* with us. If necessary, I'll keep you all as prisoners, or kill you. But I'd rather have your cooperation. Either way, Katie stays. We need her. *I* need her."

For a moment no one spoke.

Rab's face had darkened, and his eyes had a look that seemed to say he was willing to take on Cristobal and all of his men. Kayla had seen that look before, and she knew they were all seconds away from more bloodshed.

She caught Cristobal's eye and said softly, "Listen to me. This isn't the way. If you leave my friends out of this, then I might help you. Might." She reached for Cristobal's mind, tried to grasp it with hers, enclose it and quiet it. But her nearsense powers would not or could not cooperate.

Iger stood to face the group of armed men. Behind him, Rab got to his feet, and Arsobades with him.

The tension in the room was hair-trigger. Kayla was frozen. Her head was throbbing. But nearby there was a sudden blurring motion. A thin green line flashed from the gun's muzzle, and a man to Kayla's right went down gasping with pain. Arsobades.

"No!" She knew that Cristobal would just as soon have all her friends dead, anyone who might come between him and what he wanted. She had to stop him.

"You crazy bastard!" Rab started to move toward Cristobal. The rebel leader's gun came up, but before he could fire, Kayla threw herself between him and her towering crewmate. "You'll have to shoot me first, Cris."

"Katie, get out of the way."

"No."

She stared at him, thinking that she would kill him if she could. The mind clamp—if only her mindpowers were more reliable, she would use it to knock Cristobal out of commission, and she wouldn't half care if she killed him in the process. Might even enjoy it.

Cristobal glared at her.

"It's got to stop," she said. "Put your gun down. Or else shoot me."

For a moment longer their eyes met in silent anger. Then Cristobal scowled, holstered his weapon, and gestured for the rest to do the same. "All right. Whatever you want."

But Kayla wasn't listening. She and Salome were bending over Arsobades who lay moaning on the ground. "We need medics on the double!"

"Will you stay and help me?" Cristobal said.

"You son of a bitch," Rab said. "I ought to tear your head off."

"I—"

A heavyset gray-haired woman in prison drab raced into the room and gasped, "Message coming in from the station. They're giving up!"

"Put it on audio," Kayla said.

"—repeat. We agree to your terms, *Lovejoy*. Cease hostilities. The landing bay in pod seven is open."

* * *

Bryce Station's main dome was riddled with old fractures untidily covered by a constellation of round stasis patches. Kayla stared up through the yellowed circles at the blurry light of distant stars.

"What a dump," Rab said sourly. "Just how old is this place anyway?"

"One of the first of the orbitals," Cristobal said. "Probably should have been scrapped years ago. But Karlson finds it useful to let people work off their debts here, and as long as he thinks it's useful, we'll use it."

"It's the ass-end of the Alliance."

"What better place to stow his prisons?" Cristobal said. "Or prisoners?"

"We want a general assembly," Kayla told the sweating official who had met them. "Everybody on-station, right away. How long will it take?"

"Half an hour."

"Make it less." She watched as the man hurried away. "The sooner we can eyeball everybody, the sooner we'll know what we're up against here."

She thought of Arsobades, asleep in the Lovejoy's sick bay, his injured shoulder plasmed and set. The rest of the *Falstaff*'s crew had accompanied her to the station.

Within twenty minutes, all Bryce Station personnel—residents, crew, and inmates—had been assembled in the auditorium. They filled the hall to near-crush capacity, murmuring, nervous, restive. Thin, hungry, overworked folk in worn and faded clothing too large for them. A roomful of frightened faces.

And why not? Kayla thought. *We fired upon them, knocked out their defenses and communications, demanded their surrender. They know they're helpless and isolated.*

"You have a simple choice," Cristobal said. "You can join us, or you can die."

No one stirred, no one blinked. A sea of faces were upturned, every eye upon Cristobal and wide with fear.

"We're moving against Karlson," Cristobal said. "Come with us."

That isn't going to do it, Kayla thought, *not at all. We want their hearts, not their anger. Their hope, not their fear.* She stepped up beside him. "Karlson took away our livelihoods," she said. "He made it impossible for us to earn honest wages, and then he imprisoned us." She looked from face to face, staring at them, reaching out to them with nearsense, making them feel her sadness, her scars. "He took our lives and then he took our dreams. Let's take them back. Join us."

"He destroyed our hopes, and those of our children," Cristobal said, smoothly picking up the thread. His voice was deep and mellow as he warmed to the task of recruitment. "This is your last chance, your only chance, to change things, to grab hope, to live. Join us. We saved others like you."

"There are a thousand of us ready, with more on the way," Kayla lied. "Soon no Alliance force will be able to stop us. We'll walk right into Vardalia, right up to the Crystal Palace, and in. Imagine it! Don't you want to see that day? Don't you want to be there with us?"

As she spoke, she noticed a slight movement beside her. Cristobal had jumped as though an electric shock had gone right through him. He was staring fixedly at a man near the front of the room, a tall thin man with bristling ginger-colored hair and a wispy beard, who was glaring back at him. Their gazes locked for along moment. Then Cristobal looked away.

She wondered what that was about. But there was no time to pay attention to it now.

"Join us," she said. "I know what you've been through. I've been there, too. I've made mistakes and suffered for them. But does that have to be a life sentence? Come with us. Save yourselves. Re-make your lives. . . ."

Before she could finish her appeal, members of the audience began to stir. Murmurs turned into shouts, and every voice, every word, was a re-sounding, "Yes, yes we will join you, yes we hate Karlson, yes, we want revenge, yes, yes, yes." People were on their feet, stamping, clapping, screaming.

"We did it," Kayla murmured to Cristobal. "We've got our army."

He nodded and smiled weakly. But he seemed strangely subdued, and before Kayla could say another word, he again glanced uneasily at the man in the audience and rushed from the stage. What in the galaxy was bothering him now?

Rab, Salome, and Iger clustered around her, watching the uproar in the hall with outright amazement.

"You really got them," Salome said. "I can't believe it, but you grabbed their hearts."

Rab surveyed the scene with a jaundiced eye. "Congratulations, I guess. You've certainly gotten what you wanted—why exactly you want it is beyond me."

"Nice performance," said Iger, nodding. "What are you going to call your army?"

Kayla thought for a moment and smiled. "The War Minstrels," she replied.

"What kind of name is that?" Rab said.

"In Arsobades' honor. We'll be the War Minstrels."

Chapter Five

A core group quickly formed around Kayla, Cristobal, and the *Falstaff* crew: lean, coppery-skinned Oscar Valdez, who could plot course and mine asteroids; heavy-muscled Mepal Tarlinger, good at security and guarding backs; graceful and elusive silver-haired Evlin; and shy, diffident Martin Naseka of the blue-black hair, an engineering genius.

The first test of the newly assembled War Minstrels came sooner than any of them might have expected. Whether by coincidence or because someone had gotten the alarm out, an Alliance police cruiser was detected within half a jump of Bryce Station. Kayla and Cristobal watched the progress of the ship on the viewscreen, a small flickering point of light, moving infinitesimally closer, but moving just the same.

Kayla started to attempt a farsense scan of the ship. Then she remembered that her powers would no longer reach that far, and hadn't, not for years, not since her defeat of Pelleas Karlson's groupmind, back in Vardalia. That seemed ages— centuries—ago.

Rab strode in and peered over their shoulders. "What in nine hells is that?" he asked, watching the small light on the screen grow larger.

"Alliance troopers," Kayla said. "A cruiser moving in our direction. In a hurry."

Rab swore. "Bloody swell. Salome, we're getting out of here. Now. Call the clinic and tell Arsobades to hustle. You coming, Katie?"

"No!" Cristobal cried. "You can't just walk out on us. We need you!"

"Leave him alone," Kayla said. "He can do as he pleases. They all can."

Cristobal's face turned red, contorting with rage. For a moment Kayla feared that she would have to have him physically restrained. But just as quickly he seemed to recover his equilibrium. His face calmed, cleared.

"All right," he said bitterly. "Whatever you want. But you'd better leave now if you're going."

"Katie," Salome said. "Come with us."

Kayla felt torn in two. She wanted to be gone from this place, to leave with her friends and go pursue the Mindstar. The last thing she wanted to do was face a squad of Alliance troopers. But she had a responsibility to these people she had swayed. She had helped to lead them here, to convert others to the cause. How could she desert them?

And without them she would never achieve the revenge she wanted. Wanted desperately.

"Salome," she said. "You get the *Falstaff* to safety. I'll take the *Lovejoy* and intercept them. At the very least, we can draw off their fire. Cris, you'd better start somebody working on repairing the station's defenses."

"Good idea," he said. "Martin, take some people and see what you can do up there."

"Right." The heavyset engineer beamed, shouldered his way through the group, and headed out the door.

"Where's Oscar Valdez?" Kayla wanted to know. "He's our best pilot."

"On the *Lovejoy*."

"Tell him I'm on my way." Kayla turned to go.

"I'll come with you," Iger said. Beside him, Third Child bleated plaintively, as if the dalkoi were casting her vote with his.

Kayla hadn't expected that, but it warmed her to have them by her side, facing the threat with her. She flashed a quick smile. "Thanks. C'mon, we'd better get moving."

They pounded over the rubbery tube into the *Lovejoy*'s air lock and up to the bridge.

A skeleton crew had been left in place to keep the ship running, and a group of former inmates to keep watch that nobody sabotaged the systems.

Oscar Valdez was sitting at the navboard. He looked at her, his coppery face impassive. But there was an expectant twinkle in his dark eyes.

"We're leaving dock," Kayla announced. "I want full shields and I want them now. We've got to intercept that damned police ship."

Valdez nodded, his hands flying over the navboard, plotting their course. The rest of the crew moved swiftly to follow her orders. It seemed natural to her to sit in the captain's chair. Iger found the First Officer's slot, and Third Child stood beside him, grasping the chair with one of her feet.

Slowly, maddeningly slowly, the huge ship pulled away from Bryce Station, came about, and put out into the darkness to face the enemy.

Hurry, Kayla thought. *Hurry!*

"Oscar, can't we move any faster?"

"Not at subjump speeds, in-system," he said.

"Get every one of our lasers trained on that cruiser," she said. "Iger, monitor its every movement and keep those lasers tracking it."

"They'll notice we're armed."

"Let them notice. They haven't identified themselves yet. Until they do, officially, for all we know, they're pirates." Kayla spun to face the com officer. "Tell me as soon as they contact us. But make no response."

"Aye."

The *Lovejoy* drove deeper into space, engines purring. Behind them the small speck of light that was the *Falstaff* orbited out and away from Bryce Station and vanished behind a red/orange gas giant at the edge of the system.

"Katie," Oscar said. "We're closing with the Alliance cruiser now."

"We're receiving a signal from them," Iger reported.

"Put it on audio."

"*Admiral Lovejoy*, acknowledge. This is the *Devon*, First Officer Lieutenant Commander Schmidt. Acknowledge, *Lovejoy*."

Kayla turned to the com officer, Nelli Chow. "Do it, and no tricks."

Chow glared back at her but complied. "*Lovejoy* acknowledging," she said. "Com Officer Nelli Chow here."

"Chow, why the hell didn't you answer our first signal an hour ago? Are you looking for a torpedo up the rear?"

Damnit, Kayla thought. There'd been no report of a previous signal. Was Chow trying to sabotage her? Kayla leaned over. "Tell them we've been having communications difficulties after passing through an ion storm. Iger, keep an eye on her. If she makes one move out of line, shoot her."

Chow cast a rebellious glance in Kayla's direction but complied.

"Ion storm?" said Lieutenant Commander Schmidt. "We show no record of one."

"Ignore that," Kayla snapped. "Ask him what they're doing here and what they want."

"*Devon*, are you here on a routine mission or some special assignment?"

"Routine. We were told to rendezvous with you

at or near these coordinates. Do you require escort, *Lovejoy?* We note that your lasers are fully armed."

On the bridge no one moved.

Slowly Kayla shook her head.

"Negative," Nelli Chow said.

"Then why haven't you deactivated them?"

"Tell him it's a malfunction. We'll have it fixed at Bryce Station."

Chow did so.

"We'll have to report those lasers, *Lovejoy.*"

Kayla shrugged. "He can do whatever it is he damned well pleases."

"Understood," Nelli Chow said.

"Then we're turning back for Vardalia, and I don't mind saying we're looking forward to getting home."

"Safe trip, *Devon.*"

"*Devon* out."

Kayla drew a hand across her throat, signaling to Chow to cut the com board. "Thank the gods and get us back to the station pronto."

"Incoming signal," Chow said.

"From the *Devon?*"

"No, another ship. A light cruiser. *Falstaff.*"

"What is it?"

Salome's voice suddenly filtered onto the *Lovejoy's* bridge, reedy and thin. "Katie, there's a bad situation developing on-station."

Kayla stared at Chow. "Can the *Devon* read that?"

"No, they're out of range," the comm officer replied. "We're barely picking it up. I've already boosted our receptors." She flicked on audio once again. "*Falstaff*, can you strengthen your signal?"

"Negative."

"Salome," Kayla said. "What's happening?"

The captain of the *Falstaff* appeared onscreen, golden hair flowing over her shoulders. Her amber-colored eyes were fixed in a hard glare. "We've been monitoring the station. You'd better get back there, fast, and I mean *fast*. It's that fool, Cristobal. He's started to kill people."

* * *

The station was indeed in chaos. People were swirling through the fly-specked corridors, running frantically from doorway to doorway, everybody searching for something that might be a safe hiding places. Kayla grabbed at a running man. "Have you seen Cristobal? Where is he?"

The man stuttered, pulled away, and was gone.

Kayla raised her voice above the din. "Has anyone seen Cristobal?"

"The assembly hall," a woman shouted. "Don't go in there. Anybody who does gets killed."

"We'll see about that." Kayla reached for the disruptor which she now routinely wore at her belt. "Iger, you'd better get yours out, too."

"If that son of a bitch waves a gun anywhere near us, I'm going to kill him." Iger's quiet voice contained real vehemence. "And it'll be a pleasure."

Kayla stared at him in surprise. "Kill him? That doesn't make any sense. We'll stun him."

"Look, Katie, just because he's your new lover, you can't treat me like some old dog. . . ."

"Iger, don't be an idiot! I'm not going to pretend that Cristobal and I didn't sleep together. But that's not important to me."

"Isn't it?" His blue eyes bored into her.

She wanted to slap his silly face. "You weren't there. You don't have any idea what that prison ship was like."

"Nobody told you to go."

"Iger, if you don't know what you mean to me by now, I'm not about to waste time—and lives—right now trying to explain it. Come on." Disgusted, Kayla turned and strode down the corridor.

The assembly hall was eerily quiet and dark. Only the stage was illuminated, and a very odd play was taking place thereupon. Cristobal was moving along a row of prisoners, questioning, prodding, pulling one or two from the line and handing them to guards. A pile of bodies was spread over one side of the stage.

"Hey!" Kayla shouted. "What's going on here?"

Cristobal spun around, his mouth open. "Katie. You dispensed with the police so quickly?"

"I convinced them that their presence wasn't needed." Kayla held the disruptor out where he could get a good look at it. "What the hell are you doing, Cris? Why are those people dead?"

"They were informers for Karlson's government. We couldn't afford to keep them alive. I'm almost finished here—only a few more to go." His voice was as neutral as though he had just ordered a cup of coffee.

Kayla glanced at Iger. He rolled his eyes.

"I see." Kayla said carefully. "And just how did you decide who was a mole and who wasn't?"

"Oh, I can tell."

She stepped onto the stage. "Then let me finish the job for you." She leveled her gun at Cristobal. "All of these people are innocent. I can tell."

Cristobal stared at her in obvious disbelief and anger. "Katie!"

She began to weave a coercive mindnet around him. —*Calm, calm.* But before she could finish it, the doors at the back of the room swung open and Mepal Tarlinger appeared, her beefy hand locked around the arm of the ginger-haired man whom Cristobal had stared at during the first all-station assembly.

"Here he is, Chief, just like you wanted."

"Kill him."

"No!" Kayla shouted.

The man shook off his captor and calmly faced them—and Cristobal—down. "So now you're murdering, Cris? Somehow I didn't expect that from you."

"Shut up, MacKenzie."

"You know each other?" Kayla said.

"Yes, Madame Bitch," MacKenzie said. "We served together in the Trade Congress. And fell together. But now, apparently, Cris prefers that I fall . . . separately."

"He's dangerous," Cristobal said, and a pleading note entered his voice. "Katie, we can't trust him."

But Kayla was watching something else—the way the other prisoners looked at the man named MacKenzie. There was something about him that compelled attention and respect. Obviously, there was bad blood—very bad—between him and Cristobal but, just as obviously, he was a leader who could help them marshal their troops. "We'll have to."

"But—"

"Let him go."

MacKenzie gave her a disdainful look. "I don't want your mercy."

"You're not getting it." Kayla tried to keep the irritation out of her voice but failed. Something about this man rubbed her the wrong way. Nevertheless, she trusted her instinct. MacKenzie, whatever his personality flaws, was somebody who could be useful. "I'm thinking of our move against Karlson. You can help us keep everybody in order. That's the only reason I won't let him slit your throat. And don't you forget it."

MacKenzie nodded thoughtfully. "At least there's somebody around here with brains."

"What do you happen to know about running a space fleet?" Kayla said.

"Nothing."

"Then I suggest you start learning. My friend Iger here will be glad to help you." She grabbed Cristobal's arm. "I want to get the *Falstaff* back here. They can help with fleet training. Get Oscar Valdez to begin checking the records on-station to see who else has pilot training."

"MacKenzie," Cristobal said. "One wrong move and I'll have you killed."

"Right." MacKenzie managed to drawl the word out until it sounded like an insult. His hazel eyes glowed. "If I don't see you first, Cris. You always were a little slow."

"Get going," Kayla snapped. "All of you clear out. Mepal, get those bodies out of here. And Cristobal, you and I are going to have a chat."

She drew him into the wings, away from the others, and waited until they were alone. "What is wrong with you? We didn't come here to kill people."

"Katie, listen . . ."

"No, you listen, Cris! I've agreed to stay and work with you to shape these people into an army. But I can't keep cleaning up after you. One more crazy move like this and I'm through with you, finished."

"You don't understand."

"I don't have to. You stay away from MacKenzie. And keep your goddamned gun in its holster."

Cristobal started to say something, then stopped, nodded, and walked away.

Kayla watched him go. He was too mercurial, too dangerous and unpredictable. She was going to have to have somebody keep tabs on him. Someone she could trust. Who? She ticked off down the list. No one from the *Falstaff*—Cristobal wouldn't let them near him. Not Mepal Tarlinger either. She was definitely under Cristobal's spell. Oscar Valdez? Lost in his star charts, he wouldn't know what she was talking about. Perhaps she could ask Martin Naseka . . . but there was one other.

Silver-haired Evlin, the androgynous dancer. Yes. Instinctively, she felt he was reliable, that they had a bond. Perhaps it had started when he had taken care of poor, lost Shotay. Whatever the reason, she knew that Evlin was the one.

She found him in the clinic, staring into a screen on which a column of orange numbers flickered.

Casualties.

No, she wouldn't think about that. Not right now.

"Evlin?"

"Boss lady."

"I wish you wouldn't call me that."

" 'S the truth, isn't it?" He spun in his seat and fixed his pale gray eyes upon her. His eye makeup was comparatively restrained, two green thunderbolts radiating from the edge of his eyes to his hairline.

Kayla beckoned him toward her. "Come for a walk. I want to talk to you."

He was out of his chair and beside her in a moment. "Lead on. What do you need?"

Grateful for his directness, Kayla launched into her dilemma. "I want you to do me a favor."

"You have but to ask and it is yours, milady."

They were in a secluded corridor, nobody around. Kayla pitched her voice low. "Evlin, I want you to keep an eye on Cristobal for me."

The corner of the dancer's mouth quirked as though he were amused. "And just what should I watch him for?"

"Anything like his performance today, killing people he suspects of spying."

"And if I see this behavior?" Evlin's pale eyes glittered strangely. "What then?"

"Come get me."

"What if you're not available?"

Kayla paused. How far could she trust this man? Her instincts told her he was good and steady despite his dramatic tendencies. But could she give him license to kill? She didn't really want to do that. "If I'm not around, find MacKenzie. Between the two of you you can probably subdue him."

"And what if we can't?" Evlin's strange eyes were fixed on her relentlessly.

Kayla took a deep breath. "All right," she said.

"Then shoot him. But only as a last resort. And then only to stun. So help me, Evlin, if you use this as an excuse to kill him, I'll send you for a space walk. One-way. I mean it."

The dancer clutched his chest in mock pain. "Oh, Katie! You don't trust me?"

"Yes. But only to a point."

He smiled, all pretense suddenly gone. "That's probably wise. You know why I was on the *Lovejoy?*"

Kayla shrugged. "I don't care."

"Murder, boss lady. I do know how to kill." His smile died and his gaze turned inward. "But I don't like it."

"Good. Neither do I. Remember that." So now she had her spy. It left a sour taste in her mouth. How soon, she wondered, would it be before she would need a full security escort of her own? Absently, she patted Evlin's arm and left him to stare after her down the long, empty hallway.

Chapter Six

They had two weeks of training at Bryce Station before the Alliance police cruiser *Devon* returned, its lasers fully armed and ready.

The newly repaired com system blasted Kayla out of a dead sleep. "Battle stations! Incoming warship. This is not a drill. Repeat. Not a drill. Red alert! Incoming Alliance warship. Assume battle stations!"

Half-awake, Kayla leaped from her bunk, pulled on her stretchsuit, and raced out the door. She nearly collided with Iger in the hallway.

"Who's running station defenses on this shift?" she demanded. "Cris?"

"No, MacKenzie."

"Mac? Alone? Let's get up there. He'll need help."

On the third level of the main station pod MacKenzie was the still center of a storm of activity. Nearly wrecked by the *Lovejoy,* the station defenses had been jury-rigged back together. Two laser decks had been rewired and were being run by trainees. A third was being worked upon by a feverish team. Iger checked the boards and nodded grimly.

"Looks good," he said. "Screens are at seventy-eight percent and holding."

MacKenzie gave him a sharp glance. "Can we handle a direct hit?"

"Probably."

"That's not good enough," Kayla said. "How much firepower do we have?"

"Ninety-five percent capacity."

"Good. How far away are they?"

"Half hour, tops, and closing fast."

"They're signaling us now," said a young woman with pale green eyes. "They say that they want to talk to the captain of the *Lovejoy.*"

"We won't be able to bluff them this time," Iger said. "We'll have to shoot."

"We're ready," MacKenzie said.

"How many fighter ships can we get out there?"

"I've got pilots scrambled for four of 'em," MacKenzie said. "I can call more."

"Have the rest stand by. But get those four launched."

"Right."

"Where's His Majesty?" MacKenzie said. His hazel eyes were full of challenge.

Kayla knew who Mackenzie meant, but she kept her tone neutral. "Who?"

"Cristobal."

"How should I know?"

"Just wondering." He gave her a sly glance. "Thought you two were thick."

Iger threw an angry look her way.

"Mac, why don't you keep your mind on that cruiser?" she said evenly. Gods, the man was annoying! "We're wide open here. Are those fighters launched yet?"

"They're off," Iger said. "Approaching the *Devon* fast. It's stopped dead."

From the *Devon* came the announcement: "Bryce Station, lack of audio response will be considered a direct threat and hostile act. The launch of armed fighters is a hostile act. This is your last warning."

Iger glanced up from the boards to gaze at Kayla. "Can they wreck the station?"

Kayla nodded grimly. "Remember what the *Lovejoy* did? And this is a fully armed warship. They've got enough firepower to level a small planet."

"Damn," he said. "We'd better hit them now."

"Agreed." MacKenzie leaned toward his com board. "All pilots, acknowledge. Fire upon the *Devon,* shoot to destroy. Repeat, shoot to destroy."

The acknowledgments came flooding in. And, as Kayla watched on the roomscreen, four silvery birds converged upon the *Devon.* Wherever they pecked along the ship's silvery hide, dozens of white flowers sprouted.

The Alliance ship returned fire, blasting at them with its laser cannon.

Two fighters went spinning away in fiery wreckage, trailing glowing fragments like tiny comets.

The remaining two ships cut across the warship's bow, dangerously close, and poured a white-hot stream of laser fire directly upon the *Devon's* bridge and engine room.

A massive explosive flash blazed on the screen, and a moment later a slow-moving yellow and orange cloud began to envelop the *Devon,* cloaking it from view. When it had dissipated, there was nothing left of the warship but pieces of twisted metal and plasteel dust.

"Gone." MacKenzie said, slapping his armrest in satisfaction. "Very nice shooting, boys and girls."

"Did they have time to get a message off?" Kayla said. "Anything to warn the Alliance?"

"No."

"Good. Scan the area and if there's nothing else out there we can step down to yellow alert until morning." Kayla looked around her at the exultant faces flushed with success and wondered why she didn't share their pleasure. "I'd like to know what brought the *Devon* back here." She paused, remembering Nelli Chow and her rebellious stance. "Get hold of the *Lovejoy's* com officer—I want to question her—and check the com log, too. I'd bet you anything that she called the *Devon* when she thought nobody was looking and told them to come back. Get somebody to relieve her until we know for sure."

* * *

Kayla's uneasiness seemed to be catching. Despite the successful defense of the station, it was a grim bunch of inner-circle War Minstrels who met soon after the *Devon*'s destruction to discuss the station's status. Kayla, Cristobal, MacKenzie, Oscar Valdez, Salome, Rab, Iger, and Arsobades stared across the table at one another, all of them sunken in gloom. All but Cristobal.

He glanced from face to face with obvious bewilderment. "Hey," he said. "What's wrong with all of you? We destroyed them, didn't we? They never even had a chance to send off a message."

Rab fixed him with the look he reserved for imbeciles. "I don't care if the *Devon* got a message out or not," he said. "The point is that somebody is going to come looking for that warship sooner or later. There's bound to be a record of its last reported course holding, aiming it right at Bryce Station."

Cristobal shrugged. "So we'll deal with them— whoever they are—when the time comes."

"*We* are not going to do anything," Rab said. He pointed a massive finger at Cristobal. "But I'd suggest that you move your army, Mister Revolutionary. Unless you want to be a sitting spaceduck for the next round of warships."

The com line beeped. "Message coming in. Several small ships off the lee side of the station.

Leader's name is Merrick. He's requesting a parley. Says he recognized the *Falstaff* and he wants to talk to Salome."

Salome's amber eyes grew huge. "Merrick the Blackbird? That Merrick?"

Kayla felt an odd twinge at the name. *Merrick the Blackbird*. The years peeled away, and she remembered a burly bounty hunter who had briefly caught her and tried to claim the price the Kellers had put on her head when she had run from Styx, her home world. "He's a spy," she snapped. "Probably working for Karlson. Let's blow him away before he gets any closer."

"Now who's paranoid?" Cristobal said.

"I know him."

"So do I," Salome said. "And I'm with Katie. He's bad news, and worse. I won't talk to him."

"Why don't we find out what he wants before we shoot him?" MacKenzie said, grinning tightly. "We can always shoot him later."

Cristobal nodded. "I hate to admit it, but you're making sense, Mac."

"Thanks a lot." MacKenzie managed to make it sound like an insult.

The two old enemies stared at one another, blood and thunder ready to erupt.

The com line beeped again. "Merrick on link three, awaiting response."

"I'll take it," Kayla said. "Merrick, this is Kate Shadow speaking."

A voice out of the distant past, deep and grating, boomed from the speaker as, on-screen, the dark and shaggy visage of Merrick appeared. "Nice to meet you, pretty lady. Who's in charge?"

"I am." Obviously, the old bounty hunter didn't recognize her. "You deal with me. What do you want? The last thing we need is bounty hunters. Or smugglers."

"How about space worthy ships and seasoned crews? Saw what you did to that warship. Liked it. Want to sign up."

"Isn't this a bit out of your line?"

A deep chuckle. "Anything is my line these days. Had a few deals go sour on me. Yates Keller, that filthy bastard, screwed me around and stuck me with dead shipments. Busted me, is what he did. Is Salome there? She'll know what I'm talking about. She knows business. If she's in this, I figure I should want in, too. Better than starving, right? And you look like you could use some help."

"Why should we trust you?"

The only answer was a long, loud guffaw.

"Are you offering to join up?"

"How much does it pay? I'm looking to be hired."

"Mercenaries," MacKenzie said disgustedly. "It's risky, but we need the numbers, God knows. And he's got ships. Those we need even more."

Kayla looked at the others. Everybody was nodding. "All right, Merrick," she said. "You're in. We'll discuss payment and brief you in the morning. We'll want a full accounting of all ships with you, personnel, armaments, and so on. In the meantime, maintain radio silence. Anything besides ship-to-ship will be seen as direct treason, and we'll blast you out of the sky without waiting for explanations."

"Gracious me, you are one tough lady."

"You better remember that. Bryce out." Kayla shut down the com link. "Well, that's a few more warm bodies. Provided we can trust him."

"That's a big if," said Arsobades.

"Let's get on with it," Kayla said. "What did we learn from the *Lovejoy*'s com log?"

Iger leaned toward her. "The log showed that a message had gone out. I've got Nelli Chow cooling her heels outside. Do you want to see her?"

"Bring her in."

Mepal Tarlinger led the dark-haired com officer into the room. Neither of them looked happy about it.

"Sit."

Nelli Chow took the chair in front of Kayla. Her dark eyes were hard with anger. "I've already told your female goon here that I didn't send any message. How many times do I have to repeat myself?"

"A message was sent to the *Devon*. We have proof."

"Maybe so, but not on my watch."

Kayla paused and glanced at the records. That much, at least, was true. "Who else has access to the board?"

Chow shrugged. "You can check the personnel records."

"Who?"

"Bera Bertold and Nate Dubrovnik, for starters. Look, we've already been through this. The message was sent during Nate's shift. Why aren't you bothering him instead of me?"

"We've already questioned him. He doesn't know anything about it."

"Maybe he's lying," Chow said. "Or maybe it wasn't sent from the com board, or even from the bridge. Did you ever stop to think of that? All you've got is a record of a signal. Sent from somewhere on that ship."

Damnit, Kayla thought. *The woman is right.* But was Nelli Chow telling *all* she knew? She tried to probe her but failed. That dead spot in her head, at the very center of her empathic powers, sat there like an uneven wall, suddenly cutting her skill in half when she least expected it. She had never been the same after Vardalia. Never. It was humiliating: the famous tripath Kayla Reed, struggling to make a simple nearsense probe and failing.

Some of her chagrin must have filtered through, because Chow smiled nastily and said, "You pirates have a little problem, don't you? Somebody sent a message, but you don't know how or why. And if you think that I'm going to help you find out, you can forget all about it. You can kill me the

same way you did my captain before I help you."
She crossed her arms defiantly in front of her.

"Get her out of here," Kayla said. "But don't let
her back on the *Lovejoy*. And keep her away from
those boards!"

She watched as Mepal hustled Chow out of the
room. *This is no good,* she thought. *We're becoming
the wardens, creating our own prison. Meanwhile,
we're no closer to our real targets, Karlson and
Keller.*

And I'm no closer to finding that Mindstar.

"Now listen to me," she said to the assembled
group. "We've got a spy loose somewhere, either
aboard the *Lovejoy* or on-station. Someone with
access to the bridge or with a hidden com board. I
want a sensor-scan. I want all incoming and out-
going communications monitored. Find him—or
her. Until we do, everything and everyone here is
at risk."

"How do you know?" Cristobal said.

"If you spent more time on operations and less
shooting people maybe you'd know," Iger said.

"Shut up, you!"

"Both of you shut up, will you?" Kayla snapped.
"I want to know how close we are to moving
against Vardalia."

"Vardalia? Are you crazy?" MacKenzie said.
"We've barely begun training. Half of the people
here don't know which end of a laser to shoot
with. It'll take us months."

"We don't have months. Rab is right. The Alliance will come looking for that warship. We've got to be ready."

MacKenzie's face reddened. "And if we send people out there without enough training—or support—they'll all die, and probably finish us as well."

"Yeah," Oscar Valdez said. "We barely know who we are, much less what we're doing."

"I think we need more people," Cristobal said. "Like that Merrick. We should recruit more from among the Free Traders." He eyed the *Falstaff*'s crew disdainfully. "I expected that you would handle that."

"I don't take orders from you," Salome said angrily. "I'm not even sure we should be here at all, Katie."

Kayla ignored the implication. She needed the *Falstaff*, needed Salome's cooperation, and more.

"We've got to have more ships," Cristobal said. "Many, many more. And firepower."

"We could probably detach some of the station defenses," Martin Naseka mused. "Maybe retrofit the fighters and the *Lovejoy*. Bring over some hardware."

"But you can't just advertise for revolutionaries," Arsobades said. "It would be like waving a bright red flag in front of the Alliance."

"The people who want to join will find us," said Cristobal. "I've no doubt of that. Once word spreads, our comrades will come running."

"And so will the police," Rab said. "How are we going to protect ourselves against moles?"

MacKenzie leaned closer. "Or defend ourselves against a bigger attack?"

Kayla felt her patience evaporate. "Why not worry about that when the time comes, okay? What I want is for us to double up on our training shifts right away. I want twice as many pilots available, and a plan of attack for approaching Vardalia. If necessary, send out two fighters to trader outposts and spread the word among the Free Traders. Rab, Arsobades, I'd appreciate it if you'd go with them."

She was about to say more, but suddenly a high, keening voice was slicing through the air like a laser, cutting off her concentration.

—Yes I did, yes I did, yes I did . . .

Damnit, that was annoying! Didn't anybody else hear it?

—Katydid, Katydid, Katydid . . .

Only Iger seemed to notice her discomfort. He leaned closer and put his hand on her shoulder. "What's wrong?"

"Don't you hear it?"

"Hear what?"

"That terrible sound? Like somebody tuning a mechlute the wrong way, singing nonsense words."

Arsobades was gazing at her, concern written across his ruddy, bearded face. "Are you going space-batty on us, Katie? I don't hear anything. And you know how good my hearing is."

Each of her friends and colleagues in turn confirmed what Arsobades had said. Yet that maddening sound was there. For her, anyway.

—*KATYDIDKATYDIDKATYDID*.

If anything, it was growing in intensity, vibrating through Kayla's skull down to the very roots of her teeth. The narrow green walls of the room seemed to be moving in and out with every pulse of her heart. The pounding noise in her head was getting louder, sharper. And she was cold, suddenly, terribly cold. Dizzy.

"I'm sorry," she said. "I can't—I have to go. We'll continue this later." She hurried from the room with Iger on her heels and Third Child right behind him

"Katie!"

—*KATIEKATIEKATIE*.

She clawed at him weakly. "Iger, leave me alone! I've got to get away from whatever it is." And as she pushed him away, she realized that the source of her problem was not in her ears, it was in her head.

Something was causing the thoughts of hundreds of people to ricochet through her consciousness, maddening her. She needed a mindshield.

Desperation gave her strength, but it was slow, sweaty work to construct one. *Concentrate,* she thought. *Come on, concentrate, damnit!*

It hurt to think. She grimaced as she pulled strength from deep inside herself and painstakingly fitted the shield together piece by piece.

Slowly it took form, an invisible dome within which all was safe, all was blessedly silent. *There.* Kayla leaned against the wall, weak with relief, sweat beading her forehead.

"What's happening? Katie, tell me!" Iger's arms came around her and she clung to him, resting her head on his shoulder. "Should I call a medic?"

The dalkoi chirped and prodded Kayla with one of her long-toed feet.

"It's gone," Kayla said. "Gods, that was the worst yet." She wiped her streaming eyes.

"You've heard it before?"

"Never quite like that. It's always been more like other people's thoughts at random, as if I were trolling through a crowd. The first time I heard it I just thought it was some sort of strange bleed-through."

"Bleed-through? You've never complained about anything like this before."

Kayla smiled weakly. "Look, Iger, you know I've never really been the same since we tangled with Karlson's groupmind on Vardalia. My powers are much weaker, more unreliable now. Something got burned out of me back there."

"Maybe so, but consider the benefits. At least you don't get jump sickness any more."

"I know. It's a fair trade. Or so I thought, until this started. But I'm having a harder time shielding people's thoughts out. Pieces of them keep breaking through."

"And you think that it's because there's something wrong with you?" His blue eyes were filled with concern.

"I don't know what it is." *And I'm scared. I'm scared and I don't know what it means.*

"I thought you said that what you heard this time was a noise, different than before."

"Yeah. But it had to be part of the same phenomenon. What else could it be? And, otherwise, my mindshield shouldn't have been able to cut it off."

"I don't know," Iger said. "But what if it isn't you, Katie? What if it's something that's happening somewhere outside and you just happen to hear it?"

"That's even more frightening." But he had given her something to think about. What if it were something outside? Something she had been looking for?

"C'mon," Iger said.

"Where are we going?"

"For once, don't ask questions. Just come."

He kept his arm around her as they walked through a dim corridor, around a bend, into an open doorway. A tube, hissing in descent. Rubber under their feet. A bright wall, painted with strange calligraphic shapes and portraits. Slogans. A woman with golden hair like candle flame rising above her perfect dark face, her coinlike golden eyes. Beneath that face, the legend: "The Mother of Us All." Salome.

The *Falstaff*. Good old ship. The familiar smell

of recycled air mingled with the tang of hydroponics. Home. Kayla took a deep, appreciative sniff of it.

She allowed herself to be led, like a child who was half asleep, to the room which she and Iger had once shared. He sat her down upon the bunk.

"Wait here."

Iger pressed a wall dispenser keypad and, moments later, handed her a cupful of steaming liquid.

"Drink."

She swallowed the fragrant stuff gratefully. "Choba tea. Gods, that's good. It's been so long since I had any."

Iger sat next to her, waiting patiently while she finished the cup. When she had wiped her mouth and tossed the cup into the recycler, he took her hand. Earnest blue eyes stared deeply into hers.

"Talk to me, Katie," he said. "I don't understand. What's happened to you? All these people, these ships. What's going on? What are you doing?"

She gazed at the familiar face and felt an aching sense of loss. He was loyal and he would follow her anywhere, but he didn't understand what drove her. Iger came from a family of bambera herders and a planet—Liage—to which he could return at any time. He had chosen to walk away from it. He was rich, so very rich, in his family, his choices. He could return, anytime. If only she had had the luxury of such a choice.

It was tempting to sit here on the *Falstaff,* safe

in Iger's embrace, and forget about everything else. It would be so easy to stay, to wait for her friends to return and just sail away with them. She couldn't let herself soften that much.

She sat up and away from him. "I've told you. You know why I went to that prison ship."

"It was a damned crazy move."

"Yeah? Well, I got what I wanted, didn't I? I got information on the Mindstar." *And thanks to what you said before, I've got an idea of how to home in on it.*

"Then let's go find it. Why are you bothering with all these people, this station, and that guy?"

Again she felt the void of understanding that separated them. "These people will be useful," she said sharply. "I'll need them after I find the Mindstar."

"Useful? For what? You don't really care about them or what happens to them."

"Oh, Iger, I don't know what I feel about them. Do I have to love them all? Haven't I given them something they want? Freed them? Don't they owe me some allegiance for that? I've helped them. Why shouldn't they help me?"

"But all they wanted were their lives back."

"That's all I want, too!"

"And you think that if you overthrow Pelleas Karlson and maybe kill Yates Keller that you'll get your old life back?" He stared at her in obvious disbelief. "That you can buy it back with this Mindstar or bring it back with guns? And after that, I suppose you'll try to bring your parents back to life, too, won't you? Wake up, Katie. You're dreaming."

"Bastard!" She swung at him, trying to slap the doubting look out of his eyes.

He ducked the blow and caught her hands in his. As she began to struggle, he pulled her down beside him on the soft bunk. "You don't want to hear the truth, Katie. Just like you don't want to know how I feel about you, or anything that distracts you from your cause. But sometimes even Kate N. Shadow has simply got to listen."

Despite her struggling, he pulled her closer and kissed her. Hard.

Kayla was even more infuriated by his kiss. How stupid was he, to think that any disagreement between them could be resolved by a kiss? As soon as she got free, she would smack some sense into that thick skull of his.

Iger kept kissing her.

She had forgotten how nice his lips were. Forgotten, too, how pleasant it was to lie beside him and feel his hands upon her, moving beneath her stretchsuit, bringing her back to him, to them, through touch. Nice, yes.

Maybe she wouldn't kill him right away.

She began to pull at his clothing, suddenly eager, ravenous to feel his skin against hers. Gods, it had been too long, too long since she had last been with him. Something in her cried out, desperate for release. *Hurry, touch me here, there, ev-*

erywhere. Was that her voice calling Iger's name, gasping as fiery waves crested through her again and again? *Don't stop,* she thought. *Don't ever stop.*

* * *

She awoke with Iger coiled around her, and Third Child at the foot of the bed. As she started to disentangle herself, Iger stirred, awoke, and clutched her tighter, murmuring, "Stay. Stay here."

"Can't. Wish I could, but there are people waiting for me." She half expected him to argue with her. Instead, he sighed and released her.

He sighed. "Go, then."

It was complete relinquishment and she knew it. Part of her yearned to turn and crawl back under the covers with him. But she forced herself to get up, dress, and walk toward the door.

"I'll see you later."

He gave no sign of hearing her. The dalkoi made an inquisitive chirp, rustled, and settled down once more.

Silently Kayla took her leave of the most familiar place she had known in years, the only home she had had since Styx.

I'll be back, she swore. *After the Mindstar, Iger. I'll come back to you, and the* Falstaff. *I promise.*

Chapter Seven

Kayla's boots echoed solidly against the floor of Dome E, the War Minstrels' new headquarters on Kemel. She could hear the cries of trainees, busy nearby in mock battle, and the hoarse shouts of Mac and Merrick the Blackbird, urging them on.

Their new home was an abandoned mining compound near the Bitter End, close enough to the major space lanes to attract new recruits from the edges of the Alliance—and any Free Traders who were traveling in the quadrant—but far enough from the center of things to avoid Alliance spies.

The mining camp provided camouflage, a place to house their troops, and space in which they could conduct training. Radar-reflective domes that had once housed mining mechs now gave shelter to a private army.

So the War Minstrels had abandoned Bryce Station and moved to a safer location. The transition had come about only after much discussion and consulation.

*   *   *

"We've got to move," Mac had said, his gingery hair waving about his head like sandy tentacles. "We're too exposed here, we're asking for trouble."

"Mac, you've been agitating around this for weeks," Kayla said. "I agree, Bryce Station is a poor hiding place—"

"The only place worse would be the plaza in front of Karlson's Crystal Palace," said Arsobades.

"—and if you'd let me finish, I'd say, okay, if you're so smart, then find us a better hideout."

Arsobades cocked an eyebrow at her. "Why hide at all? Why are we even here?"

Kayla ignored him. "We can't sit and wait for the Alliance to find us."

"What about Styx?" Rab asked. "I don't think anybody's using it right now. Just think, we'd have all those nice comfy tunnels to settle down in."

"Serious ideas!"

It had been Rab, finally, who remembered the deserted mining station on Kemel, and Salome who, with her connections, had cleared rights to use the place. Kayla had been pleased for several reasons. Foremost among them was that this new location took her closer to what she had determined was the Mindstar's hiding place.

The War Minstrels had packed up their guns and moved, a bumpy process as Kayla had quickly discovered. It would have been a whole lot easier to move a pod of hungry, curious dalkois through the capital city of St. Ilban at midday than to get a bunch of squabbling rebels with hair-trigger tempers to cooperate on anything, much less move quietly—and quickly—from one hideout to another.

* * *

Now, watching Merrick the Blackbird calling down changes on the War Minstrels' new pilots, Kayla was amused to see what a fierce trainer the bounty hunter had become. His experience was considerable and he shared information freely, training pilots in doubling-back, tipping wings, and other lifesaving maneuvers under fire. But it hadn't come easily.

The Blackbird had driven a hard bargain with them, damned hard, demanding escalating fees contingent upon their success. Finally, after considerable haggling, Merrick had agreed to work for a steep price, to be paid at some later time. Like most merchants, he had balked at delayed payment. But in the face of Kayla's stubbornness, he finally had gone along with it. He was no fool and knew that the War Minstrels were his best hope for the future. In the meantime, he would receive free meals.

Once Merrick had signed up, word must have gone forth, for Free Traders came flocking in from

all over, eager to join, pledging their ships, personnel, and firepower. Before Kayla had had half a
chance to look back, the War Minstrels' numbers
had swelled to over a thousand men and women,
and thirty-five ships with jump capacity.

"If only we could get ourselves twenty-five
more," MacKenzie said. "Twenty-five. Then I'd
feel better about taking on the Alliance troops."

"No matter how many we have, you'd still want
twenty-five more," Cristobal said. "We're ready to
go now."

"Soon," Kayla said. "Soon we will be."

* * *

Most nights, the Minstrels gathered in Dome C
to share home-brewed ale, sour wine, and tales of
their past. Once or twice a week Kayla attended
the party, more out of a sense of duty than actual
desire.

The crowd roared at her entrance.

"Katie! Come sit by me!"

"No, me!"

"I'm buying her drinks."

"You bought them last time!"

"Listen to this new song, Katie. I wrote it just
for you."

A bald man and his bald mate began to strum
twin mechlutes. Arsobades laid down a deep bass
rhythm behind them, and a fourth Minstrel, a thin
man with a high, sweet voice, began to sing:

"Katie saved us. Katie loves us. Katie, our dar-
   ling, our favorite, our own.
She killed seven men with her bare hands alone.
Took us from prison and led us to freedom,
Katie, our Katie
Our mother. Our home.
Give us a target, give us a quest,
Some way that we can return the favor.
Katie, who saved us. Katie, who loves us, who
   freed us,
Our darling, our leader, our own."

A great cheer went up, and cries for more, for
additional choruses, immediately.

Kayla forced herself to smile despite the thick
lump in her throat.

"Drinks all around, on me!" she said. The crowd
roared one more time.

But then the roaring faded as a strange, pulsing
beat began to overwhelm her. So it was happening
again. Her mind was flooded once more with fragments of words, of thoughts, although none of
them were intelligible, overriden by static. Was
this some sort of bleed-through from mindsalt addicts? What was going on? What was she hearing?

Before Kayla could even attempt to get a fix on
any of the thought fragments, they faded to silence. The roar of the room enfolded her once
more.

Rab loomed over her, a drink in his hand. "Why
so silent, Katie-my-dear? Dalkoi got your tongue?"

He hugged Salome against him, sloshing both her drink and his. "Who would have thought that our own Katie would become a famous jailbreaker? And that everything she knows she learned from us!" He and Salome raised their glasses in a toast, laughed, and wandered back into the crowd.

Who would have thought it indeed? Kayla mused. She watched Mac and Merrick sitting in a corner trading war stories. The two were like oil and water, and yet they were drawn toward one another.

An impromptu tattoo session had started up near the door; each War Minstrel in the room seemed eager to sport the sign of their movement, a black starburst, the Free Trade sigil. Even Cristobal was drunkenly submitting to a having small tattoo applied to the back of his right hand.

Arsobades began to strum familiar chords, gathering the Minstrels around him for a chorus of "Free Traders Living Free." They yelled out the song, then repeated it.

On the third time around, Kayla decided that she had had enough. She didn't want to sing or drink; she wanted to get moving, to find the Mindstar, to squash Yates Keller once and for all.

She was halfway out the door when she felt a hand gripping her arm.

"Want some company?"

Whipping around, she was about to tell the speaker where to get off when she saw who it was. Iger.

His blue eyes implored her. She could feel the ice inside melting. She smiled. Yes, yes, she wanted his company very badly. "Please," she said, and together they moved out into the night.

* * *

The next day, the inner circle of the War Minstrels held court in the mess room of Dome E, de facto center of operations in their new base. Now they sat around the wide table, Rab, Salome, Kayla, Cristobal, Iger, Evlin, Arsobades, and the rest, staring at their cups of cooling spice coffee. Evlin took a sip and pursed his lips in displeasure.

"I never thought I would grow nostalgic for prison food," he said. "But this stuff is nearly as rancid as what they served us on the *Lovejoy.*"

"The *Lovejoy*'s dining facilities are still available, you know," Rab said acidly. "If you don't like the grub here, then I suggest that you arrange for other accommodations. We're not running a restaurant."

"Maybe you can even get your cozy old cell back," Arsobades suggested. "We'd all be willing to put in a word for you with the management."

Evlin said nothing, merely gave the two of them an evil look from purple-shadowed eyes.

"Knock it off," Kayla said. "We've got work to do. I want to know if we can take Vardalia with what we've got. We know what our figures are.

What are theirs? How many ships? Orbital defenses? What will we be going up against?"

These were questions she asked herself constantly.

Her days were taken up by the hard facts of equipping and training an army. Drills. Arsenals. Tactics. Planning. Kayla found that she was better suited to the work than she had dreamed. MacKenzie and the others consulted her regularly, often seeking out her approval and opinion rather than Cristobal's.

"You're just easier to work with than he is, Oscar Valdez said. "You give a definitive answer."

"And you don't try to second-guess."

Privately Kayla agreed with their estimation of her coleader. But she didn't want to undermine him. Twice now, Evlin had warned her of extreme behavior on Cristobal's part, behavior which could have ended in violence and disarray of the growing army. In both instances, Kayla had managed to intervene in time. But sooner or later she would not be available at a crucial moment. Then what? Would Evlin—or MacKenzie—shoot Cristobal? And would that, in turn, start a riot, ending her quest before it had really begun?

I can't worry about everything, she thought. *The future will have to take care of itself.*

She was monitoring training maneuvers when she heard a grating mental mutter that she took to be the subvocalizations of the War Minstrels trainees. It took her a moment to realize that she did not so much hear thoughts per se as feel a certain compelling mental force, an emanation.

The Mindstar. Could it be? The strange mutterings and static? Were they emanating from that one source?

Her heart beat faster as she attempted to use the emanation itself, bearing down upon it to triangulate and find the Mindstar's location.

It was somewhere nearby. Kayla felt it in her blood, pounding double-time. It was a reverberation in her skull. She held tight to it, battling to sharpen her directional focus on it. And gradually she developed a sense of the emanation's actual point of origin.

Yes. Yes, the star maps merely confirmed what she had managed to work out. The asteroid cluster that Shotay had told her about, the one she had been searching for, that had been so maddeningly elusive, was indeed in this quadrant, at the far end. A fast cruiser could reach it in a few days.

Kayla's spirits soared. *The Mindstar!* She had to go, right away, this very instant. But whom could she confide in? If she paused to explain, Cristobal and the others would just try to stop her, delay her. They would argue endlessly, throw foolish obstacles in her way.

The only one who understood was Salome. The *Falstaff*'s beautiful dark-skinned captain had backed Kayla all along. Salome, yes.

Kayla found her in the *Falstaff*'s ops center, playing Transolitaire with the ship's knowbot.

"Salome," she said. "I'm leaving."

"It's about time." Salome blanked the game screen and turned to her with expectation in her amber eyes. "I'll get Rab and the others. What's our heading?"

"*We're* not going anywhere. I'm going. It's the Mindstar. I know where it is."

"Don't be silly, Katie—"

"I know where it is. Really."

"Really?"

"Yes," Katie said. "I have to go."

"Well, then, we'll all go."

"No. I can't take a whole crowd with me. I have to concentrate. No distractions."

"I see." Salome looked annoyed. "And what shall we do while you're off concentrating?"

"Ride herd on Cristobal. Don't let him kill anybody."

"Thanks a whole frigging lot."

"I mean it, Salome. He's a loose cannon. If I leave, I've got to know that someone I trust is keeping him in line."

"You can't expect him to listen to me."

"He will, though. Especially if he realizes it's the entire crew of the *Falstaff* that's talking. You, Rab, Arsobades, Iger, and me, *in absentia*."

"I don't like it, Katie. But I'll do it. And if you're not back in two weeks, I'll come looking for you."

"It's a deal." Kayla grabbed Salome in a quick hug that left both women flustered and embarrassed. "Gotta go."

She rushed from ops, thinking hard. She needed a ship, fast and maneuverable. But where? As she moved past the ship berthed next to the *Falstaff,* her eyes fell upon the *Antimony.* Sleek and spaceworthy, it was built to outrun a Trade Police squadron. Perfect. It had come in under Merrick's protection, captained by Vlad Karinovksy. A beautiful ship, and empty. Karinovsky and crew were running Merrick's *Blackbird* while he was training new recruits for the War Minstrels.

Kayla knew that she could pick the *Antimony*'s lock, override ops control, and have the ship up, running, and away from dock before anybody had a chance to sound the alarm. She could already feel the *Antimony* under her, cutting through space. . . .

"I'm coming with you, Katie."

It was Iger, blocking her way, and Third Child was at his side. Kayla felt the dalkoi attempt to make telepathic contact with her, but she brushed Third Child aside. She didn't have time for that, not now.

"No." She tried to slip around Iger, but he sidestepped neatly to cut her off.

"Katie, I heard what you told Salome. If you're going out on a wild goose chase, you'll need somebody to run the gun board at the very least."

Kayla bristled at his nervy assumptions. "Why were you eavesdropping on me? And just what makes you think I'll need help with defense?"

"You never know what—or who—you'll encounter out there. It's stupid to go it alone."

"No, Iger. Absolutely not."

"This isn't open to argument." He folded his arms in front of him. Kayla had never seen him look so determined.

"I don't care—"

"I'll knock you down and sit on you if I have to." Iger said it pleasantly but with steel in his voice. Third Child chirped, casting her vote with his.

"And," he continued, "if you try any mind tricks on me, I'll just come after you. I'll follow you, Katie. I swear it. You're not going alone."

Kayla opened her mouth to protest and surprised herself by saying, "All right. I can't stop you. But you'd better not slow me down."

"We're ready whenever you are."

"We?"

"Third Child is coming, too."

"Terrific. Anyone else?" She didn't wait for a reply. As she set off down the corridor Iger and Third Child were right behind her.

* * *

It was a quiet and careful group of three—two humans and a dalkoi—who crept down to the docks at midnight, pried open the latch on the *Antimony*'s air lock, and left dock without warning, all engines on full.

"We're pulling zero-g," Iger reported. "A nice, neat getaway."

The com board beeped frantically, and flashed angry patterns but Kayla ignored it. "They don't know who we are," she said. "Let's leave it that way. It's cozier."

"What if MacKenzie scrambles fighters to chase us?"

"He won't. I left him a message. Only he knows what's going on. He and Salome."

"Clever."

The worshipful tone in his voice irked her and she pulled a face at him. To her relief Iger began laughing. She didn't want him to become a distant admirer. She wanted him closer, able to argue with her, laugh at her, and even to occasionally threaten to knock her down and sit on her.

"Karinovsky will be fuming," Iger said. "I can just see the bloody look on his mug now."

"I'll make it up to him." Privately, she doubted it. The *Antimony*'s rightful captain was a stout, choleric man, as ugly as his ship was beautiful. He would never forgive Kayla for running off with his pride and joy. Well, she would worry about that later. Right now she had a course to plot.

"You have selected the shield option," announced a shrill mechanical female voice.

"What the hell is that?" Kayla said.

"The *Antimony*'s knowbot."

"It sounds like someone's crabby great-aunt."

Implacably, the 'bot droned on. "This ship is

equipped with multishield capacity. Please make your selection of partial, total, or multishields now."

"Can you cut that thing off?" Kayla said.

"Trying."

"Attempts to disconnect this circuit will not be successful," said the knowbot. "You must register your passcode to gain access to ship's logic. Repeat: You cannot disconnect this circuit. Please make your selection now."

"Damn." Iger punched a series of commands into the keypad. Still the 'bot lectured them. Suddenly the 'bot's voice jumped and there was an odd tone as though a spacebat's sonar had become audible. The knowbot cut off in mid-sentence.

"What'd you do?"

"Created a selective power surge that shorted out its speech circuits," Iger said. "We might be able to turn that thing on again if we need it."

"Nice. Let's hope that we won't need it." Kayla turned her attention back to her own screen and was happily lost in the star charts once more.

* * *

The *Antimony*'s passage did not go unnoticed. When Vlad Karinovsky found out that his prized possession had been taken, he invoked every curse he knew and gave orders for Merrick's *Blackbird* to trace the engine's trail and follow. Only Merrick's physical intervention—with Rab's help—had kept the maddened captain of the *Antimony* under a semblance of control.

"Goddamn you, Merrick, get off of me," the smaller man shouted. "That's my ship somebody's got out there."

"We'll get it back," Merrick said.

"In a dwarf's eye. You wouldn't be so calm if somebody had taken the *Blackbird.*"

"Damn straight. And I'm sitting on you so that we can prevent that from happening."

Karinovsky struggled furiously, to no avail. He tried to kick Rab, who was perched on his legs.

"Relax," said Rab. "You'll get your ship back." He pulled a cigar out of his tunic. "Care for a stogie? Very calming."

"Damnit, Rab!!"

Something glinted in Merrick's dark eyes, something cold and unamused. "Shut up, Vlad. You're my crew and you do what I say, understand?"

"I quit."

"You can't, crankhead, not until you repay the loan I gave you for that bad shipment of erfani grass."

"But, Merrick, my ship!"

"Pipe down. We'll get it back. Not you. We. In the meantime, I suggest you help us convert that damned prison barge into a fighting machine or else we'll never get out of here."

* * *

"What are we looking for?" Iger said.

"The Argentum Cluster. Leave that to me."

"Are we there yet?"

"Getting anxious?"

"No, but Third Child is."

"Well, tell her to ease up. We've got a whole half of a quadrant to cross yet."

"Katie?"

"Shhh!"

"Kayla?"

She spun, glaring at him. "I told you never to call me that. I'm Kate. That's all."

"I thought that was your real name."

"Was. And the only people who called me that are dead." *Or should be.*

* * *

Cristobal raged through the corridors of Dome E, pounding on wall plates, kicking at doors. "Where is she, damnit? Where is she, Salome?"

The captain of the *Falstaff* stayed two steps ahead of him, striding hard as though she were doing exercises in null-g.

"I've told you, Cristobal, I don't know."

"I don't believe you."

"That's too bad."

"You know why she left. You know where she went. Bring her back."

"I'm not Katie's keeper."

"I can't do all of this without her."

"You seem to be managing." Salome checked her chronometer. "In fact, aren't you supposed to be surpervising training in Dome C right now? Better hurry, Cristobal, or you'll be late for your own revolution." She made little shooing motions with her hands. "Off you go."

He glared at her. "You're a steel-plated bitch, Salome. Only Katie understood the importance of what I'm trying to do. I need her. She's got to come back."

"She will, Cristobal. Now, for the gods' sake, shut up, and get away from me or I will put a dent in your hide."

* * *

A silence and a waiting had come to an end in the deep, airless void. A signal was sent with no reply expected. Other eyes were watching, other hands were reaching for the Mindstar. And another ship, silent and shielded, unnoticed, set out for the Argentum Cluster.

Chapter Eight

Iger stared into his screen and swore. "Alliance cruiser just hove into view. It's gaining on us."

"What?" Kayla said. "Here? It's impossible."

"See for yourself."

The image on-screen was undeniable: The black arrowhead-shaped ship was unmistakably an Alliance troop cruiser, heavily armed, moving closer.

"They're signaling, requesting our ID."

"Damn. I don't know what Karinovsky's cover is."

"The knowbot would."

"No time. Tell them who we are—give them the *Antimony*'s serial numbers and pray to all the gods that Karinovsky isn't on their most-wanted list."

"*Antimony*," the cruiser thundered. "Come about."

"Stall them," Kayla said. A nearsense probe— working for once—gave her a fix on the pilot of the police cruiser. She would have him send his ship for a sudden journey into deep space.

Wouldn't they be surprised when their jump engines came on and ran away with them?

Focus, she needed to focus.

A wave of pure mental energy came flowing softly toward her, a strange disruption of neural signals and thought fragments. Was it a pulse from the Mindstar, even at this distance?

It had to be.

Dammit! I can't afford this now. I need all my energy to focus on that Alliance cruiser.

Kayla rode out the wave and regained her control.

Another pulse.

"Katie, they're aiming their guns at us."

Kayla tried to get her bearings on the police pilot once again. But the emanations of the Mindstar had scattered her focus, filling her mental field with glittering fragments and distortions.

She opened her eyes and swore softly. "I can't do it, Iger. We'll have to get out of here. Get me a minute to plot a new course."

She was dimly aware of Iger's voice as he stuttered out a hesitant response to the police request, and of the repeated demand by the Alliance cruiser. But she was submerging into the navboard interface, looking for a quick, clean, untraceable getaway course.

Damnit, where was the jump interface? The configuration of the *Antimony*'s nav system was an unfamiliar jumble of routes, all of them strange. Which path should she take?

That way, between those narrow crimson pylons? No, that one would land them near the Salabrian System. What about over here? A bounce and two twirls past a silvery pyramid burning under a purple sun. No, wrong again—that was the first jump for the Cavinas System.

"*Antimony,* repeat, *Antimony,* prepare to be boarded."

There was no time left. Kayla took them into subjump, forcing the engines to move from their near-idle condition to jump ready in a compressed, much-too-short load sequence.

Ships could be lost this way, jumping blind. Had been.

Better to die in jumpspace than be captured before I've had a chance to find that Mindstar!

The nav indicators were moving through the spectrum, red-blue-green-purple. When all lights were shading toward yellow, Kayla hit the jump switch.

The engines screamed. The ship bucked.

They were here and then they were not-here.

The no-space of jump was uncomfortable for most sentient species, producing strange paranoia, half-seen phantasms, and feelings of suffocation. Years ago, jump effects had nearly killed Kayla. But events had intervened to alter her mindpowers— and her vulnerability to jump sickness. Now she tolerated the space-between-space easily, and came away with hardly anything more than a vague ache between her eyes.

There was no time in jumpspace and therefore Kayla had no sense of how long she had been locked into the navboard. Had the police managed to follow them? She wouldn't know until the *Antimony* dropped back into realspace.

Kayla slowed the ship and watched the jump indicators make their rainbow journey back to subjump red.

Realspace came back, bright with stars.

There was an odd grainy rumble to the engines that she hadn't noticed before, but she reminded herself that she was unfamiliar with the *Antimony*. A ship this fine, this new, shouldn't run so roughly, but she was a pilot not an engineer, and no expert on the *Antimony*.

She jacked out of the navboard and was back in ops with Iger beside her. He turned, saw she was looking at him, and smiled hugely, his blue eyes signaling his relief.

"Nice piloting. We left those cops way behind us, breathing our space dust."

Kayla leaned over and grabbed him by his long blond ponytail. Pulled. "Of course it was nice piloting. What else did you expect?"

"Just one question."

"Shoot."

"Where are we?"

Kayla peered at the screen and saw a swirl of unfamiliar stars. "Uh-oh."

"I was afraid you'd say that."

She scanned the star charts frantically but could

find no point of correlation. She retraced their trajectory and tried to plot likely routes through jumpspace. Nothing made any sense.

"Try the radio," she said finally.

Iger sent out a broad-band appeal for assistance and information. The only response was a faint ping. "Nobody seems to be in the neighborhood," he told her.

Kayla sighed. "Guess it's time to turn the knowbot back on."

"I'm keying its switch, but it's not responding."

"This just keeps getting better and better."

"Let me take a look at it." He bent over the 'bot's station and began fiddling with the controls, muttering to himself. After what felt to Kayla like far too many minutes, Iger sat up and shook his head.

"I think the problem is a faulty power coupling. It's not receiving enough juice."

"Where's its power source?"

"Solar collectors and storage batteries. Panels must have been damaged in transit just now."

"Can't we fix that?"

"Not unless you feel like taking a space walk."

Kayla stared at the screen and the cold stars stared back at her. "Do I have a choice?"

* * *

The pressure suit fit as though it were a second skin, snugly but with enough give so Kayla could perform a somersault if necessary. She hoped that the necessity would not present itself. Beneath her feet were white lights, the same as above her head. If she gave herself enough time, she would work up a real case of disorientation. A touch of the jets on her pack kept her from drifting.

The *Antimony* was a sleek silver bird beneath her feet and the universe was a million brilliant points of cold fire scattered about in velvety darkness. The gods' jewelbox had been spilled all around her, above and below.

Kayla had maneuvered ships through the void on a hundred missions, plotted courses, roamed the interstices of jumpspace, but nothing had prepared her for the giddy terror of setting one foot and then the other out of an air lock and having nothing between her and space but a thin pressure suit.

She felt her skin prickling with fear. And yet, beyond all sense of dread, there was something oddly exhilarating about being outside the ship.

"Magnets on." Through the soles of her boots Kayla felt the steady pull from the *Antimony*'s hull. So long as the laws of physics prevailed, she wouldn't float away. In fact, the worst thing that could happen would be that she would trip and fall on her face. Well, maybe a sudden swarm of grain-sized meteors would be worse. But not by much.

"I was brought up to crawl through tunnels," she muttered. "Not float around in space."

The solar collectors were set into the *Antimony*'s hull at regular intervals all the way around the ship to maximize exposure. They were a dull black that made them easy to identify against the ship's shimmering skin.

Walking the length and the perimeter of the ship took time. Kayla didn't want to move too quickly and miss a panel. Luckily, the only movement which her boots afforded was slow and almost stately steps.

Sure enough, five adjacent panels were cracked. Kayla used the patch kit Iger had given her and triggered the release of the bonding salve. She laid down neat lines of it in slow motion, watching it sink and merge with the ceramsteel plates. Slowly she bonded the panels into a thick row of salve and receptors. It was careful work, and she was soon sweating into her pressure suit but she forced herself to continue.

Another touch here, and here.

Just as she was beginning to feel the strain of her efforts in her shoulders and hear the whisper of the stars in her headset, Iger's voice came through, startling her.

"All set."

It was an odd sensation to stare into the inhuman void while listening to her companion's familiar voice.

"Good job," Iger said. "You're a natural. Maybe you should have been a maintenance jock."

"Thanks, I think."

"That 'bot will be powered up in no time. Have you had enough space yet?"

"You don't have to ask me twice."

She used the jet packs to position herself, strode in slow-motion to the air lock, and let the autofeed sweep her into the moist, warm atmosphere of the *Antimony*. The welcome pressure of gees pulling at her reminded Kayla that she had a body with both weight and bulk. Gratefully, she stripped off her pressure suit and brushed her sweaty bangs out of her eyes.

When she got to ops, she found Iger bending over the knowbot, his face knotted in a frown. Third Child was perched by his side, quirching softly.

The 'bot wheezed and groaned, muttering nonsense syllables. Iger made another adjustment and then another.

With a whirr the knowbot came back to life.

"Course heading?" it demanded. Its voice was at least an octave lower than before, a pleasing baritone.

Kayla settled herself at the navboard. "A little rest seems to have done that thing a world of good."

"Course heading?" the knowbot said again. "I repeat, course heading?"

"I see that its attitude hasn't improved."

"I didn't promise miracles."

Kayla fed the information she had to the

knowbot and waited while it digested her bad news. "Okay, genius," she said. "Where are we?"

"Location unknown," the knowbot announced.

Iger rocked back in his seat. "Oh, great. Just flikking great."

Kayla wanted to kick the knowbot, badly, but she controlled the impulse. "Let me think," she said.

A small voice in her head began screaming: *"We're lost in uncharted space. We'll never find our way back, never!"* Kayla forced herself not to listen. She remembered the tales that her vid cubes had told her about people who had journeyed upon the water surfaces of worlds in boats—sailors. When uncertain of their locations, they had taken sightings from the stars and triangulated a course. Well, that wouldn't help her. Every star in the vicinity was unfamiliar.

What else had the cubes told her?

When uncertain of the depth of the water, the lost sailors had taken soundings.

Soundings, yes. That might do it. But of what? There was no interstellar space chatter on the radio, no passing ships, nothing much nearby. With what would she sound, and off what?

—*The Mindstar.*

Kayla paused, wondering. She was so far away, separated from her target by how many lightyears? How could her mind alone even reach the Mindstar, much less hear an echo from it?

—*Not alone.*

It was Third Child. The dalkoi was addressing her directly in mindspeech.

—*We shall combine to search.*

Mindlink with the dalkoi? She had done it before and found it an unnerving experience. Touching a truly alien mind was always unsettling.

The dalkoi was a wise little creature, a native of Liage, bonded to Iger. Her lack of speaking apparatus did not prevent her from communicating with Kayla now. Kayla felt the vibrant power of Third Child's mind, the odd resonances, the strange mental configurations, and, for just a moment, she recoiled from her embrace.

—*Kayla?*

She was lost in bittersweet memories, of a time when she had been a truly remarkable tripath with towering mental abilities that had been the envy of her peers. She had had mastery of not only near and farsense but also the unusual mind-numbing shadowsense. But her linkage with a group of dalkois on St. Ilban had changed all that forever.

Once more she remembered the noise and madness outside the Crystal Palace, the Alliance police, Rab on the ground, dying, and herself already suffering from a mind wound. Desperate, she had forged a mindlink with the dalkois in order to save Rab's life. The linkage had also cauterized her own injury, but the healing had left a dead place, an opacity in her powers.

It had been necessary at the time, a price to pay for a comrade's life. And with the dulling of her powers had come her ability to endure the space-between-space of jump. An acceptable tradeoff. But the memory persisted of treasured abilities lost when she had mindlinked with the dalkois, and that negative association was forever cemented in her memory.

—*Kayla? What is wrong? Why do you hesitate?*

The dalkoi's query was gentle, almost timid. Kayla was immediately ashamed of her unreasoning fear. This was Third Child, dear Third Child, her friend. There was nothing to fear, nothing to lose. Nothing.

Kayla's mind reached out fully toward the dalkoi and found Third Child waiting to embrace her.

Ah, the pleasure of linkage. The melding of the egos, the release from the prison of the single mind with all its needs and wants, its nattering concerns. Kayla stretched, reveling in her freedom. But she had little time to enjoy it, for she was suddenly being pulled through hoops of fire, massive, near-molten gateways that led—was it really possible?—to the deepest heart of the universe.

Kayla's mind shrilled with alarm. —*Third Child, where are we going?*

—*Through jumpspace.*

—*Are you mad? We can't do this. No mind can. It's a matter of physics. Of speed.*

—*It is a matter of mind.*

—*No empath has ever even attempted this before!*

—*Regardless, together we can accomplish what one alone cannot do.*

The rings of fire began to narrow, and Kayla grew afraid that they would close around her, trap her mind and the dalkoi's in the empty limbo of no-space.

—*We'll die, or want to.*

—*Put your fears to rest, mindsister.*

The rings came closer. Closer. Kayla imagined she could feel flames licking at her mind.

—*Third Child, how are we doing this?*

—*Don't try to understand that now.*

A pulsing wave of mental energy caught them up and carried them out of the path of the rings and away. In the distance Kayla sensed a deep and shimmering well of light, a liquid jewel. Or was it heat? Color? Taste? Every sense was crazily jumbled here.

Kayla heard—or did she taste it—a note stringing itself into a strange chord, swelling, coming closer. The orchestra added instruments: now the strings, now the horns, building a structure of arpeggios, higher and higher, toward a wild crescendo. Was it music? Water, thundering down a hillside, wearing boulders to pebbles and ruts into canyons? There was a sense of wild power, of uncontainable force, eternally replenished, inexorable.

Minds. It was the universe of thought, coming closer.

Eager now, famished for contact, Kayla rushed forward. How long had she and Third Child been alone together? How long in jumpspace? It felt like many many lifetimes, all of them desperately lonely.

The universe was a distant chorus, a brimming symphony of thought and sound and sensation, beckoning her closer, promising connection, warmth, love.

—*Be careful.*

—*Of what? Come on, Third Child. Hurry.*

—*There is danger.*

—*What danger?*

Heedlessly, Kayla plunged into the soaring chorus and was borne upward and away from Third Child, high, higher, laughing wildly, swimming through mind after mind.

It was extraordinary. She was riding a delirious wave of joy.

But the chorus shifted into a minor key, and the flow of minds became a flood, too much, too strong. Wave after wave of them pounded her, forcing her back, battering her against the hard edges of other minds, other notes. Kayla floundered, struggling for a foothold.

—*Third Child?*

Too late she understood the dalkoi's warning. An impenetrable wall of thought had formed, cutting her off from Third Child, and from the way by which she had come. She was stranded now in the midst of millions of unfamiliar minds.

—*Third Child?*

The push and clamor of the minds around her dominated her awareness.

There was bitterness here, sorrow and regret, anger enough to curdle one's soul. Failed love, business reverses, deaths of friends. It was a web that would ensnare one for a lifetime. Kayla could feel the strands being spun over her own mind, seeking to trap and imprison her. She struggled, broke free, and staggered from one mind into another.

A woman giving birth, keening at the pain.

Her newborn child, a welter of conflicting sensations and signals.

A different woman, grieving over the loss of her mother, tormented by guilt and remorse.

A man and woman making love.

—*Momma, forgive me, I couldn't take you in.*

—*The pain, the pain, I can't believe the pain.*

—*Fear. Noise, Heat, Light.*

—*I love you, I love you so much, I love you.*

—*The rats, the rats with teeth in their eyes, every night they come closer and they look at me. Every night. They look at me with their teeth.*

The contradictory welter of roistering, wailing, lunatic humanity threatened to tumble Kayla's senses to microscopic bits with its cruelty, desperation, fear, kindness, love, bravery, madness, cowardice, greed, and charity.

It's too much, she thought. *Third Child was right. I can't bear it.*

She wrenched herself away from the mind of a man who was having a psychotic episode and curled her awareness into a tight, defensive ball.

—Third Child, where are you?

Fear was a strange coppery taste, a sour sensation in her mind. She was as lost here as she had been before. But if she didn't find Third Child's mind, she would never get back through jumpspace, back to her own body.

What was that?

There. A single glowing source of light—not a mind, no, not exactly. Filled with strange energies and wisps of thought. It was the Mindstar, could be nothing else. She had found it, and found the way back.

Tentatively, she bounced a probe off the light source.

Her probe came echoing back at her, loud in her mind, and she sensed other minds around her, cringing, but from the dalkoi there was no response.

Kayla sent forth another probe, and another. She ringed the Mindstar with probes, webbed it carefully, fixing its location deep in her mind.

—Third Child? Can you hear me?

Hadn't the dalkoi heard the call?

—Third Child?

Again the echo, the harsh reverberations, dying away to a whisper and then nothing.

—Third Child, you've got to hear me. I know you're out there somewhere. Listen, I've found it!

Finally, faintly, as though from a great distance, she caught the dalkoi's mind signature.

—I hear you, Kayla. You say that you have found the Mindstar?

—Yes. I know how to get back now.

—Let us go, then, quickly.

Cling mind to mind, Kayla and Third Child made the perilous journey back through the long loneliness of jumpspace, coursed between the rings of fire that marked the transit point between real- and nonspace, and emerged into time and space.

Kayla opened her eyes.

She was sitting in her webseat in ops. Iger hovered anxiously by her side.

"Gods," he said. "You were out of it for almost a day. You and Third Child. What happened?"

Shakily, she reached for his hand and pressed it to her cheek. *Iger, dear Iger.* The touch of flesh against flesh was good. Later there would be more.

"Kayla, are you all right?"

She didn't even mind that he used her real name. "Now I am." She squeezed his hand once and sat up. Third Child chirped quietly and scuttled off to a well-cushioned wallseat. "Now I am," she said. She released him with reluctance.

"And you know how to find our way back?"

She nodded and picked up the navboard jacks. "Prepare for jumpspace."

Kayla plugged in, set the engines growling softly, and submerged into jumpspace. She knew that between those pylons and around that yellow spiral was a route back toward known space. She remembered the Mindstar blinking like a beacon and, following that memory, brought the *Antimony* back.

Chapter Nine

Slowly Kayla piloted the *Antimony* into sync with the Argentum Cluster, a cloud of rocky fragments that, aeons ago, had comprised a planet.

"Deflectors on full," Iger reported. "Gods, that's a lot of nasty stuff out there. Just listen to it singing against our shields."

"A regular asteroid chorus."

"Rab says it'll drive anybody stark raving spacemad in three days."

"In three days' time we'll be gone."

"Optimist."

The binary asteroid that they were looking for was at the heart of the Cluster. It took some delicate maneuvering on Kayla's part to bring the *Antimony* into synchronous orbit with the smaller twin. The larger asteroid circled them in a perilous *pas de deux,* its pitted face so close that they could count the craters.

At first she had thought that what she heard—and felt—was merely another, higher note in the asteroid chorus. But it emerged from the din and became a solid, solo tone which drilled steadily into her consciousness, one steady note shrilling "*Mememememe.*"

The Mindstar was calling to her. Tendrils of telepathic force tickled Kayla's mind.

"This is it," she said. "I can feel it. The Mindstar is here. Prepare the pod."

"It's ready to go," Iger said. "All powered up. I'll bring the suits."

"Suits? Iger, you've got to stay here."

"Forget it. You think I'd let you go down there alone after I've seen the way that thing can affect your mind?"

"But I need somebody on board to monitor me."

"The knowbot can do it."

"I thought you fried it."

"Only its voice."

She decided not to argue. "Better hope that 'bot doesn't hold grudges."

They suited up quickly, sealing themselves into the exoskeletons which would provide life-sustaining artificial environments for them for twelve hours.

"Let's go."

With Iger at the controls, the pod detached from the belly of the *Antimony* and took them on a teeth-rattling ride to the scarred red surface of the small planetoid. All the way down, the Mindstar's voice was loud in Kayla's mind, and she was glad of Iger's anchoring presence, of his steady hand on the pod's navboard. She was beginning to see things, to feel things that she knew were not real. Ghostly presences accompanied her in the pod, red and green outlines of figures in motion, whispers in her ears. Shadows of Kate N. Shadow: She left trails through the air whenever she moved, odd fluttering shades of blue and green. Could Iger see them? He was leaving his own trails, orange-purple, as his hands moved over the landing board.

"Landing in two seconds."

Whump!

The pod rocked for a moment, reverberations dying away as the engines stilled.

"We're down," Iger said. "Not much to look at, is it? What are we searching for?"

"A casket about the size of a cot."

Iger fiddled with the screens. "Three-hundred-and-sixty degrees: nothing. This place isn't that big, but I don't see any indication on the screen of a good-sized box."

"Use the sensors. Shotay said that the casket was magnetically charged."

"Scanning." He paused, peered into his screen once again. "Nothing yet."

Kayla was growing impatient. The Mindstar was here, she knew it. She could feel it thrumming in her feet, luring her out onto that rocky, desolate plain. She was tempted to start walking, trusting her instinct to find the stone.

But she didn't want to exhaust her suit's power,

and she knew that the Mindstar could be elusive. "Come on, Iger. This place isn't that big."

Iger bent over the board, puzzling. Then he looked up. "Got something."

"Let me see it! How far is it?"

He turned and showed her the reading. "I'd say it's about a kilometer from here."

"In which direction?"

"Down."

Her eyes met his. "We are down."

"I mean it's down." He pointed through the floor of the pod. "As in down there. The Mindstar isn't *on* the surface of the asteroid, Katie. It's inside."

She stared at him, dumbstruck. Inside? Inside this planetoid? She had never suspected it. She didn't have any digging equipment or any of the proper tools ... or wait. Did she?

"Scan for any natural openings in the surface," she told him. "If we don't find one then we'll have to use the *Antimony*'s lasers to blast a hole."

It was Iger's turn to gape. "Are you crazy? Have the *Antimony* shoot at this asteroid while we're still on it?"

"It'll be a pinpoint laser," she said. "Like the kind of big laser cutters my father used in the mines on Styx. We can do this the same way, with a narrow cutting radius and a short burst. Unless we're sitting right on top of the Mindstar, the laser won't come anywhere near us."

"Katie, your father was using cutters, not cannons."

"A laser is a laser, Iger. It's all in how you decide to use it."

"If you say so. But remember, if something goes wrong, we've left Third Child by herself in the *Antimony*. She can't pilot the ship alone. Or rescue us."

"She'll be all right. That dalkoi's got twelve lives. At the very least."

"Well, I still don't like it. We don't know how stable this asteroid really is. What if it splits open like a dry log the minute we start cutting on it? Who can tell what's going to happen?"

He was beginning to annoy her. "I knew I should have left you behind," she said.

"Yeah? And I think we should go back to Kemel and get Rab and Arsobades to help control the lasers."

"After what we've gone through to get here?" She gave him an outraged look. "Are you crazy? That'll take too much time. Besides, we can handle it. I know we can."

"Wish I were as confident as you."

"Take a deep breath, Iger, and shut up, please."

She programmed the *Antimony's* lasers by remote board and set them to drill a hole into the closest of what the pod's sensors showed was a series of shallow tunnels.

"Put the pod deflectors on," she said, waiting for him to shield them. Once Iger had given her the thumbs-up sign, she triggered the *Antimony's* laser banks and hoped that she hadn't been overconfident.

Narrow beams of bright lime-green light poured down from above onto the asteroid's rust-colored skin, and wherever they touched the asteroid a great gout of dust reared up, pink and spinning. When the dust had dissipated, a neat hole could be seen in the asteroid's surface, big enough for one—or even two—people to crawl through.

Kayla pressed the pod door trigger. "Come on," she said. "Last one out is a burnt choba omelette."

* * *

The caves inside the asteroid were nothing at all like those on her home world, Styx. There the cave walls and floors had been full of dark somber crystal that seemed to absorb light and feed it back in strange flashes of green and bronze. But here, everything was brightness, white light, a flamboyant cathedral of glittering crystals and strange, smooth walls from which crystalline growths extended like arms and legs, tentacles frozen into strange lacy patterns.

Despite the differences Kayla felt memories throb and ache like old scars. *Morning in the mines. . . .*

A split opened before them in the tunnel: two paths. "You go left, Iger. I'll take the right. Meet you back here in ten minutes."

"Ten minutes or I'll come after you." He was a

fading, wavery shadow in her headlamp, half un-
real and already far behind her, moving farther
away every minute.

Silvery walls studded with pale green gems.
What were they? Kayla's fingers itched to find out.
Old miners' instincts never die, she thought. But
she kept walking.

And the past walked with her. Flowing over the
silvery walls like familiar shadows were the images
of people she had known, places she had been.
The Mindstar, she thought. *This is just an effect
of the Mindstar.*

Shotay peeked at her from around a stalagmite,
but when Kayla turned to look she melted away.
Greer smiled up at her from the path beneath her
feet.

Keep walking.

And there, two faces, two dearly beloved faces
she had not seen in years. *Mom. Dad.*

Kayla ran toward them, arms outstretched. "It's
so good to see you," she called to them. "I never
thought I would see you again."

"We've been here, waiting," her mother said.
She gave her a kiss.

Her father hugged her. "We knew you would
come. Take a look at this cave wall, Kayla-girl.
Isn't it something?"

She couldn't believe it. She was back in the
mines with her parents, probing a crystalline out-
cropping with her beloved father at her side. Tears

began to trickle down her cheeks. She would never leave her parents again, never let them go.

She saw a sudden reflection of her own face—not Kayla the child but Kayla as a woman, older, much older, her face drawn, flesh thin, hair lackluster and gray. Lines rayed out from her eyes, and deep creases furrowed her forehead. Old, she was so terribly old. The pupils of her eyes swelled until they were huge, until the green of her iris was obscured. And then she was looking into empty sockets. A skeleton grinned back at her with jagged broken teeth. A skeleton with her name.

Kayla gasped.

Her parents, beside her, were two gaping, grinning skeletons crumbling to dust.

Kayla looked quickly away. When she looked back, they were gone.

The Mindstar effects, she thought. *They're getting stronger. I must be coming closer to it.*

Was that somebody behind her, coming closer? No, it must be the Mindstar hallucinations again. But surely those vibrations were from footsteps. Iger, checking up on her before ten minutes had elapsed? Didn't he trust her?

She spun to confront him and found herself face-to-face with the man she hated most in the entire galaxy.

"You!"

Instinctively, she reached for the disruptor she wore at her hip.

Yates Keller. Yates-Goddam-Keller. Kayla had

felt him ticking in her mind like a slow-fused bomb, and knew that her heart was the detonator. Each beat, each breath, each thought drew her closer to an explosive concussion.

Keller smiled, white teeth flashing. He was as maddeningly attractive as ever. His low voice came over her suit headphones, teasing and seductive. "There's no need for that gun, Kayla. Put it away."

"Bastard!"

"You're very resourceful, Kayla. Be reasonable, too. I think we can work together. Why not? We can split the proceeds of the Mindstar and live like royalty."

"Is that what you're after?"

"We belong together. A team."

"Still singing that same old song, Yates?"

"Yates?" he said. "Who's that?" His handsome face blurred, widened, spread to become a space helmet revealing a familiar visage within. Wide nose, high forehead, small piglike eyes. It was a face that Kayla knew, but not the one belonging to Yates Keller.

"Mogul! You?" Kayla stared in disbelief at his broad ugly face. It wasn't possible. How could the prison guard responsible for Shotay's death be standing, grinning, before her? It was another Mindstar hallucination, had to be. "You're dead. You died on the *Lovejoy.*"

He nodded with evident satisfaction. "That's what I wanted you to think. When the rebellion came down on the *Lovejoy,* I knew I'd buy it if I didn't hide. So I played dead until there was nobody around, then hid out in the farthest cells."

"You miserable son of a bitch!"

"Just following orders."

"Whose?"

"Somebody's. Somebody important who wants that Mindstar. And I figured you knew where it was. So I followed you."

"It was you who radioed that Alliance police ship, the *Devon*, and brought it in after us," Kayla said, comprehension dawning. This was real. Mogul was actually here, right now, alive and talking to her. "You. You're the one who did it."

Mogul's face was a sneering mask. "Sure. I thought maybe I might need some help. But you took care of that. Blew them away. Don't care who you kill, do you? You and your army of pathetic bastards."

"You mean I'm becoming like you?" She stared at him, remembering again how much she hated him. "Shotay died because of you. Don't talk to me about killing."

To his credit he looked slightly uneasy. "I didn't want to kill her. Just wanted to find out what she knew." He paused, mouth working. "But you did, instead."

"I don't understand how you could land on this asteroid without our sensing it."

"I didn't land on it. I landed on its larger twin and used a flare pack to span the distance between." Mogul paused for a moment. "Well, girlie, you know what we're both here for. Where is it?"

"Where is what?"

"Don't play games with me. The Mindstar."

"Think I'd tell you?" She wanted to drain his mind of thought, peel the smug and sickening expression right off of his face and hand it to him— here, Mogul, look at this. Her mind reached for his like a hand stretching out to extinguish a candle flame. Reached. Reached harder, but something was in the way, blocking her. Kayla trembled, gave it her all, but she couldn't bridge the distance between them.

The Mindstar, she thought. *It's interfering, controlling everything that happens here. I can't use my empathic powers, they won't work.*

"You should have died on the *Lovejoy,* Mogul." She pulled away from him, finding footholds, backing into darkness. The headlamp on her suit was a dead giveaway, but she couldn't find the switch to blank it. She slapped her hand over it and faded back into the shadows.

"Girl! Where are you? You can't get far. I've got sensors, I'll track you." For the first time his voice was tinged with fear.

Mogul shifted position on the brittle floor, groping for her, crushing rock beneath his feet. Crystals cracked and a few showered down from the walls of the cave.

He doesn't know how to move underground, Kayla thought. *But I do.*

She turned and ran, her feet falling lightly upon the cave floor. She had to use her hands to push herself off of walls whenever a leap took her too high. Her suit-generated gravity was sufficient to keep her grounded, but she felt as though one good jump would put her through the ceiling.

In moments she had outdistanced Mogul, leaving him behind her to flail in the darkness. Born to a life in the underground mines, Kayla moved swiftly and easily through the tunnel. She had a sense that the Mindstar was nearby. But did she dare try to recover it with Mogul coming after her, trying to track her every move?

She began to lose her bearings. That was no good. She might walk right into Mogul's outstretched arms. Cautiously, Kayla uncovered her headlamp. The reflected light nearly blinded her.

She was in some deep inner cave of the asteroid, a vast arching space awaiting a benediction— or a sacrifice. Spears, stalks, crystal plumes, and chandeliers hung from the walls. Stalagmites reached up for her, shimmering in her suit's lamplight, beautiful, delicate, deadly. Behind her came footsteps, slipping yet relentlessly, following.

* * *

It was morning and she was trundling along behind her parents in the caves. Her father turned to smile at her, to point out a stump of good dark crys-

tal. Someday he would let her get her own cutter.
Someday. . . .

* * *

The shadows flickered and crystalline daggers
crashed to the slick floor, whispering past vulnerable
flesh. Good. Kayla knew where she was now. She
remembered life in the dark, in the tunnels. She
would play with the shadows and the light, in and
out, between the shadows. She was a shadow. And
she felt the footsteps coming fast on her trail.

Kayla slipped and slid but kept moving forward,
nimbler than her pursuer, faster. A crevasse split
the floor and she leaped, spanning its treacherous
gap as though she had wings. In her headphones
she heard a curse, a crash, another curse, as Mogul landed awkwardly. But she was around a knob
of crystal and out of sight before he had regained
his feet.

Silence.

Where was he? What was he doing?

She peered out of her hiding place, but the cave
was too dark to show much. Cautiously, she extended a nearsense probe. It bounced around
oddly but finally homed in on Mogul. He was
caught in a cul-de-sac, feeling his way along the
crystal-sharp walls as he slowly tried to follow her.

Behind him, the crevasse cut deeply into the
floor of the cave. If only he would edge a little
closer to it. Kayla tossed a crystal. It bounced off

a shimmering wall behind her and drew Mogul's attention.

He spun wildly on the slick floor, scurried forward, and, too late, saw the chasm. He scrabbled, tried to stop, but his momentum, coupled with his suit's auto-g, took him plunging over the edge.

Kayla moved forward, uncapping her headlamp. She peered into the split in the rock.

Mogul was splayed against the crevasse wall, balancing desperately upon a small crystal escarpment. He looked up into the glow of her lamp and his eyes through the faceplate were terrified.

"Help me." His voice quavered.

"First tell me who sent you here."

"Keller. It was Yates Keller."

"Not Pelleas Karlson?"

"Nobody deals with Karlson anymore. It's Keller. He's Karlson's eyes, arms, and legs."

Mogul shifted his position slightly. The blue and green crystal around him began to splinter and calve.

"Help me!"

Despite herself, Kayla extended her hand. "Hold still," she said. "Don't make a sound."

He stretched toward her and his gloved fingers grazed hers, just out of reach.

With a monstrous groan the shelf upon which Mogul was perched sheared away from the cave wall. His voice tore itself, shredding upon the cathedral's frigid walls as he fell, echoing in Kayla's headphones. A thousand daggers descended in tribute as, howling, Mogul plunged away into darkness.

Kayla watched the place where he had been and shivered at his ghostly green outline as it decayed to brown and disappeared. She could imagine him, grinning and silent at the bottom of the chasm, a jagged ice spear protruding through a hole in his abdomen. A spreading wet spot dyed the front of his pressure suit deep, deep red. A few droplets of blood escaped and froze into crystals, floating up from the body, released from the gees generated by Mogul's suit.

* * *

—*You don't care who you kill, do you?*
—*But I didn't kill him.*
—*No, but you would have.*

* * *

I won't think about it. I don't have time.

Her thoughts were loud but the Mindstar was louder. She was getting closer to it with every step that she took.

* * *

She was webbed into her seat in ops aboard the Falstaff, *running the navboard as they outraced an Alliance gunship.*

"Faster," Salome commanded.

"I'm right at the edge of subjump now," Kayla said.

"What's the nearest two-jump port?"

"Voorhays."

"Lay in a course and go."

Kayla's hands flew over the board. She was jacked in and ready, linked with Iger as backup. She coasted through the canyons of the board interface with no fear of jump, not anymore. Elated at the thought, she triggered the engines. "Jump in two minutes."

* * *

Where was she?

Kayla looked around herself and saw nothing that she recognized. A jumble of rocks, darkness beyond the puddle of light cast by her headlamp. How long had she been wandering? Had she dreamed her encounter with Mogul? Was Iger hurrying to meet her? Was he even here at all?

* * *

"Come here," her father said. "There's someone I want you to meet."

Kayla came obediently to her father's side and saw that he held a fabric-wrapped bundle in his lap. It was squirming oddly, as though something inside it were alive.

He grinned at her. "Don't be shy, darling. Come and meet your new sister."

"Sister? But I don't have a sister."

A flap of blanket fell away from the bundle. Bright eyes stared out at her. Lavender eyes.

Kayla started to back away. "I don't understand, Daddy."

Third Child sat in Redmond Reed's lap, toes curled happily. She gave a chirp as Kayla looked down at her.

"But I don't have a sister. . . ."

"Dad said you'd react like that." It was a familiar voice, coming from a familiar face.

"Iger!"

"Hi, Sis."

She pulled back and away. "I'm not your sister."

"Don't be ridiculous," Redmond Reed said. "You're talking nonsense."

"But—"

"We've gone along with your odd behavior long enough, Kayla." He was using a tone she recognized, the one that said, "Don't push me any farther."

Kayla looked helplessly from face to face. Iger, her brother? Third Child, her sister? It was wrong, all wrong, but somehow she couldn't explain why.

* * *

She was in a rock cave, kneeling before a metal casket. It had smooth sides and seemed to absorb light right into its matte green-black surface. And it was whispering to her. Softly at first, then with increasing volume, voices seemed to pour out of the casket into Kayla's mind.

One mind prevailed, one louder than the rest, but not hers. And she was looking out through strange eyes, seeing an alien landscape, speaking a peculiar language that she nevertheless understood. Someone else was thinking with her mind.

* * *

Sitting in a floater parlor with three other hard-faced men at the table, holocards being dealt upon the thick blue plasfelt surface. A quick hand. Winner take all, and weapons parked at the bar. A black-hearted bunch, but I can beat them. Sis is running the scanner. She's steady enough. Still, if they knew I was wired, they would frag me. . . .

* * *

Whose mind was this? Whose memories?

Names and faces swept over her, voices, stray fragments of conversations long past, tinkling lost arpeggios, the ghostly clink of glasses from some long-ago dinner party, a symphony in which each life was a leitmotiv neatly joined, one to another, and all caught within the cold heart of the stone.

She was a young mother clutching her dead child.

A haggard man staggering backward, a bloodied dagger in his hand.

A skin-covered skeleton but somehow alive, moving, talking, thinking. And thinking was the worst.

Partial lives, Kayla thought. *Perhaps they're moments, fragments from the lives of the Mindstar's previous owners.*

The lid of the casket gave when she pushed it, telescoping back into itself to reveal an orb of velvety blackness. Kayla palmed it and the top sprang open. Within, pillowed upon iridescent silver fabric, sat a marvel.

It was the size of a man's fist, bronze and green, purple and red, and it made a faint sound, as of a bell ringing, when Kayla touched it.

The Mindstar. Finally.

She held the smooth glowing ball in her hand and wondered at its splendor. Never had she seen such a magnificent mindstone. She hefted it happily. It was huge, and much heavier than it looked. Who had found it and mined it? When? Why had they cut it as a cabochon, without facets?

Kayla gazed at it with admiration. The polished golden swirls were like sunlit clouds above a lush purple world. She blinked, looked closer. Were the clouds moving? She could almost swear that they were. And then she was floating down through those clouds, down through twilight, submerging into the very depths of the mindstone.

Chapter Ten

The world inside the Mindstar was a hot and airless space. The press and murmur of people crowded Kayla into a claustrophobic panic. A ghostly touch upon her arm. A whisper in her ear. Kayla jumped.

"Who?"

No one was there.

"Where am I?" she called. "Is there anybody else here? What is this?

She could hear vague mutterings, sense the movement of minds all around her. Whose?

There *were* people in here. Strange faces watched her impassively, flickered, changed. Kayla knew without asking that the voices in the stone had come from them.

They neither welcomed her nor warned her off. There was a weary look of inevitability in their faces, a resignation that made her want to back away from them, to flee that strange darkness. But she was in an enclosed space, caught between minds. There was no place to run.

"You'll get used to it," said a thin, pale man with a face like a boy's. His name was Golias.

The name struck Kayla with peculiar force. Could this be Shotay's brother? This pale manling?

"I don't believe this," Kayla said. "I don't believe you're—we're—all trapped in this mindstone."

Golias' mouth curved upward in a sad smile. "There's no place left for us to go, even if we could."

The others around them stirred, faces shifting like leaves in wind.

"No," they whispered. "No, not so."

"Her body," said the faces. "She still has a corporeal body. We could have it, take her body."

"Just try it," Kayla said. Her mindpowers came on full, brimming, potent. She was flanked on both sides, no, surrounded by the remnants of people who had tried to control the stone. She felt them reaching for her, trying to hold her. They were flimsy dry spirits, without force. She could brush them aside, crush and flatten them.

But this place, this darkly terrible, oppressive place—she could push the spirits back and away from her but she could not fight her way free of the stone. It was like running on quicksand. Was this what happened to all of those who had tried? Had they been absorbed into the stone when they died, a part of them living on, dreadful ghosts, within the gem that they had purchased so dearly?

Did this mean she was dead, too? No. No, it couldn't be.

"That's not going to happen to me," she said. "I'll find a way out of here even if I have to use every scrap of mindpower I have."

"That won't do any good," said Shotay's brother. "You have formidable powers, that's obvious. But they're no use to you here."

"We'll see about that." Kayla lashed out at the hungry minds around her, blasting them in a pre-emptive strike. But they had more resilience than she had expected and fought back hard. Before she knew it, she was engulfed, drowning. So many lives and memories, pounding her mind like surf against sand.

—She was splayed upon a table, stomach huge, straining, gasping, screaming with the effort of propelling new life out of her body and into the world.

—Tasting her first piece of land-grown fruit, an apricot, ripe and tangy on her tongue, all of its sweet pulpy goodness, its earthbound sweetness, melting in a golden sunset glow.

—Running from the police, breathless and laughing.

—In tumultuous rebirth, laughing with joy, weeping with awe and fright.

—Cradling a dying woman, weeping: "Momma, Momma. Don't go. Don't leave me."

—Hiding, shivering behind a sack of machine

parts as men with guns wrecked the room where her family had lived.

—Feeling the cool wind ruffle her hair.

There was pain, yes, but there was pleasure as well. The loss of self, the release from her earthly concerns, was near ecstasy. She could look back, pityingly, upon poor Kayla, bound to the flesh and its weakness, its limitations, its needs, bound to a single finite lifetime.

Give them her body? Yes, of course. Why not? They were welcome to it, welcome to her poor timebound shell. She would remain here, pure mind, immortal, to savor the many rich and varied lives arrayed before her, a feast of experience which one lifetime could never offer.

Shifting atmosphere, swirling clouds framed a spectral opening. A figure moved slowly, uncertainly, through the rift between worlds. Kayla tensed and stood ready to defend herself against this new threat.

"Katie! There you are." White teeth in a tanned face. Blue eyes.

"Iger."

It was an effort to pull herself back, swim up through the layers of selves to be the Kate N. Shadow who knew him, who loved him. But, yes, she remembered, and her doubts about him— about them—fell away and shattered like crystal. She loved him. Iger, sweet Iger. "How did you get in here?"

"I don't know." His outline wavered, solidified.

"I've been getting these weird flashes of things. Hallucinations. I don't know what's going on."

"It's not possible," she said. "You'd have to have empathic powers to penetrate this stone."

He said nothing, merely stared at her in dismay.

"Gods, you do, don't you?" She remembered being linked to him through the navboard, watching his piloting skill growing, and wondering at his latency as an empath. It was true, then. Something in the Mindstar had kindled Iger's mindpower, expanded it. But how? And how strong was he?

"Katie, we don't belong in here. Come back with me. Come on."

"You're afraid, aren't you? But, Iger, you don't have to be afraid. Don't you see? This is a different place. A better one. We can stay here."

"And be trapped like the rest of them?" His gaze took in the leaflike faces arrayed around them. "No, thanks. I want the real world, or what passes for it. And if you weren't so caught in their web, you'd want it, too."

She couldn't convince him with words. Instead, she reached for him, enfolding him in her essence until there was no difference between them, until they were two glowing souls linked by mind, by love, bonded in ecstatic communion. "See?" she said. "It could be like this forever."

Together they drifted in a timeless space, ghostlike, wrapped one around the other and their minds and hearts were as one. She read his mind, knew that he wanted to keep this connection, that he loved her and wanted to stay bonded to her. But because he was Iger, born to roam a planet and later a galaxy, he struggled. He couldn't help struggling against confinement, even in a golden prison. And because they were so linked, he drew her into his fight. And saved her.

This wasn't a paradise, it was a tomb. She saw that, suddenly, and recoiled in disgust. Parasites! These pathetic vestiges of dead personalities which had somehow persisted within the Mindstar, pretending to lives and memories, had nearly captured her, entombed her with them. And she, in turn, had nearly dragged Iger along with her. She had almost condemned the person closest to her to slow death and terrible afterlife. Her fury mounted at the thought. And her mind struck out with ferocious intent.

Light blazed in the darkness, blood red and jagged. The assembled mind fragments of the stone's former owners stirred uneasily. A fierce wind gusted suddenly, swirled out of the darkness to pull at the leaf faces, to push and worry them, pressing them one against the other.

Kayla bore down upon them.

They called out in protest.

The wind drowned their cries.

Red lightning raked the skies of the strange inner world. Orange clouds, dark and sulfurous, boiled up. The wind howled like a mad thing gone hunting, rushed up out of the darkness, and caught the leaf beings as they attempted to flee.

NONONONONO. . . .

The wind swallowed their remnant minds, their fragmented lives, their hopes, their memories, their protests, and carried them away.

Alone in the darkness, Kayla and Iger faced one another, their bond nearly torn asunder.

"We've got to get out of here," she told him. "This Mindstar is much harder to control than I ever dreamed it would be. You were right. Its emanations are so powerful that they're interfering with my mindpowers. I'm trying to fight it, but it's so damned powerful."

She pushed back, tried to press the Mindstar's force in upon itself. The world rocked around her. Each move she made caused deafening reverberations. There was no reality to any surface, any dimension. Did she and Iger hang upside down? Were they inside the stone? Outside of it? Furiously she battled and the Mindstar fought back.

The surface beneath their feet shifted, twisted, tried to buck them off and away. They were slammed against a cold, hard wall as a wild spectrum of light and hue flashed around them, a storm of color broke over their heads.

How could this stone fight them so? Could it be alive? Kayla was staggered by the thought. The Mindstar a sentient form? A crystalline mind, transmitting murderous thoughts in pulses of light, of pure mental energy?

Something floated in midair before them, and Kayla tensed, expecting an explosion.

A bubble, lit from beneath by a greenish light? No, not air. Not a bubble. An inclusion. A flaw in the stone, a small, liquid-filled cavity, sealed off for aeons. The Mindstar *was* a stone, *just* a stone. Not alive. Never alive.

A wild gush of emotion—a flood—engulfed them. Kayla wept, laughed, fought back panic, floated on euphoric waves. Beside her Iger struggled in the torrent, gasping.

It's an emotional magnifier, Kayla thought. *Everything we feel comes bouncing back at us at twice the power. We'll be battered into idiocy by our own feelings. Got to stop it.*

Trembling, she commanded herself to be still. Plunging deep within her own resources, she found strength, found the will, and used them both to summon a mindshield, spinning it from the depths of her being. But it was a flimsy defense, weak, buckling at its seams, and it nearly disintegrated as a huge wave of despair broke over her.

"I don't know how I can do it alone," she said. And then she thought: *I don't have to.* Iger was here with her. Together, joined by nearsense, they might be able to hold off the Mindstar. They had to!

His mindpowers were not as developed as hers, not nearly. But they would be enough, she hoped.

Kayla reached in, bonded Iger to her again with nearsense, and fed upon his energy. His mind was strong, not as strong as hers but surprisingly resilient, filled with burgeoning empathic power. She fed upon that lodestone of strength, and as she funneled his energy through her, the mindshield firmed up, a strong and solid barrier. Kayla slapped it over them both.

"Hold on," she said.

The air before them flashed red, then molten white. The floor melted and ran. Time dissolved.

When Kayla could see again, she was standing, clad in her pressure suit, in the cave by the Mindstar's casket. Iger stood beside her. Their eyes met through their visors.

"Another illusion?" she said.

Iger rapped his gloved knuckles against the box. "I'd say this one is real."

The Mindstar glittered in its velvet nest, hypnotic in its lush colors. Beautiful. Kayla felt herself being drawn back toward the thing. Gasping, she turned away. "Iger, quickly, close the lid!"

Not until she heard the click of the casket lock did she dare to gaze upon the Mindstar's cache again.

"Will that hold it?" Iger said.

"I think so."

Kayla felt suddenly giddy, buoyed up by their escape. "We should be able to manage the thing, between us. But watch for any odd effects, bleed-through and the like. So long as you stay linked to me with nearsense, our double-mind should be able to contain it, at least long enough to get it into the pod."

"And then what?"

"I'll worry about that when we get there."

The Mindstar gave them surprisingly little trouble on the way back to the pod. As they trundled through the tunnels of the asteroid, Kayla cast her headlamp back and forth before them, lighting their way. Hallucinations flickered at the edge of her field of vision: dark, armed figures, Gazanian fire rats, huge boulders rolling toward her, all of which, when viewed head-on, evaporated in the beam of her headlamp.

She and Iger made good time despite the weight of their shared burden.

"There's the pod," Iger said.

He keyed the automatic lock and it sprang open with a gush of escaping air. Moving quickly, they loaded their cargo, sealed the pod, cast off gravity, and in a burst of bright ignition made for the *Antimony*. But when they got the pod back to the ship and unloaded the casket, things were not quite so easy.

At first the Mindstar was quiescent in its casket. Kayla left Iger in charge of it and hooked herself into the navboard to plot their course back to Kemel.

They got under way without incident and were just approaching subjump velocity when fire, red and awful, exploded in Kayla's mind.

She fought to hold onto the navboard, but she couldn't move, couldn't breathe, and there was a shrieking agony in her mind that was turning her brains to jelly. It was a hundred times worse than any jump sickness she had ever experienced.

The *Antimony* began to drift, wandering farther and farther off course, moving faster and faster.

Kayla couldn't believe the pain. She was certain she would die. No one could endure such fiery torment and survive.

The jump engines came on.

—*Iger*, Kayla thought.—*Gods damn it, Iger! Look up. Notice something is wrong. For all the gods' sakes, Iger, if we jump blind we may never get back. We'll be lost forever, maybe even get stuck in jump-space. . . .*

Another mind, cool, implacable, entered her own, moved through the flames, suffocating them. Red embers danced in their wake for a moment and were gone.

A familiar mind signature greeted Kayla's probe. Not Iger, no. It was the dalkoi, Third Child.

—*Third Child, how did you do that?*

—*I cannot explain. It nearly overwhelmed me. Only by temporarily combining my own mindpowers with your mental energy and Iger's was I able to push back the assault. Iger would have assisted me more, but he was afflicted as were you.*

—*Can you keep the Mindstar under control?*

—*Unknown. It is not the Mindstar, exactly, which is the problem. It is the mental energies it has absorbed and magnified. As you correctly surmised, it is an amplifier of sorts. However, it is quite powerful without being precise.*

—In other words, dangerous.

—Exactly.

—Can we deflect it?

—Temporarily.

—By the gods, how did Shotay and her brother ever hold onto this thing?

Third Child showed her.

Kayla saw familiar faces: a thin girl with a scar on her cheek and short, pale hair, and an equally thin, blond young man. Shotay and her brother— what had she said his name was?—Golias. They were struggling with a large silver container set high upon null-g casters. It was twice as large as the Mindstar's casket.

As she watched, one of the casters began to blink with yellow-red lights, then another, and another. An alarm shrilled and the casket tipped, fell to the floor, cracked open. Within it was a smaller casket, also cracked, similar to the one Kayla and Iger had found. The Mindstar had been dislodged from its nest and could be seen spilling out purple-green radiance.

Golias threw himself over the shattered container. "Get away," he cried. "Shotay, hurry! The stone won't affect you for a few minutes."

"No! Golias, I won't go." Shotay tugged her brother's legs, but he kicked at her, forcing her back and away from him. "Please, Golias! Don't."

She stopped begging as the unearthly purple glow enveloped him, penetrating his skin, turning it purple, then bronze. He became a statue, frozen in place. Then his skin began to shift, the metallic luster dulled, thinned, went transparent, and Golias was an incandescent skeleton, all purple bones and purple grinning teeth. His eye sockets stared at her, empty.

Shotay cried out her brother's name, but there was no answer. She began to run.

—*He was absorbed by the Mindstar?*

—*Partially. Although he retained the potential for some consciousness, he was so weakened by the mental drain upon him that he was helpless. He died of starvation and dehydration. There was no way that his sister could have saved him. After his death she stayed away and used mechs to secrete the stone upon the asteroid.*

—*What is this thing? This Mindstar?*

—*I do not know. It is unlike any other mindstone I have ever encountered. Our minds, combined, are, I believe, strong enough to protect us from its more lethal effects. But unprotected minds appear to be at risk. Perhaps this is not true of all. He seemed to be especially vulnerable.*

—*Has it been tampered with in some way? Enhanced?*

—*I do not think so.*

—*How will we contain it now?*

—*Possibly a triune mind will be sufficient to keep the stone permanently controlled. Possibly not.*

—*If not then we're all space dust.*

—*There is that possibility.*

—*You don't have to sound so cheerful about it.*

—Cheerful?

—Forget it. This triune mind, how does it work? Will I be able to pilot the ship and still contribute to it?

—Unknown. That depends upon your mental strength.

Kayla felt her temper flaring. She had to pause to remind herself that, despite her considerable mindpowers, she alone had not been sufficient to master the Mindstone.

—Only a groupmind can run that thing?

—That is my hypothesis, yes.

—All right. Have you explained this to Iger?

—He has been listening.

—He's willing to try?

—Yes. Of course, we may all be absorbed by the stone in much the same way as the unfortunate previous owners.

—Spare me the speculations, Third Child. Just get on with it!

—As you wish.

Kayla felt a sudden throbbing vibration as though something was making excavations in her cerebellum. Suddenly she was part of a mosaic mind, one piece in a greater consciousness. She saw through Iger's eyes, and through those of Third Child. The multiple vision was dizzying, disorienting. That pale woman there with the bright red hair. That was her! She was watching herself through somebody else's eyes.

Iger moaned.

—*I second that motion.*

—*Shhh. I cannot be the bridge for this if you do not concentrate.*

Kayla felt power being drawn out of her mind on a long, bright cord, drawn to a nexus, there to be combined with the force of Iger's mindpower. Third Child acted as the medium, the lens through which their groupmind focused. Their power pulsed and grew. Slowly, ponderously, the Kayla/Iger/Third Child entity turned its potent attention to the Mindstar.

The mindstone was a point of white-hot light, a glowing primal spot, a burning malignancy on the periphery of their consciousness.

The moved to extinguish it.

The Mindstar would not yield.

They pressed their great weight upon it.

Still it resisted.

—*Give!* they demanded. —*Cease!*

It would not.

The triune mind pulled back, curling around itself like a spider as it began to spin out strands as thin as thought and as tough as ceramsteel girders.

Strand after shimmering strand was laid in place, and another woven into it, next to it, beneath it, all cohering gradually into a pattern, a web.

—*Will the web hold?*

—*It must.*

—*What if it doesn't?*

The web was alive with prismatic light.

Finished, it glowed softly, humming with latent power, the power to contain unimaginable energies.

Up, up the web floated, up above the Mindstar, a cloud, lighter than air. And it came down suddenly with ferocious speed, clinging, blocking the Mindstar's radiance, cutting it off behind an impenetrable barrier.

The stone glowed dully within its incandescent prison-web, menacing, promising.

Kayla stood alone, her mind clear, the mindlink cut back to a subliminal connection. Beside her Iger blinked and yawned. Third Child gave what sounded like a very relieved chirp.

"What the hell are we going to do with that thing?" Iger asked.

"Let's get it back to Kemel, and give me a chance to decide," Kayla said.

"I thought you were going to sell it."

"I might. But just shaking it at somebody and watching his face when he realizes what I've got . . ."

"That somebody being Pelleas Karlson?"

"Exactly. He wanted that star badly enough to have a spy trail me and pay for it with his life. I wonder how he'd respond if he knew I've got exactly what he wants. He just might be willing to deal."

"And what's your price?"

Kayla paused to savor the thought. Slowly she said the name: "Keller."

"Who?"

"Yates Keller. He's the one who killed my parents. If Karlson wants that mindstone badly enough, he'll turn Keller over to me."

Iger was staring at her as though she were a stranger. "I can't believe you're really saying this. You'd actually deal in a human life?"

"Yates Keller isn't human. He's a monster in disguise. A monster who killed my parents and almost killed me."

"Katie, you told me that your parents' death on Styx was an accident."

"Yes, but Yates Keller caused it. He was trying to steal our mines from us, scare us off our stake. My folks just happened to get caught by his explosives."

"Katie . . ."

"No, Iger." She steeled herself against the entreaty in his eyes. "He killed them. He will pay."

"Then you'll be as bad as he is."

"I can live with that."

* * *

She slept alone that night, and as she slept, Golias, Shotay's brother, came to her. He crept over the pale plains and green-shadowed valleys of her dreamscape, a thin figure, pale hair and eyes gleaming.

"What do you want?" she said.

"To live."

"It's too late for that."

"Shotay sent you to me. She knew."

"She couldn't have known that I was an empath."

"She sent me what I needed. She always took care of me. Always. Now you will."

"You're dead, Golias. Stay dead."

He came closer, a figure made of green moonlight. Closer. His pale eyes glittered as he reached out for her.

"Get away!"

He took her in his arms, hands stroking her skin, lips seeking hers. It was pleasant in a way, the touch of him upon her. Cool fingers, cool lips. She savored the kiss, the gentle caresses. But the stroking grew fierce and he was moving now, moving against her, forcing his way in past her defenses, into her most secret, vulnerable places.

"Stop it, stop it!"

His hands were plunging through her head, through hair, skin, bone, to grasp her brain and squeeze.

Kayla awoke, gasping and shaking. Her head was pounding, her skin felt cold and clammy. A ghostly touch lingered upon her lips. She wiped her face, trying to scrub away the chill, rub some warmth back in.

"You're dead," she whispered. "Dead."

Chapter Eleven

The *Antimony* made good time to Kemel. Kayla signaled to the *Falstaff*, eager to share the
news.

"That's funny," she said.

"What's up?"

"They're not responding."

"Rab is probably taking a nap."

"And Arsobades and Salome as well? There's
not a whole lot of in-system chatter, either."

Iger shrugged. "I wouldn't worry about it. Just
get us parked."

Kayla put the ship into an easy orbit and she,
Iger, and Third Child hastened down to the planet's surface.

It seemed curiously depopulated.

She strode past Dome A. Empty. Dome C had
been stripped. Their boots echoed loudly in the
empty building. Unease gripped her as her pace
quickened. The place was deserted. What had
happened? Where was everybody?

She and Iger pounded through the empty

domes as Third Child straggled behind them, chirping disconsolately.

"Hello! Anybody here?"

In the doorway of the last dome, Dome B, a shadow fell. MacKenzie stood there with his arms folded across his chest, his gingery hair standing up in wisps around his head, mouth puckered as though there were something sour in it.

"Wondered when the hell you'd get back here," he said.

Behind him loomed the lanky figure of Evlin. The tall dancer's face was drawn and dour, but his gold-rimmed eyes flashed when he saw Kayla.

"Evlin," Kayla said. "Mac. What happened?"

The two of them exchanged uneasy glances.

"Damnit, say something. Where is everybody?"

"Cristobal took the whole damned army to St. Ilban," Evlin said. His voice was constricted and unusually dry. "And I do mean everyone."

"St. Ilban!" Kayla couldn't believe it. "You're joking, Evlin, aren't you? You've got to be." She waited for the telltale twinkle in his eye, the familiar smile.

Evlin's eyes remained opaque and unreadable. "Cristobal said that you had betrayed him— deserted him—and that he had to move right away, before the War Minstrels realized that you were gone."

"They can't do that," Iger said, voice rising in alarm. "Cristobal's gone completely out of his mind."

"Amen," said Kayla. "We're not ready for St. Ilban. Not even close. When did he leave?"

"Six days ago."

"That idiot. Where's Salome? Rab?"

Again the two glanced uncertainly at one another.

"Damnit, tell me!"

MacKenzie shook his head. "Alliance police came sniffing around and Cristobal sent the *Falstaff* out to decoy 'em. Then he radioed the cops with details of your friends' specific location. While the cops were busy with them, Cristobal scrambled everybody else and jumped to Cavinas."

Kayla could see MacKenzie's mouth forming the words but there was a second of delay between hearing and comprehension. She forced herself to ask, "And the *Falstaff*? Where is that, now?"

"Taken. Probably already sold as salvage."

"And Salome? Rab and Arsobades?"

MacKenzie sighed. "Most likely your friends have been arraigned, charged with piracy, convicted, and assigned to a damned prison barge."

"No!" She was aware of the hiss of Iger's breath and his muttered curse. Fury boiled up in her. She wanted to kick out, to knock down walls, smash in doors but she felt Evlin's restraining hand upon her shoulder. And in her mind, a cool voice from out of her dreams said,—*That's not the way. Plan. Always plan. Wild destruction is never an end.*

Kayla took a deep breath to calm herself. "How many ships are left?"

"The one you came in on and a merchant cruiser."

"That's all?"

"Old Cris was pretty damned thorough," MacKenzie said. "Would have taken that cruiser, too, if I hadn't threatened the fool. One bit of good news, though. Vlad Karinovsky took a fighter and vanished during a solar flare. Couldn't get over your theft of the *Antimony*, I guess."

"Poor bastard." A new thought occurred to her. "Why didn't you go with Cristobal, Mac?"

He gave her a cool smile. "He and I aren't exactly the best of friends, Katie. You know that. It would've been way too easy for an 'accident' to happen to me in jump. And I thought that somebody ought to be here to greet you with all the good news, if and when you returned."

She nodded her thanks. "Then let's get moving."

"St. Ilban?"

"You know it."

The boarded the *Antimony* and, with engines roaring, began the two-jump journey that would take them to the Cavinas System, to the purple gas giant Xenobe, its habitable moon, St. Ilban, and the realm of Pelleas Karlson.

They came out of jumpspace into a storm of cosmic debris, the floating remnants of what aeons ago, had been a planet, still faithfully orbiting the distant double star of Cavinas. More than one ship had met its end at the outskirts of this system, caught unawares and holed by razor-sharp meteorites.

"Flying gravel," Iger said in disgust. "It's not even meteorites, really. More like chunky sand."

"Get those deflectors up," Kayla told Evlin. "I don't want us to become a statistic. At least not before I get my hands around Cristobal's neck."

"Maintaining hull integrity, ma'am." Under different circumstances, Evlin's clipped, mock-formal accent might have struck her as funny.

"Damned messy outer system," MacKenzie said. "Karlson should have spent some of the money he stole in taxes to clean up all of this crap."

"Now who's dreaming?" Iger said. His smile faded as he stared more intently at his screen. "Alliance cruiser coming up on the port side."

"Move away steadily," Kayla ordered. "We're just a merchant vessel heading for a little stopover at Brayton's Rock. We've got every right to be out here."

Iger's hands were steady on the backup navboard. Conversation in ops ceased as the crew concentrated on the Alliance warship visible on their screens, lights flashing.

It came closer, so close that Kayla could swear that she could see the faint outline of the individual plates that had been welded together to form the cruiser's outer skin.

The Alliance cruiser passed them by without comment and continued on its heading out of the system.

"See you later," Iger said.

"Not if we're lucky," said Kayla. "Keep scanning. And don't forget, we're looking for the *Lovejoy.*"

"Do you really think Cristobal is hiding the fleet somewhere in-system?" MacKenzie asked. "Pretending to be an asteroid swarm or something? Even he isn't that stupid."

"I don't know what he's pretending, Mac. I just want to find the s.o.b."

"Scanning," Iger said. "Picking up the usual garbage at system's edge and . . . hello, what's that?"

"What have you got, Iger?"

"A small foreign body surrounded by even smaller ones, all seeming to move together."

"On-screen."

The specks of light that Iger described were difficult to make out. Were they ships? A renegade prison ship and its ragtag fleet? Kayla licked her lips in anticipation.

"Nope, sorry, false alarm." Iger frowned at his board. "It's one of those Cargillan pod ships with its dependent ships swarming."

"Damn! Where can Cristobal be hiding?"

"How 'bout right out in plain view?" Evlin said. "Sometimes that's the last place anybody thinks to look, you know."

Iger gave the dancer an evil glance. "Oh, sure, they'll just be parked in orbit somewhere for everybody to see . . . hold on." His eyes slid back to his board. "Hey, I just got a reading on something that looks mighty like the *Lovejoy.*"

"Are you sure it isn't just another pod ship?" Evlin said. "Maybe two?"

Iger ignored him. "it's the *Lovejoy*, sure enough, and two fighters. I'd put credits on it."

"Show me." Kayla frowned into the interscreen linkage and her eyes grew wide. "You're right. He's parked it in a wide orbit near Brayton's Rock with a bunch of smaller ships, too. We've found them."

"Cristobal is even stupider than I thought," Iger said. "Sitting out here like a blinking target, just begging for one of Karlson's mega-armed police cruisers to swoop down and blow him out past Brayton's Rock."

"He's too confident," MacKenzie said. "Always was, always will be."

"Then let's use it against him," said Kayla. "Iger, close with them, but do it slowly. On my signal." She summoned a narrow nearsense probe, determined to begin searching for Cristobal's mind signature. But the probe faltered and Kayla cursed loudly. Had she overtaxed her mindpowers on the Mindstar?

The probe sputtered again, flared, and firmed up. Uttering a relieved sigh, Kayla swept over several familiar minds and cut through a horde of unfamiliar ones. She felt as though she were moving through a mountain of soaked bread: Every mind she encountered had a spongy, too-soft feel to it that made her want to draw back in revulsion. Mindsalt had been at too many minds here for too long and made them squishy to the touch.

A deep note sounded at the base of Kayla's spine and vibrated up each vertebra. —*Aha! Found you, Cristobal.*

She focused her probe and scanned his thoughts. To her horror she saw that Cristobal had some half-formed plan to attack St. Ilban. If he failed, he would take hundreds of innocent people down with him. Desperately, Kayla grabbed at his mind, funneling all of her considerable mental energy into seizing control of her former partner.

At her initial mindtouch Cristobal bucked and fought with surprising strength. Try as she might, she couldn't keep a solid grip on him.

—*No good,* said a cool, detached voice in her mind, the mindvoice of a stranger. —*Why don't you try to immobilize his speech center instead?"*

It was a good idea and perhaps the only workable solution. If she could manage to keep Cristobal quiet long enough to take his ship . . . but that effort was beyond her faltering powers. He slipped away even as she was attempting to reach his speech center. Disgusted, Kayla gave up.

"Hail the *Lovejoy,*" she told Evlin. "But scramble it. Tell them to maintain their neutral stance. All orders will be coming from the *Antimony.* As of this moment I'm assuming command of the War Minstrels."

They came alongside the ponderous ship, a sleek silver minnow slipping up next to a dark gray whale.

"Cristobal is squawking," Evlin said. A grin lit his face. "He demands to talk to you."

"Tell him he can come over here and talk to me. Otherwise, I'm busy."

"Aye, Your Highness." Evlin turned back to the com board, eyes twinkling.

"Try to at least get the status of the War Minstrels," Kayla said.

"Cristobal refuses to talk to me," Evlin said. "He doesn't seem real eager to come over here either."

"Then try to tap into their data banks. I want to know about their firepower and any estimates they have on Alliance forces. Has there been any noise out of St. Ilban? Any sign that they know we're out here?"

"Hold on," Evlin said. He worked over the board, fingers flying. "Hmm. The *Lovejoy* is putting out fake ID so the St. Ilban port authority thinks it's a private merchant out of Salabria."

"At least Cristobal was smart enough to think that one up. Now see if they have any information on the whereabouts of the *Falstaff*."

Again, Evlin's fingers danced over the board.

"No sign."

A cold lump began to form in Kayla's stomach. "What about the crew?" she said, hoping against hope. "Salome? Rab? Arsobades? Maybe they've been rescued and dispersed throughout the War Minstrels?"

"No. They vanished before the force set out."

"Damn the man to Karlson's deepest dungeon!" Kayla cried. "If anything's happened to them . . ."

The stranger's voice in her head cut in smoothly.

—*There'll be plenty of time for that later. Right now you have an army to run and a battle to plan. You can't help your friends if you get caught out here by the Alliance police. Head back to safety and train them properly.*

—*But my friends are in trouble. What if they need my help right now?*

—*Are you going to go careering off after them and abandon all the people here? They need your help, too. You have no idea where your friends are. Perhaps they're light-years away. You'll find them later.*

The soothing voice made sense. Yes, she would find Salome and Rab and Arsobades. Later.

"All right. Tell Cristobal and Merrick that I want a meeting on the *Antimony*."

"For what?"

"Strategy."

* * *

Kayla should have been happy to see the familiar faces: dark and glowering Merrick the Blackbird, coppery-skinned Oscar Valdez, beefy Mepal Tarlinger, diffident Martin Naseka flashing his shy grin. But she was much more aware of who was missing. The room felt empty without her old friends. And the man responsible for their absence was walking toward her, reaching out his arms, and smiling.

"Katie," Cristobal said. "I knew you'd join us."

She stiff-armed him, shoving him against Mepal's broad chest. "You and I will talk," she said. "Later." Pointedly turning her back on Cristobal, she faced the others. "It's only a matter of time before the Alliance investigates this little party here, so let's not waste any time on small talk. I want us to return to Kemel, pronto, and plot some sort of coherent battle strategy. You can follow my lead."

"I don't see how you can walk in here and just start giving orders," Merrick said. He glanced across the table at Cristobal. "I thought he was in charge."

"There's been a slight change. He *was*. I am." Kayla's eyes flashed with fire but her voice was icy steel. Was Merrick going to be difficult? A little nearsense nudge might encourage his obedience. But she held back, deciding to wait. Merrick was unpredictable. First try reason, then charm, and if all else failed, coercion.

Cristobal's eyes darted toward her and back to Merrick. His face was crimson. "You can't treat me as if I don't even exist, Katie!"

"Be quiet," Kayla said, "or you won't." She could feel the blood lust rising in her, heating her throat, turning her mind to fire. *Selfish bastard. So help me, if any of my friends have been hurt because of you* . . . "Where's Salome?" she said. "Where're

Rab and Arsobades? On some prison barge? How could you do that to them? How? You bastard, I ought to kill you right here, right now." Hands balled into fists, she pulled back to hit him, but before she could swing, Iger grabbed her wrist.

Cristobal backed away from her. "Katie, it was a mistake. I can explain everything."

"Oh, I'd like to see that," she said sardonically. She shook herself free from Iger. "I'd really like to see how you can explain to me how you happened to hand my friends over to the Alliance police. By mistake."

"I'll make it up to you. I'll personally lead a battalion. Give me a hundred soldiers!"

"What I should give you is a one-way trip out of the *Antimony*'s air lock."

"We'll surprise them," Cristobal said. "Remember what we did on the *Lovejoy*."

"That was one ship and a lot of luck. We're not ready for St. Ilban, no way, not yet. I'm taking us back to Kemel."

"No!"

Her self-control evaporated. "Cristobal, if you're so bloody eager to attack St. Ilban, you may have the honor of doing so. In fact, I insist."

"That's more like it."

"I'm glad you agree," Kayla said, smiling with all of her teeth. "I'll let you fire the first shot personally. You'll get to make the first pass at St. Ilban."

"Great. How many fighters should I take with me?"

"One should do it."

"One? Just one ship?" His smile faltered. "I don't think I understand. How many are going to back me up?"

"None." She rounded on him. "Alone, Cristobal. You're going to do it all by yourself, since you're in such a goddamn hurry to launch this war."

"But that's a suicide mission."

"Not if you're as good as you seem to think you are."

The others were staring at her, eyes wide in dismay. Only MacKenzie, half-smiling, Iger, and Evlin seemed to be enjoying the show.

"Now hold on," Merrick said.

Martin Naseka leaned forward. "Katie, perhaps you ought to reconsider."

"I'll go with Cristobal," said Mepal Tarlinger, ever-loyal.

Cristobal's face fell even farther.

"It's decided," Kayla said. "Alone."

"Nothing's decided," Cristobal snapped. "You bitch! After all I've done for you."

Evlin shoved him, not gently, against the wall. "You don't talk to her that way," he said. "Want me to wrap my leg around your lousy throat? Maybe crack your jaw? It's your choice: Be a hero or an asshole. Your choice, Lord Cristobal, sir."

"Every one of you has taken her side," Cristobal said. "You're all against me now. But you'll see. I'll make you see." He turned and strode out of the room.

The rest of them eyed Kayla warily. After a pause, Merrick grunted. "If you're serious about attacking Vardalia—and I think you've gone space-batty to even consider it—we've got to get pilots scrambled and backup crews."

Kayla met his gaze without flinching. "You were ready enough to follow Cristobal into action."

"I was trying to argue the damned fool out of it."

"And what do you think of our chances?"

"Zero."

"I hate to find myself agreeing with you, Merrick, but I do. No, we're not going to attack St. Ilban. We're going back to Kemel, with or without Cristobal."

"Kayla," Evlin said. "Ops reports that a single fighter is moving out of formation, pulling away. It won't respond to our hail."

"Cristobal?"

"Who else?"

"Let him go. Get our course plotted. . . ."

Third Child came rushing into the room, chirping loudly.

"What is it?"

—Kayla, the Alliance forces have detected us and have launched warships against us.

"Let's get out of here," Iger said.

"No," said Kayla, making a lightning decision. "Let's fight them."

"Are you crazy, too?"

"There's no time to argue. Mac, I want you and Merrick running the squadrons. Send in a couple of fighters high and low, and make it look like a suicide move."

"That won't be hard," said MacKenzie.

"Flank the Alliance ships, and when they're diverted by the fighters, come in shooting and slam them between you."

Merrick glanced at his fellow squadron chief and nodded. "All right. Might just work if we're fast enough. Carve 'em to pieces before they realize what's going on, that's the ticket."

"Do we have numbers on their ships?" MacKenzie said. "A breakdown of their fighter to warship ratio?"

"They've launched three ships at us, class-N warships, with five accompanying fighters."

"Okay, everybody, here we go." Kayla took a deep breath. "Battle stations."

* * *

The Alliance forces came at them in a wedge formation, right into the space between MacKenzie's and Merrick's battalions. And like two wings, MacKenzie's and Merrick's forces closed upon the Alliance ships.

The War Minstrels came in fast, at subjump speeds. The ferocious velocity, unheard of in-system, was intended to frighten the Alliance troops and force them to concentrate upon the dangerous possibilities of collision.

Between MacKenzie and Merrick, the enemy

fighters were crushed. Ships blazed with silent and terrible fire, falling to ashes and space dust. One of the War Minstrels' fighters was lost with its pilots and one was disabled.

But that left three warships aimed right for Kayla and the remaining War Minstrel forces. Kayla scanned the screens and knew the odds were against her. "Withdraw," she said. "Mac, Merrick, get in behind them. I'll pull back beyond the edge of the system and see if they follow."

The voice in her head was clamoring for attention, but she had no time to listen and shoved it back into silence.

The War Minstrels pulled back to the edge of the system. The Alliance forces followed.

"Two minutes to system boundary," Evlin said.

The Alliance forces were gaining on them.

"One minute."

A shot exploded off the bow of the *Antimony*. The vacuum behind them lit up with fireworks as the Alliance ships peppered them with gunfire.

"Crossing the boundary," Evlin said. "Alliance forces are slowing."

"Keep moving," Kayla said. "Draw back. Don't return fire. Tell all ships to stop shooting."

"Alliance forces have come to a full stop," Evlin said. "I don't get it. Why aren't they following?"

"Who cares?" Kayla said. "Just get us well past Brayton's Rock."

"They're falling back, turning around. Guess they just wanted to chase us out of the system. Port authority's hailing us. All but one of the cruisers are returning to base."

"Ignore them. I want us to regroup and see how many of us are left."

The number of remaining ships came to forty-two cruisers and thirteen operable fighters. Two other fighters were maneuverable but badly in need of repair.

"Let's salvage what we can from the two," Kayla said. "See if we can set them on autodrive and load them up with explosives, maybe launch them at the radar buoys."

On-screen, Merrick's face turned pale. "You're planning to go back in? With less than we had before? You're crazy."

"No, angry."

Merrick opened his mouth to argue, but Kayla couldn't hear his words. She couldn't hear anything other than the mindspeech of one very familiar mind.

—*Have they sold the* Falstaff? *Ground it down as salvage? Those bastards. I don't think I'll be able to stand it if they've junked my ship.*

Salome. Kayla's heart began to pound.

—*Salome? Can you hear me? Where are you?*

She stopped her flood of mindspeech, suddenly remembering that the captain of the *Falstaff* was extremely sensitive to empathic contact and might convulse if probed too hard. But Salome was somewhere nearby, of that Kayla was certain.

—*Third Child, help me scan for Salome. Do it gently, you know how sensitive she is.*

—*I shall attempt it, Kayla. However, this will prevent me from maintaining control of the Mindstar.*

—*It's been pretty quiet. I think it's safe. Let's try to find Salome before she moves out of range.*

Together they cast their minds in a wide arc, searching for familiar mind signatures.

—*She was here. I heard her. I know it.*

—*Perhaps it was merely an echo. . . .*

—*No, there! Coming from somewhere near Xenobe. An orbital, perhaps.*

—*Kayla, I'm not certain you're correct. It is most difficult to read mind signatures across these distances.*

—*Of course it's her. We have to go after her, Third Child. Help me, please!*

—*Kayla. . . .*

Kayla withdrew from the mental connection and plugged into the navboard of the *Antimony*. She plotted a course for Xenobe, and the *Antimony* began to pull away from the other ships.

Merrick was on the com link in a flash. "What are you doing?" the Blackbird demanded.

MacKenzie chimed in. "Katie? Katie, answer me. What's your heading? Do you want us to follow?"

Iger leaned over her shoulder. "Katie? Aren't you going to answer them?"

Kayla brushed him off. She was fixed on a course that would take her to Salome, Rab, and Arsobades. She could still sense the source of that mind whisper and knew she had to find her friends, to free them before they were exposed to the horrors of a prison ship or an orbital penal colony.

Merrick was on-screen, roaring something about crazy determination. And in her head, that small, alien voice asked, —*What about the War Minstrels?*

Later. Everything else would have to wait. She would sacrifice a hundred troops, a thousand, to rescue her friends. With her lieutenants squawking protests over the com link, Kayla brought the *Antimony* around and advanced on Xenobe.

"MacKenzie and Merrick are following," Evlin reported. "Mad as hell."

"And right on our tail, in fact," Iger said. "I hope you know what you're doing, Katie."

She barely heard them, concentrating on locating the *Falstaff*'s crew.

—*Salome? Rab? Where are you?*

Was that the faintest trace of a familiar mental echo? Rab's? Kayla probed after it. There, on St. Ilban's orbitals, the fourth colony. That had to be the source.

She scanned for enemy craft. Nothing, just a few merchant freighters.

"Merrick, MacKenzie, now listen to me. Salome and Rab are on that colony, somewhere. Arsobades, too. I'm going in there after them."

MacKenzie sighed. "Then I suppose we're going in, too."

"On my signal. Three. Two. One. Now!"

Chapter Twelve

St. Ilban glinted green and gold like a piece of rounded gemstone glowing in the reflected purple light of its mother world, Xenobe. Somewhere on that orbital colony were Kayla's friends, and she was going to find them even if she had to scan the place inch by inch.

"Heads up," Iger announced. "Here comes trouble."

"What is it?"

"One, two, no, make that three warships coming up fast from the far side of Xenobe." He stared in blank-faced shock. "Look at all of those bastards. Like they were just waiting for us to come close enough."

"We've got to get through them, somehow," Kayla said. "Red alert."

Iger bent down to confront her. "Katie, we've got to pull back. Even if Rab, Salome, and Arsobades are all down there, we'll never reach them this way. It's crazy."

Kayla stared at the forces arrayed against them,

a silvery constellation of warships and fighters. She heard the tinny complaints of the War Minstrels over the radio and in her mind, reporting the ratio of their ships to those of the enemy. They were outnumbered, outgunned. Common sense dictated that they leave. But she had the Mindstar.

—*Third Child? Can you hear me?*

The dalkoi's mindspeech replied immediately. —*Of course, Kayla. I have had no luck in locating any of the other crew members of the* Falstaff.

—*Never mind that right now. I want you to unwrap the Mindstar.*

It took a long moment for the dalkoi to reply. —*Is that wise? With all of these vulnerable minds here, and all the trouble we had with the stone before?*

—*I have no choice. Something is going on here I don't understand. I've detected the thoughts of my friends, but I'm too far away to reach them alone, and you can't find them either.*

—*I would caution you, Kayla.*

—*Don't. Just do it, and link with me and Iger. We're going to beat those bastards out there and save our friends.*

—*As you wish.*

"Iger, prepare for mindlink," she said. "Evlin, take over for him."

The silver-haired dancer nodded, staring at her in confusion, but she had no time to explain it to him now. She reached out to Iger, opening herself to him.

The contact was immediate, almost sexual in impact, the tingling connection between her and Iger like some unseen umbilicus. She reached out to include Third Child, to form the triune mind that once before had successfully managed to contain and control the Mindstar.

The incredible power of the gem surged through their union, a blast of pure energy so potent that it nearly broke the bonds between them.

Kayla called to the others. —*Hold on! Concentrate. Don't let go or this thing will eat the minds of all of us.*

Third Child held steady, a solid, reassuring force. Iger wavered, wobbled, unfamiliar with the shifting wavelengths, the eddies of mindpower, struggling, stumbling.

Kayla supported him, showed him how to channel his energy, to meld it with hers and with Third Child's into a strong, unwavering stream.

The Mindstar flared suddenly, battering at their controls. Iger dangled helplessly at the end of the mindlink as Kayla and Third Child battled to keep the thing from throwing them off completely. The stone burned with strange fires, with old fragmentary dreams from fading remnants of dead minds.

—*Don't let go!*

Bucking like a live thing, the Mindstar drained power from their union into its hidden recesses. Kayla forced herself to concentrate on her mindlink with the others, shoring it up, forming a bulwark with which to guide and channel the Mindstar's wild energies.

Together the three of them held, held and turned the Mindstar's awesome power outward, sweeping it on a broad arc through the heavens, casting it in a circular, ever-widening scan.

—*Rab? Arsobades, where are you?*

Kayla strained, longing for the answer. And it came. *Something* came. She had heard them! She knew it.

That note, there.

—*Rab? Can you hear me? Arsobades?*

But instead of the familiar, longed-for mind signatures, a flat, mechanical resonance answered her probe. A simulation of mindvoices.

A lure?

A trap.

The mind echoes: They were a cunning imitation of her friends' thoughts, magnified and looped, projected back at her. But by what? And then Kayla knew.

A groupmind.

The simulations of her friends' thoughts had been projected by a group of mindlinked empaths. And Kayla knew of only one such groupmind, the same one that she had once before encountered— and nearly been destroyed by—in Vardalia, years ago.

Then her mindpowers had been awesome and, with some help, she had defeated the groupmind. But now it was twice as strong. Its questing tendrils reached out for her, sensing her empathic powers, drawn as though magnetized toward her mind and those of her friends.

To her horror Kayla felt herself being pulled out of the triune linkage with Iger and Third Child, her awareness stretched thin, thinner, and fine as a sparkling wire, a pulsing artery between two vital organs.

She tried to fight it, to cling to her friends, to use the Mindstar's power to shield herself. But it was no use. Despite her best efforts, she fell, almost as though the Mindstar had greased her path and pushed her feet out from under her. She grappled vainly for a mindhold, sliding away from her comrades down a long, shining pathway that emptied into a vast and bottomless darkness that snapped shut behind her.

* * *

Silence. An emptiness in the mindfield that could only be explained as absence.

—*Kayla?* The dalkoi, drifting, queried, searching for the familiar mind signature which must be somewhere in the misty mindfield.

Iger searched also, his disquiet growing. —*Katie, where are you? Why don't you answer?*

Instead, a cool, strange, third voice replied, drifting into their minds as if borne on a nonexistent wind. —*She's gone. I don't know where. Something came and took her away.*

—*Who the hell are you?*

There was a pause. A small dry sound that might have been two bones rubbing together or one mind laughing.

—*My name is Golias.*

—*What are you doing in Katie's head?*

—*He is esnnimm, Iger.*

—*A what?*

—*An unwanted passenger.*

—*A hitchhiker? How'd you get in here? Did you do something to her?*

—*No. It happened during the Mindstar event on the asteroid. I had been trapped in the stone. Now I'm trapped in Kayla's mind. On the whole, I prefer it this way.*

—*Yeah? Maybe I'd prefer it that you take a hike.*

—*Calm yourself, Iger. Until we can relocate Kayla's mentality, we must at least keep her body animated and this stranger—*

—*Golias.*

—*. . . will at least be able to maintain her.*

—*Like she's been possessed? No way.*

—*I'm afraid we have no choice, Iger.*

—*Shut down that damned Mindstar, then. Maybe that'll get rid of this guy and bring Katie back.*

—*What if it cuts us off from her forever?*

—*Don't be ridiculous. We're not in touch with her now, are we? And without Kayla we can't use it, can we?*

—*No. Without her mindpowers, we can barely rein in the stone's power.*

—*Wait. You must listen to me. I'm at least capable of keeping this body animated while its owner is gone. But you have to help me.*

—*Help you walk around like some zombie in Katie's body? It's obscene. No way. Absolutely not.*

—*Iger, he may have a point. We don't know just how long Kayla's body can be sustained without her consciousness being within it.*

—*Are you crazy, too, Third Child?*

—*Hardly. You must calm yourself. This stranger can provide an important service to our friend. I recommend that, temporarily, we accept his offer.*

—*I don't like it.*

—*You don't have to.*

—*How do we control him? What if he just takes off with Kayla's body?*

—*I admit its a temptation,* the stranger told them. *But I don't have the mastery of this body yet. I don't think I could move it very fast if I tried.*

—*You won't get the chance. You're going to spend some time in the* Antimony's *clinic, under guard.*

—*And if your friend Kayla never returns to her body?*

—*We'll deal with that if we have to, later.*

* * *

—*Iger? Third Child? Hello, can anybody hear me?*

Kayla knew that she was in trouble, knew that

she was caught someplace far from her friends, cut off from the mindlink, alone and confused.

Really alone.

Her own thoughts echoed loudly within her very own mind cave. She paced the length of it, hammered futilely with her mind against its impervious walls. Imprisoned. This was as bad as any jail cell, perhaps worse.

But there were windows in this cave. High up— parallel ports which she could just reach if she strained. Kayla peered through them and saw a huge jumbled scene of glowing colors, fantastic shapes, strange angles. Slowly the shapes realigned and resolved into recognizable objects: the lights on a navboard, the scanners of a warship.

It took her a moment to realize that she was looking out through somebody else's eyes.

She was in somebody else's brain.

Cautiously she searched her new environs, but there was nobody else in this head with her, no hint of even the vestigial fragments of a former personality. The body did its work, the autonomic and other physiological systems functioned, but how? Blood pumped through the heart's muscle and out again, air moved in and out of the bellows of the lungs. But where was the body's controller? What was propping it up? And how had any of this happened?

Mindsalt. Her own mind curled around the thought and pulled back in revulsion.

The mindsalt had done its sinister work, burrowing through her host's nervous system, burning out neural pathways, exalting and then numbing the senses, altering the thought processes so gradually that the addict was not fully aware of losing his mentality.

Mindsalt hollowed out its victims until they were little more than automatons encased in flesh. Any empath with even a fledgling ability would be able to control them. A powerful groupmind could keep a squadron, a platoon, even an army of healthy mindsalt zombies moving—and attacking—almost indefinitely, as long as the bodies lasted.

Pelleas Karlson's groupmind had controlled the body Kayla sat in. It was trying to reach it even now. She cut off its attempts, shutting out its seductive whispers by slamming down her own mindshield, cloaking it to echo as though it were just another receptive empty skull. She had dueled with the groupmind before—and won—but she had no desire to do so again, especially alone and unassisted.

A coruscating field of purple and orange diamonds danced across her vision. It faded slowly, and Kayla peered out through the eyes of her host to see the slack, dull faces of the other officers on the bridge of this ship. Dimly, she could hear the orders of the groupmind being issued. If only she could send this all back through Iger to the War Minstrels! Who would have ever suspected that they were fighting an army of literal zombies, zombies made docile by mindsalt?

The groupmind went off like an all-ships bulletin, brash and loud: —*You will destroy all traces of these rebel fighters. They have been lured here and now they must not be allowed to leave. Surround them and destroy. Destroy!*

In spite of herself, Kayla found that the compelling, powerful mindvoice was getting to her. She became aware of the body she was in shifting slightly in position as it worked what she realized was a weapons board beneath its fingers. In a moment she would be firing upon her own comrades, and there was not a thing she could do about it. She felt her own will fading as the voice droned on and on.

—*Destroy. Destroy them.*

A sudden shift in timbre, a different voice, brought Kayla back to attention. A voice from her past, from old, unwanted memories and bad dreams.

Yates Keller, addressing his troops.

—*We've drawn the rebels into our trap. Let's finish them now. Close upon them and blast them away.*

No. She wouldn't do it, couldn't allow this to happen. She felt her anger growing and she fixed upon it, used it as a source of energy and power. *Get up!* she told her prison-body. *Get moving, damit.*

She forced the torpid limbs to shift, the numb

backside to slide forward in its webseat. The body was sluggish, as though it had been sitting for a long, long time.

Where was that bastard Keller? If she could get a fix on him, she would turn his own troops against him and use one of his own ships to blast him out of the skies, so help her.

She struggled with the body that imprisoned her. And slowly, ever so slowly, it began to obey her commands.

* * *

Aboard the *Antimony*, Iger came out of the mindlink to find his face covered in sweat. He gazed uneasily upon Katie's body, possessed now by the entity called Golias. Its shoulders were slumped, the muscles of its face were slack. It nodded at him in what was surely intended to be a reassuring manner but succeeded only in unnerving him further.

Here we sit, he thought, *in the flagship of a rebel army under attack and our leader has just been possessed by—for all I know—a demon.* A demon named Golias who was barely able to make Katie's body move. But how long would that last? How long before he gained real control? And what if anybody else saw her like this? Evlin had obviously noticed something odd and was trying to catch his eye, to ask all the questions Iger didn't want to have to answer.

It was time to take some action, fast.

Iger switched on his ship-to-ship scrambler. "MacKenzie? Mac, can you hear me?"

A faint and reedy reply. "Who's that? Iger? Let me talk to Her Highness."

"No good. You're it, Mac."

"What are you saying? Kate's been hurt?"

"Uh, yeah, sort of."

"How badly?"

"I don't know," Iger said truthfully. "She can't talk, at least not right now. So you're in charge. Start calling the shots, Mac, and hurry. That armada is getting closer every second that we wait."

"Right. I'm switching to all-ships." MacKenzie's voice disappeared into static and reemerged on a slightly different frequency. "War Minstrels, pull back," he said. "This is Mac, assuming temporary command. Pull back past system boundaries and plot course for Kemel. Use subjump if you have to, but I'll frag the first clown who has a collision."

The War Minstrels, bloodied and torn, began to retreat.

* * *

Helpless, horrified, Kayla watched her friends pull away and heard the orders to pursue them issue from the mind of the man she hated most in the universe.

—*Follow and destroy them!* Yates Keller said. —*Don't let them get away.*

They'll chase them all the way back to Kemel, she thought. *They've got the War Minstrels outgunned and outnumbered. I've got to do something to stop this. Got to find a way to interrupt this massacre.*

A beaker of pink stuff, mindsalt in frothy liquid, was placed at her elbow. If the troops needed more of the drug, then they were probably at their most vulnerable, at lowest ebb. Now, was the time to strike at them! Oh, if only she could reach Third Child and, through her, access the Mindstar. If only she had more power, she could finish that goddamned Yates Keller, once and for all.

The thought sent a jolt along the spine of the body she was in, a spark of hope that quickly died. She was too weak, the body too enervated. There was no way she could reach Third Child, not now.

But in a few moments, when the first flush of the mindsalt reaction was spreading throughout the troops, what about then? Yes, perhaps she would be able to ride that mindsalt surge as far as it would go, reach out, searching for Third Child and Iger. It just might work.

She forced her prison-body to pick up the beaker, raise it to numb lips, and drink the wretched stuff. It went down cold and clammy and sat, a chilled rock in the stomach.

Another few moments, she thought. *Be patient.*

Sure enough, she could feel the mindsalt beginning to work upon the body, beginning to sing in its blood, sharpen perceptions, deepen colors and sounds. And the energy—dear gods, it was roaring up through her, from the feet to the head. Suddenly Kayla felt as if she could lift a starship single-handedly and toss it right into the heart of a supernova. The mindsalt was a vibrating electrifying current pulling her into the enormous circuit that was the Alliance army.

As the groupmind began issuing orders, Kayla felt the energy peaking within her. This was the moment. She climbed the crest of the mindsalt surge and reached out, rising, rising ever higher, climbing up above the noise of the groupmind, above the sounds of the warships, surging toward Third Child, toward Iger and the War Minstrels.

Perilously balanced upon the energy surge, Kayla opened her mind on an intimate, narrow mode.

—*Third Child. Third Child, please hear me. Please! It's Kayla. I'm aboard an Alliance vessel.*

She waited in eager anticipation, but there was no answer. The silence was complete, as though she had never mindspoken another being, let alone linked with them.

Kayla was trapped in the body of an enemy, surrounded by troopers on an enemy's ship, about to attack her friends. She had never felt so alone.

* * *

Iger watched Katie's body slowly pull itself to its feet and walk—stagger, really—the length of ops.

Instead of the light-footed grace he remembered, he saw to his dismay that she strode with a heaviness that made her seem drunk or drugged, a clumsy figure. Her eyelids drooped at half-mast and her hands hung limply at her sides, swinging slightly with each stride she took.

This is no good, Iger thought. *She looks like a mech. Or a dead woman.*

Tensely, he waited for her to leave the room and prayed that nobody asked her any questions. Gods help them if Golias—or whatever that thing was in Katie's head—attempted to stay and answer.

How was he going to find Katie's consciousness? His mindpowers were so weak, nearly nonexistent without her to help guide and focus them. Iger felt despair wash over him. If Katie's mind didn't make contact soon, her body wouldn't be able to keep going . . . or would it, animated by that stranger fragmentary personality? That was even worse: a Katie-not, a thing that would have to be destroyed.

The thought chilled him to his core. Could he kill Katie's body, even if he knew that what was in it was a malicious stranger? Iger didn't want to have to make that kind of decision. Desperately, he turned back to his com board and hoped that Katie would find them.

—Hurry, Katie. Hurry up! We can't wait around. Mac has ordered a retreat. There's only a little bit of time left for you to find us before we're out of range.

* * *

Katie watched helplessly as the Alliance fleet began to fire upon her friends with renewed ferocity.

—*Third Child! Iger! You've got to hear me, please! While the mindsalt is still working.*

She felt as if she was throwing messages out into the void, letters that no one was going to read.

—*Kayla?*

—*Oh, gods, thank you.* It was Third Child's blessedly familiar mind signature.

—*We had thought you were lost.*

—*Well, I'm right here, in somebody else's body. We can destroy these bastards if you can link with me and the Mindstar. I'm going to try to cause a feedback wave that will fry out what's left of these soldiers' brains. If we blow the fuses, the machine won't work, right?*

—*I cannot take part in such carnage.*

—*Third Child, these are the walking dead! What's more, they're attacking you, attacking our friends!*

—*I'm sorry, Kayla.*

—*Fine. You're condemning me, instead. I'll be trapped in this body unless the Mindstar can free me.*

—*But . . .*

—*Get Iger.*

In a moment, Iger's familiar mind signature

bloomed like a wonderful flower in her mind.
—Katie, you found us. Gods, I was worried. Where the hell are you? What happened?

—Never mind that. Just send that Mindstar power through me, fast. Third Child will show you how.

—You've got it.

The dalkoi made no further protests, and soon the thrumming, overwhelming energy of the Mindstar was pouring through Kayla as though she were a conduit.

She forced the body she was in to move, to get up, to reach across the span from the weapons board to navigation and the body sitting there. She touched it. It convulsed briefly, slumped, fell. She lumbered to the next station, touched the next body, and sent it crashing to the floor. And the next, and the next.

Now she sent the Mindstar current into the minds of those elsewhere on the ship. As they fell, she began to extend the range ship by ship, mind by mind, throughout the Alliance armada. There was surprisingly little resistance.

Bodies slumped, soldiers gasped, clutching heads in slow-motion agony. Ships went dark, hung in space unmoving.

The groupmind growled, screamed, lunged at her. Only at the last moment did she evade the attack, dodging it nimbly.

That was close, she thought, *too close.*

Kayla poured power into her mental shields. The groupmind was dangerously strong, but it was no match for the Mindstar's unique power. And, raised up by the Mindstar, Kayla could hold the groupmind at bay while knocking out platoon after platoon of its zombie troops.

She parried each thrust that came at her. But she had pushed too hard and too long for the body she was riding. A dreadful chill swept through it. It shuddered, shuddered again, and began to convulse. Kayla knew that it was beginning to die. She must escape it, or die, too.

—*Iger, Third Child, pull me back! Hurry. This body is going to go.*

Instead of the reassuring message she expected, Third Child said: —*Kayla, we can't get you. Something is interfering. Each time we grab at you, something gets in the way.*

—*The groupmind?*

—*We can't tell. Come toward us.*

—*I'm reaching for you now. Can you feel me?*

—*We're getting close. Closer.*

A quavering, building scream, a light too bright to focus upon, was pounding against Kayla, threatening to rend her body and mind, to tear her to pieces. She held, held against it, pushed, trying to keep open the way to Third Child and Iger, the only way back.

There was a sudden rending, a giving, and the light took Kayla, snapping her too fast for thought. Maddeningly, she brushed against a mind she did recognize: Yates Keller.

Stop, she wanted to cry. *Wait! I've got him. Let's take him, now!*

Her thoughts went swirling away in the interchange. She was only a drifting mote, not a mind, not a body, a mere speck caught in a dangerous moment. Revenge would have to wait.

A sudden burst and upswelling, not quite perceived as pain but uncomfortable and growing more so, a noise too loud, a light too bright, tore at her, slashing at the essence of her consciousness. She was completely exposed to the sudden onslaught and her mind screamed out for what seemed like an eternity before she was yanked away.

*   *   *

The pain had stopped. She was in a glowing space, peaceful, floating, safe. She didn't know where she was, but that didn't matter. She had escaped from something terrible, and the knowledge of that alone was sufficient.

Chapter Thirteen

"Katie, can you hear me?"

Iger stood near Kayla—Kayla's body, rather—slumped in a webseat in the *Antimony*'s clinic.

She had suddenly gone rigid, as though an electric shock had coursed through her system. Her eyes had closed, her mouth contorted into a grimace, and then had come a terrible collapse, head rolling back, mouth slack.

"Katie!" Iger had grabbed at the body, hoping that this wasn't just some new and awful game the demon possessing her was playing.

Iger had been questioning the personality called Golias, anxious to learn if the demon knew where Katie was. He had expected to find her safely back in her own skull after the mind concert between them and Third Child and had been horrified to find the stranger glaring out of Katie's green eyes at him.

"Maybe she's vanished." The voice was familiar, but the accent odd, and the words slurred as though the tongue had gone thick in the mouth.

"Dissipated. The mindforces she was fighting were formidable."

"Shut up, or I'll drug you silent!"

"That won't bring her back," the demon Golias had said.

"How do I know that? Maybe you're lying. Maybe you're really the one who's been keeping her from getting back into her skull."

Katie's face, that was not really Katie's at all, had smiled a terrible malicious smile. "You'll never know that, will you, Iger?"

The clinic was several levels below ops and the sound of the *Antimony*'s engines was a steady, roaring presence in the room. Iger had felt a similar roaring growing louder, pounding in his own skull.

Then the convulsing had begun.

He knelt, putting his arms around her, whispering reassuring nonsense syllables.

And she sat up and stared wonderingly at him.

* * *

Kayla didn't know who the blond-haired stranger was, but she liked the way he was looking at her. He smiled, white teeth in a tan face. She smiled back.

"Do I know you?"

His smile grew broader. "You did."

"What's your name?"

"Iger."

"What's mine?"

His smile wavered. "You're not kidding, are you, Katie?"

"Katie? That's me?" *Katie. Katie.* It sounded vaguely familiar, almost right. "No, I'm not kidding. At least, I don't think so."

"Third Child?" the man named Iger called. He leaned over a brightly-lit panel and spoke into it, sounding increasingly upset. "Third Child, get down here, fast."

Moments later, one of the strangest-looking creatures Katie—if that was her name—had ever seen came waddling into the room. It had a pointed head, bright lavender eyes, a tapering, rounded body, and two limbs upon which it walked. The thing came close to her, made a strange, chirping sound, and closed its eyes. Then it turned to Iger and shook its triangular head.

"What do you mean she doesn't remember anything?" Iger said. "She's got to remember."

The thing chirped again.

"Third Child, you have to help her."

So that is Third Child, Katie thought. "It's sort of cute," she said. "What is it?"

He replied brusquely, "A dalkoi. And it's a she."

"How can you tell?"

Iger opened his mouth, closed it again. "I just can. And so could you, before you forgot." He paused. "I have something to ask you that might sound a little strange."

Katie smiled at the blue-eyed stranger. He really

was nice-looking, broad-shouldered, and with all that long blond hair pulled back and tied behind his neck. He carried himself with such easy grace. "Go ahead."

"Do you remember anything? Anything at all?"

She paused, pondered, shook her head.

"Where were you before you were here?"

"I don't remember."

"Do you have any recollection of the War Minstrels? Mac? Merrick?"

"No. Should I?"

He sighed, rubbed his eyes. "Do you have any weird feelings? Like maybe there's another voice or presence in your head with you? Something that might be controlling you?"

"What do you think I am, crazy?"

"Just answer me, please."

"Another voice in my head?" She stared at him. "Why would I have that? And how would I be able to check?"

"You're an empath, remember?"

"A what?"

"I don't believe this," Iger muttered. "Golias! Stop playing games with me."

"Why are you yelling? And who's Golias? I thought you said that my name was Katie!"

A tall, thin man draped himself gracefully in the doorway. His muscles stood out in sharp definition against his gold and red stretchsuit and his eyes, rimmed by orange swirls, were a piercing icy gray.

He stared pointedly at Katie. "What's wrong with you, Your Highness?"

"What do you mean, what's wrong with me? Why call me that?" She was fascinated by his appearance, but his angry tone put her on guard. "Nothing's wrong with me. Who are you?"

He turned to Iger. "What's going on here? Why did she zombie out of ops? What's she doing in sick bay? And why doesn't she recognize me?"

"I honestly don't know," Iger said. "She's caught a good case of amnesia."

Evlin looked disgusted. "Damn! Where's the *Antimony's* mechdoc?"

"It was under repairs, left at Kemel Station."

"So you're telling me we don't have a doctor, and Katie doesn't know who she is?"

"That's about the size of it."

"I know a doctor in the Salabrian System. We'll be safe there. Iger, I'll show you the plot coordinates."

"Don't you think you should tell Mac about it? He's in charge now."

Evlin's glance was filled with icy disdain. "Why don't you tell him?"

"Hey," Kayla said. "Stop talking about me as if I'm not even here."

Iger ignored her, called MacKenzie ship-to-ship, and explained the situation. MacKenzie's reply was immediate. "I say we go back to Kemel," he said. "No sense all of us sailing around the galaxy like this. We need time to regroup."

"Right. We'll rendezvous on Kemel. *Antimony* out." Evlin turned and flashed a dark look at Iger. "Keep Katie out of sight if you don't want the troops to riot. And let's get going. You're pilot now." With that he was gone, heading for ops.

Kayla watched Iger's face flush with anger. "Would you mind telling me who's in control around here?" she said.

His mouth worked for a moment and then he said: "Good goddamned question. Wish I knew."

* * *

The transition to Salabria was not smooth. Iger sat the navboard, and although he was an experienced navigator he was a much less intuitive, graceful pilot than Kayla. The result was a stiff, jolting ride with the *Antimony*'s engines grinding through each course change as Iger brought the ship's speed up to jump velocity.

They made the passage from realspace to jump without incident, but Iger prowled the silvery pathways of the jump interface with a sense of nervous anticipation. Orange pyramids leaped out of crevasses. Lavender spheroids caromed off the wall beside his head. He felt as if he were in the midst of a blinking vid cube shooting gallery.

The floor seemed to lift up and out from under him. Wave upon wave of distortion made the walls shimmy. The jump interface features blurred into a mixture of half-melted shapes, a dangerous situation when traveling at jumpspeed, relying upon landmarks and split-second timing to make the exit from jumpspace successfully.

Another wave of distortion hit, and another. Despite the danger, Iger pulled himself out of the navboard connection while still in jump and found that ops was being buffeted by a series of strange whirling energy storms, small golden cyclones that appeared out of nowhere, descended upon some hapless crew member, and departed a moment later, disappearing, leaving the assaulted personnel immobilized and in shock.

Iger didn't know what was causing it but he had a damned good hunch: the Mindstar.

He saw Evlin staring at him in outrage and fear as a golden whirlwind spun past him.

"Get Katie up here," Iger shouted.

"Are you crazy?" Evlin said. "I don't even think I can walk through this."

"Do it if you have to crawl! I can't leave the board!" Something in his tone must have gotten across to the dancer. In one quick, graceful move Evlin was out of his seat and across the room.

Iger didn't have time to watch him. He sank back into the navboard connection, battling to keep the ship on course. The exit point for Brayton's Rock loomed ahead. If they missed it, they would be forced to use a distant star system as their exit point, come out, turn, and begin the buildup to jump speed again. There were risks associated with every single move made in jumpspace, when entering it, and while leaving it. Iger didn't want to overshoot.

The Mindstar—for what else could it have been?—was erupting so powerfully now that he came out of the jump interface momentarily to find himself holding onto the navboard with one hand and his seat with the other. Where the hell was Katie? Hadn't Evlin gotten her up here yet? He called for her weakly via mindspeech.

—Katie! Can you hear me? Hurry up!

Another dizzying wave of Mindstar energy rocked ops. Iger cursed the day he had ever heard about mindspeech—cursed, too, the day he had ever decided to leave his home world, Liage, for the excitement of space. This was all getting just a bit too exciting. More than a bit, maybe.

—Katie, damnit, I know you can hear me. You're the one who taught me how to do this! Help!

He strained to reach her with all the power he had in him, all the vestigial empathic skills that Katie had discovered and helped him to nourish and use while piloting a spaceship.

—Katie!

No answer. He felt somebody pulling at his arm and brushed them away, trying to concentrate.

Someone yanked off his headset.

"Hey!"

Evlin stood there, silver-haired, orange lines around his eyes, holding the navboard connectors and staring at him as if he were questioning his sanity. "Katie's here. I brought her, like you asked."

Iger closed his eyes briefly, ignoring the strange look Katie was giving him, and reached out to her with his mind.

After what felt like his entire lifetime passing, a quavering tentative reply came forth.

—*Iger, why can I hear you in my mind?*

—*Don't ask questions now, just link with me.*

—*I don't know how.*

—*Damnit! Third Child, can you hear me?*

His mindpowers were so very weak and uncertain, his ability to sustain mindspeech so extremely limited that he felt the connection to Katie fraying, unraveling even as he called for help. In a moment it was gone, before he had been able to contact Third Child. Disgusted, he resorted to the intraship com link. That, at least, was usually reliable.

"Third Child to ops! Third Child to ops on the double!"

Another wave of Mindstar power rocked them. The ship bucked and the ops crew members clutched their heads, battered by the wild emanations.

Iger plunged back into jumpspace and anxiously scanned their pathway. They still had a few minutes left to make it out safely into Cavinas space. A familiar sound brought him up out of the navboard interface.

"Churrip!"

The dalkoi was standing at his side, eyes bright, glancing from him to Katie and back again.

"Third Child," he said. "Mindlink with Katie. She can't do it by herself."

Third Child chirped loudly.

"She doesn't remember how," Iger said. "And I can't keep a link with her long enough. So you do it, okay? Then link with me and maybe the three of us can get that damned stone under control. Otherwise, I'm going to jettison it."

Third Child gave a squeak of what might have been dismay or protest. Her lavender eyes began to glow.

The mindlink grabbed Iger's mind like an invisible claw, making him shudder. No matter how many times he did this, he would never get used to it. He had to concentrate on jumpspace, but he also had to concentrate on what was happening here. He fervently wished that the crackerjack pilot Oscar Valdez was on the *Antimony*—if they ever made it through jumpspace to Brayton's Rock, he'd have him transferred.

In mindlink Iger felt like the third side of a triangle that was attempting to walk in every direction at once. It was even worse than usual this time because Katie—usually the linchpin of their mindlink—was flailing about and had to be contained and focused by Third Child. Iger calmed himself and waited. Slowly, Third Child marshaled their power and pushed the triune mind toward the pulsating fire of the Mindstar.

It was like trying to grab hold of an erupting volcano. By comparison, capturing the Mindstar's energy while in the confines of realspace had been easy. Trying to tame it in the jump interface was a nightmare.

The Mindstar didn't want to be controlled. It jerked like a wild animal, nearly throwing them off, and each time it broke free it tried to absorb the combined mindpower of the three of them. And if it succeeded, from there it would move on to the rest of the crew, devouring every mind, leaving a crew of dead or insane in its wake.

Had the Mindstar grown even stronger? Iger couldn't tell, but he suspected as much. It was too much to master while in jumpspace. He made a snap decision to take the *Antimony* out of jump before Cavinas.

The nearest plausible exit site took them out into a tiny system, Mantissa's Sun, a feeble and undersized green star circled by one lonely pock-marked planet. Iger had never heard of it, but he was looking for a port in a mindstorm.

As the ship's engines slowed to subjump and realspace came back all around them, Iger set the *Antimony*'s autopilot for a wide orbit around the star and gave his full attention to the battle for their minds, and their sanity.

* * *

Kayla was lost in a jumble of light and noise. Her body didn't move—couldn't. But her mind was on a strange, frenetic journey. She felt the presence of Iger and Third Child beside her in some unaccountable way. And they were urging her to follow them, to focus all of herself upon a strange storm of unbearable light, the thing that Iger had called the Mindstar. It was bright, so terribly bright. Each time she tried to turn away from it, her companions gently prodded her back.

She felt the Mindstar reaching out, sensed its hunger, its ravening desire for the mental energy of others. It unfurled a massive tendril and sent it questing toward the tall man with the silver braid, the graceful, long-limbed one named Evlin.

No! Leave him alone!

She got hold of the thing and shoved it back toward Third Child.

In realspace, Third Child hiccuped once, twice, and set to work. Powered by the triune mind, the dalkoi enfolded the mindstone, containing it within a socket of neutral energy as it wove an impenetrable web around it. The dalkoi's mindforce swelled, expanded, seemed nearly to be on the verge of exploding.

Third Child hiccuped again.

A flash of Mindstar energy lashed out and caught Kayla in its nimbus.

But the triune mind fought back. Flashes of psychic energy split the ether, silent detonations as mindpower strained against mindstone. Slowly Third Child/Kayla/Iger forced the thing back into their net. It hung there, trapped, blinking a wild spectrum of colors.

They had prevailed, but Kayla felt as if every ounce of mind energy she possessed had been lifted out of her body and transferred to the effort to contain that terrible brightness. It had been a crushing task and had taken too much from her. Slowly, very slowly, she slid away from her companions, out of the triune mindlink, and into unconsciousness.

Dreaming, dreaming, she floated among crowds of people with unfamiliar faces—or were they? Each time she was on the verge of recognizing someone the features melted, merged, and became those of a stranger. A mob of endlessly changing strangers to whom she would never belong, milling around her. But they belonged, they knew one another, they were given all the things she lacked: family, birthright, kinship, history. They knew who they were, where they had come from, and where they were going. Each one had a past, and a future. Each one possessed the very thing that had been stolen from her, stolen by someone whose name she could almost remember.

She awoke to hear the sound of a mech humming gently. The room came back around her, blue walls, white ceiling, a familiar face at her side. She was lying on a soft cot and Iger was sitting nearby. The tall dancer, Evlin, graceful as a cat, lounged in the doorway, watching her closely. Third Child drooped against a wallseat, eyes closed.

Kayla flexed her legs and arms, trying to loosen her stiff, aching muscles. A scanner band was strapped across her forehead, and she could feel it pulsing against her skin.

"Welcome back," Evlin said.

Iger grinned down at her and squeezed her hand. "You gave us a hell of a scare, Katie."

Martin Naseka loomed up beside them, smiling his shy smile. "Yeah, but you inspired me to tap the *Antimony*'s engineering data banks and rig up an autodoc." His smile widened. "Never tried it before. An interesting challenge."

"So," Evlin said. "Do you remember anything?"

A roomful of hopeful faces. She shook her head, knowing she had disappointed them.

"Mechdoc says there's no sign of traumatic damage to the brain," Iger said, reading from a portascreen. "No evident damage to the limbic system; the temporal lobes, hippocampus, and mammillary bodies are intact. No concussion. What you've got isn't post-traumatic amnesia, at least not of a physiological nature."

Evlin frowned. "What's that supposed to mean? Is there any other kind?"

"Psychological. Katie could have suffered some sort of profound emotional wound, something that caused her memories to be repressed."

"And what's the cure for that?"

Iger shrugged, tapped the mechdoc board, and scanned the readout. "It says that we can try to reexcite those regions of her brain that contain long-term memory. Sometimes that works. But there's no sure solution for amnesia. At least not in this thing's database."

"How long could this last?"

Iger squinted at the board again. "It's rare for nontraumatic-based amnesia to persist, but again, there are cases of lifelong memory loss."

Evlin kicked at the mechdoc angrily. "It can't last! We need her. Damnit, Katie, you've got to remember us."

She smiled, trying to pacify him. "I want to. Maybe I will. I'll try." She hoped that would make him feel better, but all it earned her was a look of disgust from him.

Martin Naseka began removing the mechdoc connections, freeing her. She sat up, stretching her neck, her back, and slowly rolled her head from side to side.

"What about that Mindstar thing?" she said.

Iger frowned at her. "We'll talk about it later. I think we've got it under control." He tugged at her hand. "C'mon, it's late. I've got to plot our way out of this backwater tomorrow. Evlin, you've got ops."

"Thanks a whole lot, Sir Iger."

Hand in hand, Kayla walked with Iger through the *Antimony*'s corridors until they came to Iger's bunk. Without a word they walked in, Iger shut and locked the door, and they began to undress.

When they were in bed, Kayla snuggled up against Iger, enjoying the warmth of his skin, the dry spicy scent of it. She really liked him, even if she didn't know him very well.

Gently she ran her hand down his chest, heard him sigh, and felt him shift closer to her. She experimented with touching him here, touching him there, and soon he began to run his hands over her skin, too.

He kissed her deeply and she felt his hands moving eagerly down her body. Excitement was beating a wild drum in her chest and she began to gasp as he entered her and they moved rhythmically together, faster and faster.

She felt his mind reaching out for hers and willingly opened, linking with him as the world exploded around her in spasms of hot, white pleasure.

With each delirious wave came scenes of life, of color, of warmth, love, and anger. All of these washed over her.

* * *

She was in ops on the Falstaff, *steering the ship safely past a dead ship, pulling them out of jumpspace, feeling the protection of Third Child's aura around her, preventing her from convulsing, dying.*

* * *

She was lying in bed with Iger as he told her that he loved her.

* * *

She was struggling to free herself from the arms of Yates Keller, finally using her mindpowers to break his hold and strike him, senseless, to the floor.

* * *

She was fleeing for her life, hiding in the cold night in an alley on Brayton's Rock.

* * *

She was in the tunnels of Styx, walking behind her parents.

* * *

The earth shook beneath her feet as she ran through dark tunnels, desperate and frightened.

* * *

She and Beatrice Keller, Yates' mother, stood face-to-face at the Miners' Guild of Styx, arguing.

* * *

She was running through the halls of the Admiral Lovejoy *with a mob of inmates behind her, leading them to the bridge.*

* * *

She was plotting to get the Falstaff *out of debt by finding the Mindstar.*

* * *

She hated Yates Keller. He had taken away her parents, her world, her future. She would destroy him.

* * *

And then she knew. Kayla, she was Kayla. It all came flooding back. Her life. Every shred of memory, every moment of her life, good and bad.

"Iger," she cried. "I remember."

She saw again how she had been dragged via mindlink from a dying body on an enemy ship, ambushed by the groupmind, and sent into limbo before finally landing back in her own aching skull minus her memory.

She had herself back.

But there was somebody else there, somebody else watching and remembering, savoring every bit of feeling, every exquisite shudder, every gasp.

Golias.

With a shiver of revulsion Kayla remembered the unwanted passenger, the voyeur in her head. Golias.

—*So you like it that way, hmmm? How pedestrian.*

—*Shut up, you!*

—*I've got an idea, something I think both of you will enjoy. I picked it up in the pleasure market of Nunjader.*

—*Be quiet!* Kayla couldn't bear it. She shoved him back into a tiny corner of her mind and, ignoring his squawks of protest, imprisoned him behind a thick mindshield where she couldn't hear his obscene whispers.

Mortified, she broke off her mindlink with Iger. She couldn't stand the thought that he might discover how Golias had been a delighted observer of their lovemaking.

Iger didn't seem to notice the closing down of their mental connection, so delighted was he in the recovery of her memory. "Thank all the gods," he murmured. "I missed you, Katie." He hugged her until she had to fight for air.

She owned herself once more, had taken back her joys and her pain, her history, all that was important to her. Part of that was a burning drive to right the wrongs done to her. But another part was about love. And with that realization she once more wanted that primal connection with Iger. She began kissing him, guiding him back along the path with her to frantic, radiant ecstasy.

When she awoke later, her mind was blissfully silent. There was no sign of any other entity in there with her. Golias, if Golias it had truly been, was quiescent behind the sturdy screen she had erected.

Kayla allowed herself one long luxurious sigh of relief. She stretched, nudged Iger away with her toe, and got out of bed to face the day and spread the good news throughout the *Antimony*. She was back.

Chapter Fourteen

Kayla stared at the scrolling star maps with some perplexity. Iger leaned over her shoulder, sharing her confusion. "Mantissa's Sun? That's where we are?"

"Yep."

"Never heard of it." The screen scrolled through quadrants and coordinates. "I can't even locate it in the mapmind. Sweetie, let me hand it to you. You really found us one terrific spot to hide in."

"Hey, don't blame me. I told you what was happening. I had to get us out of jumpspace."

"Yeah, yeah, I know, I know. Wait. Hold on, I think I've found us." Kayla frowned and scrolled back through two screens. "Yes. Yes, that's it. There it is."

"You mean, there *we* are."

She peered hard at the coordinates. "Gods, talk about your backwaters. There's really nothing out here. No stations, not even a fueling stop, and no people."

"Except for us," Iger said. "Well, how about it.

Can you plot a course that will get us back to Kemel?"

"Yeah, but not a direct one. It'll be a three-jump from here." Her eyes met his above the screen. "I guess you'd better go tell Third Child to prepare herself. She'll have to sit on top of that damned Mindstar for the entire trip in case it decides to erupt."

"I'd rather her than me," Iger said. "That thing caused so much trouble during our last jump that I nearly threw it out the air lock."

Kayla stared at him, dumbstruck. Was he serious? While she had been out of commission, had her dearest companion—the person closest to her in the universe—almost destroyed everything for which she had worked, even risked her life? When she found her voice, she said, "I'm very glad you didn't." She couldn't trust herself to say more. "Let's get out of here."

Jumpspace was a familiar landscape, a welcome sight despite its skewed perspective and odd geometric equivalences: Kayla took the *Antimony* past a shimmering green sphere and dodged between a stand of spiky black rods. She felt the data streaming through her, full of points and vectors.

The *Antimony*'s jump engines purred. The first jump went so well that Kayla couldn't believe they were already through it and had to review the stats to convince herself that they were on their way to the second jump and still on course.

The second jump went smooth as bambera fur.

As they built up speed for the third jump, Kayla felt an odd commotion in her mind. At first she was afraid that the Mindstar had broken free of its restraints. But then she heard an all-too-familiar voice, a laugh that sounded like dry bones rattling, and she knew.

Golias had gotten out of his prison and was whispering to her in his repellent, confiding manner.

—*Why are you so intent on this path, I wonder? You'll only lose to the Alliance, and part of you knows it. Forget this rebellion.*

—*But those people are relying on me.*

—*Forget them. You have the Mindstar, what more do you need? You even know how to use it. Unimaginable wealth can be yours. Power. Why struggle with this political nonsense? For revenge? And if you get it, then what?*

—*Shutupshutupshutup!*

—*I see. Guilt is driving you. You fear that you've lost your friends, and that it's your fault. That the very people who took you in have become victims of your obsession for revenge. Well, it's probably true. So what? These won't be your only losses, Kayla. Better prepare yourself for more. Guilt is a luxury you can't afford.*

—*Damn you! I'll shut you up for good!*

He answered her with his arid laugh.

Kayla tried to shove him back, to encase him neatly behind a mindshield once again. But he resisted. She was horrified to feel him actually fighting her, a parasite draining strength from her struggles.

The engines whined as her trajectory within jumpspace began to go wide of its mark. A crash in jumpspace? It wasn't possible. But to become lost between worlds, between jump points, to float in this nonreality forever, that could happen, had happened, according to spacers' lore. Kayla had no intention of allowing the *Antimony* to become a ghost ship. There would be no sad ballads of the lost *Antimony* for her, thank you.

With renewed ferocity she battled Golias for control of her mind. He was getting stronger all the time. What could she do? What if he tried to preempt her completely?

Shadowsense.

The idea astonished her.

Quick as thought, she spun a tiny shadowsense field and surrounded Golias' presence with it. He struggled, struck out at her, but there was nothing he could do. He was well and truly disarmed.

Once he was helpless, Kayla encased him in a mindblock three times as strong as his previous prison. That would hold him. If she ever found another empath she could trust, she would beg, plead, and bribe for an exorcism.

But there was no time now to think about any of that. The *Antimony* was about to go right past its jump point vector. Kayla slowed engines—a daring maneuver in jumpspace.

The ship shook from port to stern, but it held

together. Slipping between two enormous golden pyramids, the *Antimony* made the crucial transition.

Realspace, with stars, with planets and people, came back around them.

"Iger? Do you read me? Iger? Does anybody hear me? Anybody there? What the hell is going on? *Antimony,* do you read? Where have you been?"

It was MacKenzie's wonderfully abrasive and impatient voice coming out of the com link. Just hearing it brought a smile to Kayla's face.

"Iger," MacKenzie rasped. "Damnit, I hope you can hear this. That looks like the *Antimony.* But I thought you were going to Salabria. What gives?"

Kayla leaned forward. "Mac, Katie here."

"Kate, that you? I thought you'd been knocked out for good. What happened? Found a medic?"

"Let's just say that we found a home remedy." She allowed herself a smile until she saw Evlin gazing at her with a new and unwelcome look in his eyes. Fear. She would have to do something about that, explain something to him, soon.

"Well," MacKenzie said. "I can't say that I enjoyed my time at the helm. I'm happy to return the mantle of control to you. What's our next move?"

She remembered the tantalizing feel of Yates Keller's mindtrail, so maddeningly close.

—*Damnit, I nearly had him that time.*

"Mac, I've got something in mind. Something

that involves another trip to the Cavinas System. Come on over and we'll talk about it."

She shut down the com link. Evlin was standing at her shoulder. "Katie?"

Uh-oh. This wouldn't wait. Not a minute more.

"Katie," Evlin said. "I don't understand. "How can you be out of your mind one moment, walking around like a zombie. Then, zap, you're back, but without any memory. And then, zap again, you're fine, no problem, back at the helm and giving orders again?" He trembled slightly. "Explain it, please. Explain it to me before I go crazy."

* * *

When MacKenzie arrived, Kayla took him and Evlin into the captain's lounge, had Iger stand guard, and told both men about her empathic powers and the Mindstar.

MacKenzie nodded, having had some of it explained to him previously by Salome. But Evlin stared, furious and disbelieving, as though Kayla had somehow betrayed his private trust.

When she had finished speaking, he ran his hands over his tight-braided silver hair. His eyes, rimmed by purple spirals, were huge. "You mean," he said, "that you've been peering into our heads, spying on us, reading our thoughts, maybe making us all do whatever you want us to do?"

"No, no, nothing like that. Not at all."

He frowned. "I've heard about empaths, Katie,

and everything I've heard is bad. They only work
for the Alliance. They crack open people's minds
like bad nuts, eat what's in there, and throw the
rest away. You can't trust them."

"Stop being so melodramatic," Iger snapped.
"That's bullshit and you know it."

"Yeah?" Evlin glared at him, and then included
Kayla in the look. "You checked out on us, Katie.
Deserted us right in the middle of battle. Gone.
Mindless."

"I didn't want to go! I told you, I got trapped, pulled right out of my head. That's why
MacKenzie took over. And he did a damned good
job."

"We're not following him. We're supposed to be
following you. You're the one who freed me. You're
the one *I* trusted. What if it happens again?"

Kayla saw how close she was to losing him and
she couldn't bear it. Not Evlin. She reached out,
palms open. "Here, let me show you how it is.
Link with me. Then you'll see that you have nothing to fear. Here, Evlin, just take my hand."

"No!" He recoiled as though she had slapped
him.

"Please, Evlin, believe me."

"You're crazy." He pulled away to the back of the
room, flashing frightened looks at her that were
like daggers piercing her heart. If only she could
show him, mindlink with him, and prove that she
wasn't frightening, was still his friend Katie who
just happened to have these unusual mindpowers.

She was grateful when MacKenzie broke into her thoughts.

"Okay," he said. "So you're back from wherever it is you said that you went. Personally, I don't give a damn if your brain's still orbiting the twin moons of Galbenia, but we still have this little problem of our new recruits. While you were missing in action, I found some more warm and willing bodies to join us. But we'll need weeks to prepare them. Are you still planning this move on St. Ilban, Katie? If you can't give me at least a fortnight with these greenhorns, I want off right now."

Kayla looked at his tired, ragged face. Evlin's was much the same. Even valiant Iger had deep shadows below his eyes. What was she forcing everybody to do? Would they keep following her if she didn't ease up?

"Let's take a break and talk after dinner."

MacKenzie nodded his assent, but Evlin excused himself and, without looking at Kayla, left the room.

Kayla knew that the silver-haired dancer was sending her a message. His absence meant that he couldn't, wouldn't accept her. She would have to seek him out, to help him, when there was time for it. Not now.

She and MacKenzie proceeded to the ship's mess hall and again he told her about how green their new recruits were. He would need days, maybe weeks, to shape them up. Her absence had enabled him to send out scouts and win more people to the War Minstrels, but they weren't battle-ready, not yet.

Kayla listened, nodding occasionally, thinking that she could jolly MacKenzie along. The recruits would learn by doing, and MacKenzie had a taste for battle once his blood was up. Let him talk long enough and he would exhaust himself. A quiet dinner, some wine, and some time to unwind, and soon he would be talking about looking for Salome himself.

But the news of Kayla's mindpowers had leaked out and flowed through the War Minstrels. Instead of peace and quiet at dinner Kayla heard Merrick roaring her name.

She let him find her at a table with Iger and Third Child on either side of her and MacKenzie sitting across from her, busily diminishing a mountain of choba rolls.

Merrick shouldered his way into the room, a large, dark presence, looking every inch the bounty hunter he had once been. "So you're back, are you? Well, I don't want to talk to your boyfriend here, or your pet." He said and waved his hand at them in dismissal.

Iger and Third Child ignored him.

MacKenzie continued chewing, but his eyes flashed as he glanced at the smuggler.

"Then talk to me, Merrick." Kayla met his malevolent glare, remembering other days, other fights.

He gripped his disruptor belt in open defiance. "You're an empath, hah?"

Her answer was lazy, even insolent. "What about it?"

"Well, maybe I don't like hearing news like this last."

"You're not last. Not even close."

"No? Then what's Mac doing here? Why'd you tell him and not me? I'm a battalion leader, too."

"This isn't grade school, Merrick. So I told Mac before I told you. Now everybody knows."

He stared at her, unspeaking, obviously thinking hard. Finally he said, "It's all beginning to fit together for me, Katie. All coming back, now. I thought you looked familiar. And I seem to remember an empath I tried to collect for Beatrice Keller and her son, Yates, couple of years ago, on Brayton's Rock. She was a green-eyed redhead just like you. Fact is, I think she *was* you." He guffawed loudly and shook his head. "Haw! Bet I could get a good price for you now. Real good."

Kayla forced herself to laugh harshly at the crude joke, but she kept her eyes locked upon his. She could hear the threat beneath the jest and vowed that she would never turn her back on Merrick. Never.

"Don't we feed you enough, Merrick?" she said. "Mean to tell me you're looking for more money? Better watch out, Blackbird. If you eat too much, I just might have to turn you in!"

She took a step forward and smiled. "It's not a

bad idea, really. I don't see any of those fancy neural shields you used to carry to protect yourself from empaths. Maybe I should just turn you into a meat puppet, march you into the nearest Alliance magistrate's station, and leave with the reward."

Merrick smiled uneasily. "I'm just small change, girlie. Hardly worth the bother."

"Yeah, that's true." Her smile turned feral. "Better to simply mindwipe you. Faster. Cleaner. You've been useful, Merrick, but you're not irreplaceable."

Merrick's eyes still glowed, but now it was with fear. "Hold on," he said, voice cracking. "Wait just a minute here. I don't think . . ."

"That's right," Kayla snapped. "You don't. I do, and what I think is that you should shut up and take orders." She paused, allowed her face to soften, smiled. "Besides, we're just joking around, aren't we, boys?"

Iger chuckled mordantly.

"Sit down and have something to eat, Merrick." She paused as she saw Evlin at the door. Damn the man's timing! He come back and overheard her threat to Merrick. His face was drained of color and he looked at her with open fear. Before Kayla could do more than reach out to him, he was gone.

Merrick took his hand off his disrupter. "Sure, we're joking." He said down next to Iger. "Maybe I will have a bite. Chow's better over here."

Kayla sent him nearsense affirmations, a powerful sense of well-being. "Sure, Merrick. And remember, Yates Keller's our enemy. He's the one we should go after—together."

"She's right, Blackbird," MacKenzie said, wiping his fingers. "If I were you, I'd listen to her."

"We've got to work together, to defeat Keller and save Salome, Rab, and Arsobades," Kayla said.

Merrick nodded, suddenly eager. "Y'know, I always had kind of a yen for Salome. Was sorry that Rab saw her first. If Keller's done anything to hurt her . . ." He didn't have to finish the sentence. There was murder in his eye.

"Let's shake on that," Kayla said.

He hesitated for a moment, then extended his large, doughy hand.

Kayla grasped it, hiding her distaste. His flesh was moist, almost clammy. *So you'd joke about turning me in, you black-hearted bastard? Not if I see you coming first.*

She extracted her hand from his and forced herself not to wipe her palm against her green stretchsuit. "Okay, everybody. Let's open up the brandy and relax. We've got a lot of work to do, starting tomorrow."

* * *

Over the next month the War Minstrels trained their new recruits, plotted strategy, and searched for traces of Kayla's vanished companions.

There was a rumor that they had been sighted on a prison barge out of Voygan's Rift. Then another that put them in the orbitals of Salabria IX, and again Salome was rumored to have been sold as a rich man's plaything in the outer reaches of the Catfish Nebula.

Kayla greeted each rumor with gritted teeth and renewed hope, checked it out with care, and at the end found every one of the rumors dissolving into dust. She was impatient to return to Cavinas, to St. Ilban, and its vast Hall of Records. She would find her friends if she had to spend the rest of her life searching.

* * *

Kayla walked into ops to find Evlin dancing in the middle of the room.

Singing in a high, tuneless drone, silver braid swinging back and forth, he did high jumps over the heads of the other War Minstrels, spun, leaped, twirled, all with a drunken fervor that was both beautiful and frightening to behold. In another moment, he would probably send the navboard flying, kicked to bits by a careless gesture, and a crew member's head with it.

"Evlin," Kayla snapped. "This isn't a music hall."

He paused, eyes half-hooded, and stared at her with real hostility. "Her Majesty doesn't enjoy the dance? Perhaps she would like to take over my body and edit out all the offending passages in that last movement?"

"You're drunk. Get back to your quarters and sleep it off. Now!"

"Her Majesty commands this humble performer, and I scramble to do her bidding, before she wipes my mind." With a mocking flourish he bowed, spun on one foot, and pirouetted out the door.

Iger leaned close to Kayla. "He's losing it."

"I know." *And it's my fault.*

Somewhere in the back of her mind she could hear Golias laughing.

* * *

Five weeks after her return to Kemel, in the early morning hours, Kayla felt somebody shaking her.

"Wha—?" Her eyes flew open. "Iger, what's wrong?"

His long blond hair was loose and tangled on his shoulders. "It's the Mindstar. It's gone."

"What?" She sat up.

"So's Third Child. And Evlin."

Kayla was wide awake now. "Evlin took her. And the stone, too? How did he find it?"

"Dunno. I heard some kind of mindsqueak out of Third Child. It woke me up. Surprised you didn't hear it. So I went to investigate. And she was gone. Then I looked for the Mindstar." He shook his head.

"That poor, crazy bastard." Kayla shivered at the thought of the Mindstar and its effects upon an unshielded mind. Evlin might already be gibbering in a dark corner of the compound.

"Call a search!"

The tall dancer had been avoiding her for weeks, ever since the incident in ops. Had he finally cracked altogether? Gods, they had to find him. And she would treat him gently, she promised herself. As long as Third Child was all right.

"Iger, we've got to find them!"

How could he have gotten past Third Child and near the Mindstar without any alarm being given?

The answer presented itself in seven empty containers of choba ale scattered at the foot of Third Child's bunk. The ale was a favorite drink of the dalkoi's, and one which always inebriated her into a state of dizzy bliss. Third Child, drunk on ale, would be easy enough to maneuver around. And Evlin had been fond of slipping the dalkoi a drink now and again.

Once Third Child was out of commission, Evlin would have had no trouble at all taking the Mindstar from her quarters. The muscled dancer would have easily hefted the shielded casket in which the mindstone was kept.

But why take both Third Child and the stone? Had Evlin been plotting all this time to steal the Mindstar, pretending allegiance to Kayla and waiting until she had run the heavy risks of retrieving the Mindstar? No, not Evlin. He had had too many other opportunities to take the stone before this. No, he must have stolen it to punish her and taken Third Child along for some obscure purpose.

Kayla told herself that Evlin would not hurt Third Child. But she remembered what the mindghost Golias had said to her: "These won't be your only losses. Better prepare yourself for more."

No, I won't. I won't lose Evlin or Third Child. I can't!

Determined, she dressed quickly, buzzed MacKenzie, and apprised him of the facts, minus the missing Mindstar. She trusted MacKenzie, but only so far. She had trusted Evlin too far.

MacKenzie was quick to report back. "A small cruiser pulled out of here about ten minutes ago. I've got tracers scanning for its ion trails."

"Let me know as soon as we get a fix on it. I want everybody ready to go after him."

"Everybody? On such short notice?"

"Mac, the longer we wait, the worse things will get for Third Child. And Evlin is in danger, too!"

"Aside from ramming his cruiser into an asteroid, I don't see what sort of danger he's in. Not until we catch him."

"Look, if you want to hang back, fine, but I'm going after him."

Iger interrupted their conversation to report: "We've caught his emissions trail, but it disappears into jumpspace. Course heading logged with data central seems to indicate Cavinas."

"Oh, great. Let's move. Coming, Mac?"

"Yeah, I'll come with you, Katie. And gods help us all."

Chapter Fifteen

The ops crew assembled quickly. In moments, the jump engines were on, building from a purr to a growl.

"Jump in two minutes," Kayla announced. "Everybody strap in. We're heading off for Cavinas, the edge of the system near Brayton's Rock. We'll establish a loose orbit out there in neutral territory, and scan for Evlin."

The *Antimony* and its fleet moved smoothly through jumpspace with nary a flicker out of the Mindstar. Nevertheless, Kayla was relieved when the jump interface for Cavinas came rolling toward them.

"Exiting jumpspace now. All ships cut engines."

The *Antimony* popped into the Cavinas System, followed one by one, by the War Minstrels, some limping, some broadcasting curses, but all staying on their heels.

"What the hell?" Valdez muttered.

"What's wrong, Oscar?"

"Brayton's Rock? I can't find it."

"What do you mean, you can't find it? How in hell could you possibly lose anything that large?"

"It's gone. Gone, like somebody sneaked up behind it with a tugship and moved it to another system."

Martin Naseka's voice came out of the com link, surprisingly loud for shy Martin. "Kayla, we've got radiation readings all over the place. Really dirty stuff, too."

"Radiation? Get our shields up, Oscar. Martin, what's the locus of the radiation?"

"Right around where Brayton's Rock used to be."

"You mean . . . ?"

The ship began to bounce, and the whistle and ping of small objects hitting deflectors was audible above the regular engine noise. "What in hell is that?"

"My best guess is that's what's left of Brayton's Rock. Debris and radiation. Somebody took them out—and recently—with old style N-Ware. Nuclears."

"Gods." Kayla felt something icy stab her in the gut. She knew where a stash of old-style nuclears had been hidden on St. Ilban, years ago. Could there be a connection? It was unlikely, she told herself. No one else alive knew where those nuclears were. "I'm backing us out of here, folks, and fast. Iger, get on ship-to-ship link and tell everybody to go to maximum shields and back away. Martin, what do our sensors pick up?"

"Debris," he said. "Slag. All signs point to a big nasty explosion. Why they used N-ware, and where they got it, is beyond my understanding."

"How recent an explosion?"

"Recent enough so that if we hadn't taken that little detour on our way here we might have been seriously involved."

Kayla imagined the War Minstrels exiting jumpspace right into the heart of a planetary nuclear explosion and swallowed, hard. The Mindstar had, inadvertently, saved their lives.

"Iger," she said. "Scan the in-system com links. What are the locals chattering about? Any reaction?"

"V-e-r-y quiet. I think we've got some seriously frightened people out there who are keeping their mouths shut until they know a bit more. I see a mech probe poking around out there, probably testing radiation levels, and there's some discussion about the extent of the radiation on an Alliance wavelength: whether it will reach the inner planets."

"And?"

Iger cocked his head to one side, listening. "Doesn't look like it will. But they're discussing orbital shields, just in case. Which means they don't really know."

"Neither do we. So we'll keep our distance. Damn! What—who—could have done this? How many innocent people were killed?" Kayla thought briefly of the main arcade of Brayton's Rock. It had been years since she had been there, and it had never been her favorite place, too ugly, thrown-together, lit by a bleak garish light that seemed to permeate the place, day or night. However, it was the place where Rab had first recruited her to join the crew of the *Falstaff.* Kayla couldn't help but feel regret at seeing yet another part of her personal history vanish into dust. Radioactive dust.

"Katie?" Iger said. "Ships are requesting instructions. What should I tell them?"

"Pull back beyond system boundaries, clear of the radiation, and far away from any stray Alliance cruiser. I think they're going to be pretty busy with this little disaster, but that doesn't mean somebody won't notice a group of unidentified ships observing them."

"We could go back."

"No! We've got to find Evlin. And also Salome, Rab, and Arsobades."

"There's no sign that Evlin is even in this system. As for the others, how can you still be planning to go to St. Ilban? You really think that they're somewhere on that planet?"

"If not, someone there will know how to find them."

"And you expect just to walk right in and ask for them?"

"Iger, I intend to find them any way I have to. If that means skinning somebody's mind like a ripe fruit, I'll do it, understand? It's because of me that

they're in trouble. I'm going to get them out of it."
Kayla didn't bother to add, *if they're still alive*. She
didn't want to give that thought any additional
substance.

She tried farsensing St. Ilban, but the range was
too great.

"Katie, we're picking up a ship-to-ship hail on
an odd frequency." Iger leaned closer to his board,
listening. "Gods' eyes, I don't believe it!"

"Don't keep us in suspense, Iger."

"It's that damned Cristobal, come back from the
dead. He's hiding out near an asteroid swarm.
Wants a meeting."

"Cristobal?" she exploded. "I thought he'd been
killed! How did he survive that first attack on the
Alliance? I thought his ship was shot to pieces.
And how in nine hells did he find us?" Cristobal,
alive, was more trouble than Kayla wanted to con-
template, especially now.

"He's asking for—demanding—a parley."

"Tell him we're busy. I'll consider his request
when I have time."

"He's determined to talk to you, Katie. Now he's
threatening to reveal the War Minstrels to the Alliance."

"Let him."

Iger shook his head. "He's making a lot of noise.
If we don't get him quieted down, he'll attract attention."

"Damn him! All right, bring him aboard. But get
an armed escort down there, and make sure that

Mepal Tarlinger isn't part of it!" She didn't want any of Cristobal's former sycophants joining the party. "And do it quietly."

So it came to be that Kayla met Cristobal under armed guard in a weapons locker near air lock four.

His handsome face looked pale and his brown eyes were weary, but otherwise he appeared unchanged, and he smiled when he saw her enter the room.

"Katie, look at me! I survived!" He stepped forward and moved to hug her, but she pulled back abruptly. "Hey, aren't you glad to see me?"

"That's not exactly the term I would use. Surprised, yes. Where have you been?"

"I hid out near Styx until the first battle was over. Then I cruised around Brayton's Rock, trying to find some trace of you out there."

She didn't believe him. "Pretty dicey. And were you in orbit there when it blew?"

"No." He smiled oddly. "Timing is everything."

"I'll say. Any idea who did it?"

Again that odd smile briefly lit his features. "No. Big mess. Should keep the authorities busy for a while. This is our chance, Katie."

"Our chance?"

"Yes, we'll hit St. Ilban while the Alliance's guard is down. They won't be expecting a thing."

Kayla was chagrined to find that his plan actually made sense. Moments before his arrival she had mused over the possibility of slipping into

Vardalia under cover of the post-blast chaos. So Cristobal had had a similar idea? That didn't mean it wasn't worth having.

Her thoughts were interrupted by Iger's breathless voice over the ship com link: "Battle stations. I repeat, battle stations. Red alert. Alliance forces are approaching us. Seven armed ships coming this way. Katie to ops on the double!"

"But they were supposed to wait!" Cristobal blurted. Kayla saw the petulant, frightened look on his face and she knew suddenly what had happened.

"You did this," she said, stepping toward him. "You. Set us up, didn't you? Bastard!" She slapped him, hard, and the sound of it was like a gunshot going off in the small room. "You called the Alliance down on us! Why? Why?"

"Why not?" His cheek was bright red with the imprint of her hand. "You stole my fleet, deserted me, tried to kill me! They promised to give me back my property. But they're coming in too soon! Stop them. Radio and tell them I'm still aboard and I demand safe passage."

Kayla wanted to laugh at him and kill him at the same time. She had been a fool to allow him to get this close to the *Antimony.* "I didn't steal a thing." she told him. "These people didn't belong to you. You went crazy with power and I took over before you got everybody killed or we had another mutiny."

"That's your story. Let's see who they listen to,

Katie. If they discover I'm back, they'll flock to my side."

"You've lost what little grip on reality you ever had." Kayla turned to the guards. "He's leaving. Push him back out of the air lock if you have to."

Cristobal's petulance turned to horror. "You can't send me back to my ship in the midst of a battle."

"Watch me."

Cristobal clutched a webseat in desperation. "If you let me get killed, you'll never find the *Falstaff*—or your friends—again."

That stopped her. "Where are they? What do you know about them?"

A crafty look slid into his eyes. "Promise me safety and I'll tell you."

"All right." Kayla smiled coldly and said to the guards, "Hold him!"

Without any preparation she launched a blunt, wide probe into his mind, knowing the pain it would cause him, not caring in the slightest.

Cristobal began to shriek.

Kayla probed deeper.

She brushed past an area that held information about the destruction of Brayton's Rock. There wasn't time for her to investigate that now, but perhaps she would be able to come back to it later.

She could feel Cristobal's body convulsing as she pushed deeper and deeper into his mind.

There—that patch of memory seemed to contain what she was looking for. Salome, Rab. She had nearly reached it when the first of the Alliance's laser cannon shots penetrated the *Antimony*'s defenses.

The light went out.

Another hit. The *Antimony* rocked back and forth.

Kayla lost contact with Cristobal. Blindly, she groped her way toward where she thought the door was, only to discover that she had gone in exactly the opposite direction.

Another hit. *Damnit,* she thought. Where were the shields? Where was the secondary generator?

The lights began to flicker, to come back. Kayla saw that Cristobal was slumped against the wall in a stupor, his eyes unfocused, jaw hanging slack. She had done that to him, mind-raped him. The thought caused her a slight pang, but then she remembered the *Falstaff.* He had done worse to her friends, and betrayed her her as well.

The doors flew open and Iger stood there with a laser rifle aimed inside. "Katie! Gods, when you didn't respond, I thought something had happened."

"Now I know why those shots got in under our defenses."

"You're blaming me?"

"Yes. Now let's get to ops and stop these bastards before they blow the ship to pieces."

Iger saw Cristobal and his eyes got wide. "What the hell happened to him?"

"Nothing that he didn't deserve." Kayla brushed past Iger and out the door.

Back in ops, she scanned the front viewscreen and felt the bottom fall out of her world. There were so many battle cruisers arrayed out there—an entire armada facing her tiny fleet, red lights blinking along their sleek sides like a hundred malevolent eyes. How could they ever fight all of them? But she steeled herself, turned a confident face to the crew, and said "Get me Mac, ship-to-ship."

MacKenzie came on the screen. His expression was grim.

"Katie, it looks bad here."

"Split your forces, Mac, and flank the end battle cruisers. I'm going to lunge at them, then fade back and see if I can draw the main body with me. You close behind and finish as many from each side as you can. Just leave me two ships on port and starboard."

"Right." MacKenzie didn't bother to say goodbye and Kayla didn't expect it.

She kept her voice calm as she addressed the ops crew. "We're going in, on my signal."

Kayla took a deep breath. Let it out.

"Okay, let's go!"

The War Minstrels dashed toward the ships of the Alliance, making up in agility what they lacked in firepower.

They danced in and around, beneath and above,

staying in motion, evading the Alliance troopships' laser fire.

Kayla felt the *Antimony*'s big guns go, hammering away, white blips hitting the Alliance armada, blossoming against the sleek silver hides of their ships.

But there were smaller explosions, something odd happening to the hulls of several War Minstrel ships. Jagged black dots through which gas was escaping into space. Puncture wounds.

Kayla stared in stunned amazement. In addition to lasers, the Alliance ships were using some sort of projectiles, shooting them from massive bow projectors.

The damage to War Minstrel ships was considerable. Pilots were dying in fiery agony, navigational systems destroyed, laser systems shorting out. Yet still they came on.

Kayla knew their own guns could attack and fire on automatic, and she had no doubt about the Alliance weapons. Each side could keep firing right down to the last ship. It might be a war fought by mechs, but the casualties would be flesh and blood.

The War Minstrels may have been outnumbered, but they were fiercer, faster, and more maneuverable. As the Alliance ships wallowed one beside the other in confusion, the War Minstrels moved swiftly between them, slicing them to pieces.

The click and clatter of ops went on around her,

but Kayla might as well have been in jumpspace for all the thought she gave it. She was focused, every inch of her, on a slot between the lead Alliance ship and its companion. If she could manage to bring the *Antimony* through there, shooting from lateral guns, she might be able to take down both ships at once. It was a tricky maneuver, one that a less foolhardy pilot would not have tried. But she was determined.

—*Desperate*, said a small voice in her mind. She couldn't be certain if it was her own thought or Golias breaking through. No matter, there was no time to think about it.

She took the *Antimony* on a rolling turn to pick up momentum, speeding past the entire fleet, coming about with engines roaring, darting back into the heart of the fray.

She heard Iger shout a warning, but whatever he had to say was lost in the sound of the guns.

Mac's voice rumbled on ship-to-ship, indistinct, the words a jumble that never penetrated her mind.

The *Antimony* was a streak of light in the darkness, moving faster than the naked eye could register, at subjump speed, to shoot down the narrow alley between the two larger ships, guns blazing the entire time.

Explosions bloomed along the bellies of the ships and begat larger explosions. Escape pods rained from the larger vessels like silvery raindrops falling from deadly blossoms.

The ships were doomed.

Now, in the confusion, Kayla thought. *Now is the time to press on to St. Ilban.* She had Iger signal MacKenzie that she was going ahead, and cut off his squawks of protest.

The inner system waited before her, marbles rolling slowly around the yellow and green orbs that were the twin suns of the Cavinas System.

Past Styx, with a shiver of recognition that Kayla quickly put down. Past Liage, tawny prairie world, and up to the purple gas giant Xenobe, whose only habitable moon, St. Ilban, held the capital of the Alliance, the glittering city of Vardalia.

Kayla slowed the *Antimony* just out of range of St. Ilban's orbital defenses. "Martin," she said. "Scan the orbitals and report."

He gazed at his board and a frown creased his broad forehead. "They're fully functional, Katie. All screen up, three hundred sixty degree coverage. Ugly."

"Damn."

"I don't think I have to remind you that we can't outshoot 'em. Not with their targeting systems and range."

"There's got to be a way," Kayla said. "I can't—I won't accept that we're finished, dead in the water because of those damned orbitals."

She attempted a farsense scan of the planet, but there were so many minds down below, too many from which to cull distinct mind signatures, at least at this distance. She strained, listened, but she couldn't find any trace of Salome, Rab, or Arsobades. Damnit, they had to be down there somewhere.

"Mac is begging you to pull back before we all get fried here," Iger said. "He's afraid that you're underestimating the orbitals' capabilities."

"Tell Mac to keep his mind on that armada. I'm taking us in a bit closer." If she didn't get closer, she couldn't search for Salome and Rab, for Arsobades.

Dangerously close to the orbitals now, with shields on full, she mindsearched again. For a moment she touched Yates Keller but lost him again just as quickly. As she scrabbled after him, she brushed against the frightening power of the groupmind. It made a grab for her that sent her racing back in retreat. Frantically, she cut off her probe and rode quietly in orbit.

The groupmind hadn't pursued her. Either it had lost her scent, or been distracted elsewhere.

Cautiously, Kayla tried again.

Still no sign of her friends, nor of Keller.

And, curiously, there was absolutely no indication of Pelleas Karlson, not one single resonating thought. She would have expected an ego like that to be readable from the frozen surface of Styx.

But there, again, was Keller. Yates Keller, just waiting, asking for her attention. And that faint echo beyond him, was that Karlson? Perhaps. Or perhaps it was the echo of more familiar minds.

"That bastard," she said. "If only Evlin hadn't taken the Mindstar."

Iger gazed at her in obvious disbelief. "You'd use it on the Alliance? That thing? You can't even control it now. Gods, I don't want to think about what it took to get it back in its container the last time it got out."

"But Keller's there! I can feel him!"

"Your obsession with revenge is making you crazy, Katie. We can't get past those orbitals. Mac's right. We should pull back before we get blown to pieces."

"Warship approaching on starboard," Martin Naseka reported. "Evasive maneuvers are suggested."

Before Kayla could respond, a second warship was on their tail, firing warning bolts.

"They demand surrender," Iger said.

"Damnit, where's Mac?" Kayla cried. "Where's Merrick? Have they destroyed our entire fleet?" She was on her feet and reaching for her disruptor. She would not go back to a prison barge. Never.

"The warship reports that orbital defenses have been trained upon us as well," Iger said. "Right in sync with our course projections. They can vaporize us, Katie.

"No surrender, damnit!"

"Katie, be reasonable. We'll all die." His words were like a hard slap. She saw the assembled faces of the ops crew, the fear in their eyes. How could she condemn them to death because of her own fixation?

A sudden mutter from the ops crew and a squawk from the com board drew her attention.

"Incoming light cruiser," Naseka said. "Moving fast, too fast for in-system."

Iger was on it, nodding. "Warships demanding that it halt. It's ignoring them. Demanding parley with you, Katie."

"Put it on audio."

In a burst of static a familiar voice blurted out, mid-sentence: "—won't let them get you. Katie, I'm here. I have Third Child and the Mindstar. Hold on!"

"Evlin!"

He was a streak across their screens, moving at subjump speed, too fast for the Alliance guns to set their aim upon but also too fast to stop safely and accurately in-system.

"Evlin, you fool!" Katie cried. "You've got too much velocity. Get out of the system!"

"I won't leave you here to surrender. They can't have you. I've got the Mindstar and I'm taking it out of its box"

"No!"

"I'm holding it, Katie." His voice was coming in ragged gasps. "It's so bright. And it's cold, but it burns me. Can you see it, Katie? Can you?"

The mainscreen came to life and showed the muscular Evlin, chest heaving, holding the unsheathed Mindstar. His eyes were squinted nearly shut at its blinding radiance. Beside him, the dalkoi was quivering in agitation.

Kayla stared, horrified. "Put it down, Evlin," she whispered. "Oh, gods, quickly! Put it back in its box."

Too late. The thing seemed to ignite with a strange fire and, as they watched, its pale iridescence overwhelmed everything else on-screen.

"He'll die," Kayla said. "It'll kill him, and Third Child, too." She cast an agonized look at Iger. "We've got to help them."

"Help them? How?"

She reached out. "Mindlink with me."

"Here?"

"We'll reach Third Child, create the triune mind again."

He acquiesced and she felt his hand in hers. His mind, its familiar signature thrumming in hers. But there was another note there, discordant. A stranger.

—*And shall I join with you as well? Or perhaps I'd just as soon not.*

Golias, damn him.

Kayla could feel Iger's dismayed surprise at Golias' appearance, and she struggled to keep him linked to her. To Golias, she said:

—*Parasite! Be of use or be gone. I must control that stone. Will you help me?*

—*Why should I?"*

—*Because otherwise, an innocent man will die. Because it's right. And because you're a part of me.*

—And?

—Because you have no choice.

She did not wait to hear him agree. He would do it.

Now there was a roaring sound as of a waterfall plunging down long miles to dash upon distant rocks. But coming closer, getting louder. Not a sound, no—a force, a threat. The groupmind, homing in on the compelling radiance of the Mindstar.

"No!" Kayla wasn't strong enough to stop them. But they must not have the star. They would be unthinkably strong if they gained control of it. And if Karlson and Keller had the Mindstar in their arsenal they would be invincible.

She tried to get to Evlin, to link with him and convince him to set the Mindstar back into its container.

But Evlin had been possessed by the stone. He moved his lips but many different voices came out of his mouth.

"Glip, I didn't mean it."

"Order my car for me immediately."

"Pliss Pliss Plit."

"Let me out, let me out, let me out."

His fingers were clenched whitely around the Mindstar and the look in his tormented eyes was too much for Kayla to bear.

She forced her way into his already-over-crowded head. Evlin was ringed by conflicting personas, all of them attempting to appropriate his body. His mind was filled with a cacophony of voices. Kayla tried to enfold him, tried to repel the voices and shove them back, back, out of him.

Evlin shuddered and his eyes rolled up in their sockets.

Kayla was dimly aware of distant noise, roaring and explosions. She was needed elsewhere, she knew it. But she couldn't turn away, couldn't abandon Evlin.

—*Hold onto me. Evlin, don't give up!*

She knew that she was losing him. Blinded by fear and fury, she cried out to Iger, to Golias, to Third Child: —*Help me. Help me!*

—*Let him go*, Golias told her.

—*No!*

—*He'll take you with him.*

—*You know how to fight the Mindstar. You survived. Help me save him.*

—*I didn't survive. I'm a ghost. You said it yourself.*

—*Damnit, stop arguing with me and do something useful.*

But even as Kayla strove to direct the triune mind—with Golias' addition—to protect Evlin, all hell broke loose.

Who began the attack was never clear. But there was a sudden eruption of disruptor fire in space, ships shooting at one another, silent blooms of white destruction flowering around each ship, a garden of violence. The defense screens held, held, then began to give.

As the firing continued, the *Antimony*'s defenses

began to buckle. Kayla was in two worlds at once. On the one hand she was in the madhouse of ops, ordering Martin Naseka to shore up their defenses, plotting defensive maneuvers, listening to the whump! of their guns as they fired and fired and fired. And at the same time she was caught between minds, clinging to the tenuous link with Third Child and with Iger, striving desperately to protect Evlin, to fight off the rapacious groupmind.

Which was attacking in earnest now, drawn by the Mindstar's fire. Kayla knew that she no longer had any options. She could fight the groupmind, or she could abandon her quest now and retreat—and risk having the *Antimony* blown to bits, the Mindstar captured, and Evlin, Third Child, everybody she cared about, taken prisoner or murdered by Alliance troops.

She could feel the groupmind penetrating her mind's defenses, reaching into her and beginning to gain control.

No!

She broke free of its grip.

It came after her again, this time twice as strong as before, twice as terrible.

She struggled, desperate to free herself again.

—*Golias, help me!*

—*Why should I? You want to destroy me.*

—*If I don't get free, we'll both be destroyed. Don't you see that? Do you want some kind of life? Imagine spending the rest of eternity shackled to this*

*groupmind, unable to even think freely, let alone
live! Golias, with me you at least have a chance.*

He made no other response, but her words
seemed to have affected him. She was aware of
the mindghost moving about, rummaging through
her memories and thoughts. And then he stopped.

—*Golias?*

There was no response. Where had he gone?
She couldn't feel him at all.

But there—that odd flutter at the periphery of
her senses: what was that? Kayla had a sudden image of a shelter being erected, of wings enfolding
her, barriers being anchored all around her.

The groupmind slid away from Kayla as surely
as if Golias had greased its descent. She could feel
the burning trails of its claws as it receded, glowing in her mind like red-hot ash. Slowly that pain
flickered and died.

For a moment she could think, breathe, and
plan.

—*Thank you.*

—*Thank yourself. I found it in your subconscious.
But it won't last for long. The way that groupmind
thing is battering away at it, it'll give any second.*

Kayla thought hard. She could not defeat the
groupmind by strength: Even if she could hook up
directly to the Mindstar, there was no guarantee
that she would be able to direct its power against
the groupmind.

But what if she attacked the groupmind from
within? Yes. Yes, it might just work. If she allowed

the groupmind to penetrate her initial defenses, then pulled back, pulled way back, and drew it in right after her, right into a trap.

Remember, she thought. *Remember what you know about the groupmind. It's made up of former miners from Styx. They combine their empathic powers through a vector: one empath whose mind is unusually open and pliable. The vector provides the groupmind's binding, its focus.*

Without the vector there would be no direction. To destroy the groupmind, she had to destroy the vector. But to do that meant getting inside the groupmind, opening herself to it, and putting herself and her friends directly at risk.

—*Katie, can you hear me?*

Iger's mindspeech was surprisingly loud and vibrant.

—*Iger, I'm going to lower our defenses.*

—*You can't be serious.*

—*I'm going to let the groupmind come after the Mindstar.*

—*You'll kill us all!*

—*Not if what I'm planning works.*

—*But . . .*

—*Iger, I don't have time to explain it. Trust me. Just keep your mind open. Help me to stay connected to you, to Third Child, and the Mindstar.*

—*What about that weird voice in your head?*

—*Golias? He won't cause any trouble.*

—*If you say so. But whatever it is you're going to do, you'd better do it quickly, Katie. Those Alliance bastards are pounding the ship to pieces, and whatever they miss the orbital defenses hit.*

—*Right. Just follow my lead, Iger. Trust me.*

She didn't have time to say more. The groupmind was a looming presence, drawn by the Mindstar, voracious and cunning, determined to force its way in and somehow absorb it.

Its hunger was pitiless, bottomless.

Kayla took a deep breath and stopped fighting it.

The sensation was much like sinking beneath the surface of the sea. Eddies of thought moved her this way and that. She floated weightless for blissful moments. Then a dark and ravening force swept up from out of the depths.

The groupmind engulfed Kayla—engulfed Iger also, and Third Child—and went to work on the Mindstar.

But the Mindstar was not so easy to swallow.

Gouts of psychic energy exploded all along the periphery of the Mindstar's radiance, wherever its power intersected that of the groupmind. No realspace projectile could match this explosive force, no N-ware or laser fire could match the frightening energies that were discharged as the groupmind collided with the Mindstar.

Kayla was certain that she would not survive this. It was impossible. The powers detonating around her were too great. She could not hope to master any of it, much less direct one against the other.

The groupmind was trying to devour her completely and absorb her mind for its own purposes. She struggled with it, catching stray bits of individual thought, odd memories. She saw that the groupmind controlled St. Ilban's orbital defenses, and helped coordinate much of the troop movement in space. But she could not do much more than gape at each bit of information before she was torn away. The groupmind wanted her. Wanted her badly.

Once again Golias helped her ward off the attack. But how much longer could they hold their ground against this constant onslaught?

The separate personalities comprising the groupmind had once been her parents' friends and companions. Old miners, all.

—*What do old miners fear?* Golias whispered.

Kayla knew. It was the thing that had killed her parents, and nearly taken her as well. The single primal fear of every man and woman who had ever worked underground—a cave-in.

The crushing rock, the thunderous air, the choking grit, the darkness.

Cave-in.

Her parents had perished in a cave-in when explosives that Yates Keller had set went off with more power than Keller had anticipated. He had intended only to frighten. Instead, he had killed.

Cave-in. Cave-in. Cave-in.

Anger gave Kayla new strength, and that, in turn, was kindled by the Mindstar until her mind was set like a timed explosive to bring the greatest fear known to miners into the inner depths of the groupmind.

She pushed against their memories, but the entrance was barred. Summoning the collective strength of the triune mind, of Iger and Third Child, she held it up against the strange fires of the Mindstar. Their united power boiled, expanded, bubbled over. Fed by the Mindstar, Kayla pushed again. Pushed hard—harder—blew open a small hole in the groupmind's defenses and vaulted through.

She was in a familiar place, one that held images that she recognized from her childhood.

She searched for the groupmind's memories of time spent in crystal-strewn darkness, of time in the tunnels of Styx. She reached for those memories, and savored their nostalgic resonance, and when she had licked the last bit of them from her mind, she detonated the entire mass.

A great silent implosion, soundless but deadly.

The groupmind screamed. Its thoughts were crushing, thunderous, and suffocating.

They were choking on pulverized crystals. Crushed by tons of rock. Fragmented into shreds, dragged down, down, down into darkness.

Gone.

The darkness was profound, empty, deep. Kayla was alone, all alone, floating in the echoing gloom. And then she wasn't there either.

Chapter Sixteen

Kayla could hear Salome calling her. Sometimes the voice sounded like Rab, sometimes like Evlin.

—*Evlin? Can you hear me?*

No, that wasn't right. Evlin wasn't linked to her, had never linked. He was afraid, so afraid. He was outside.

—*Salome?*

Salome, too. She could not bear the mindtouch. And Rab, Arsobades, they also feared it. Feared her.

—*My friends are frightened of me.*

Even Iger? Gentle, beloved Iger? Did he fear her? Hate her? No. No. Perhaps he had been afraid at first, before he had tapped his own latent mindpowers. But not now. Iger understood. And Third Child. She wasn't alone. Not entirely. Golias was there, too. A whisper in the desert of the mind. She wasn't alone.

—*Did you kill them?*

—*The groupmind? I don't know. I can't hear it*

anymore. I think I destroyed its ability to function, to hold together. At least I hope so.

—A neat trick, doing to them what was done to you.

—Golias, are you comparing me to a monster like Keller?

—I'm not passing any judgment on you, Kayla. Merely making an observation.

—Save it. I don't feel guilty. They would have killed us. I did what I had to.

—If you don't feel guilty, why are you defending yourself?

—Shut up, Golias!

—Don't be ashamed. We all do things we regret. There's often no choice. The fallacy is in worrying about other people. If you care about other people, you are lost.

Before she could argue, Golias had pulled her into a whirlpool of memories, scenes more vivid than any vid cube could be. She saw a tiny cramped apartment, a mother whose skin showed the greenish tinge of breen addiction. An alcoholic father who died in a pool of vomit as his children watched. A desperate, brutal existence. Golias had learned to steal, scavenge, and fight in order to survive, even if that meant betraying those who were closest to him—even if that meant pimping his sweet little sister, Shotay.

He felt remorse, but he also understood that he had acted in the only way that seemed possible, the only way to survive. And he felt no guilt for his crimes.

—*Forgive yourself, Kayla. There are plenty of worse things than losing one's parents. Besides, you weren't responsible for their deaths.*

—*I should have died, too!*

—*That's bullshit. Survivor's guilt. Guilt is a waste of time. Your parents would have wanted you to live. Don't let guilt drive you. Or revenge.*

—*I don't need a thief to lecture me. Especially a dead one. If you're so smart, why aren't you still alive?*

Kayla regretted that as soon as she had thought it, but Golias said nothing, merely laughed his thin desert-wind laugh and faded away.

She awoke to a silent world. The engines of destruction had stopped. All was calm in ops. The crew—Iger, Oscar, Mepal, all of them—turned expectant faces to her.

She reached for Iger. Her voice was a whisper. "How long have I been out?"

"Not even a minute."

"What's happened?"

"There was a great flash of unbelievable brightness, killer light, and all the guns stopped. The ships are dead in space. No com link chatter."

"And the orbitals? The planetary defenses?"

"They're all down. As though some sort of enormous power failure had hit them."

She thought of the Mindstar. "Maybe it did.

Have you heard anything out of Evlin? Third Child?"

"Not a peep." Iger's expression betrayed his uneasiness. "I don't like it."

"Let me probe and see what I can find."

Her farsense was shaky and she doubted whether she would reach much farther than the orbitals, but she pushed her powers to their limit, reaching, reaching, calling. —*Third Child? Third Child, where are you?*

The answer, when it came, was faint, reedy, and distorted by static. —*Here. Kayla, in loose orbit around St. Ilban. The Mindstar's power flared through the groupmind and burned out the orbital defenses. Many minds have been destroyed as well. Evlin requires immediate medical assistance. Hurry.*

—*But the mindstar . . . ?*

—*It will not be a problem.*

The connection faded.

Kayla came out of the mindlink. Exhaustion seeped through every pore of her. She felt as though she could sleep for a hundred years. A thousand, maybe. But she couldn't spare Iger from the com board. Her gaze fell on Oscar Valdez. Oscar, crack pilot. She smiled at him. "Feel up to a little in-system piloting, hot shot?"

His eyes gleamed with his eagerness. "Just say where and when."

"Now. I want you to home in on the signal from Evlin's ship. Get over there and put them under tow. We've got to get Evlin to the medics, pronto."

"Let me at that navboard."

"Iger, where's Cristobal?"

He shrugged. "Disappeared during the fire-storm. And good riddance."

Mepal Tarlinger looked stricken.

"Relax, Mepal," Kayla said. "He'll turn up like bad credit. He always has before."

"Message from MacKenzie," Iger said. "He wants to know our next heading."

"Tell him, and tell Merrick, too. Tell everybody. We're going in. We're making landfall. On St. Ilban."

They made the transition to Vardalia's spaceport without trouble. The port authority was silent, the port police absent, their skimmers silent and dark.

The Crystal Palace was open, unguarded. Inside, the Alliance police sat at their posts like zombies, eyes empty of expression, limbs hanging, unmoving. Everywhere were signs of decay, of dirt that no one had cared enough to clean away. Broken things that no one had bothered to repair. Dirty goblets and cracked plates were strewn carelessly across tables in a common room. Tapestries hung in shreds across the walls. The ornate inlaid crystalline floors were coated with a dark gummy film.

Waste receptacles overflowed. Where were the recycling mechs? Garbage spilled out into hallways, crunched underfoot. The grim signs of neglect were everywhere. Kayla felt disgust mingle with anger. How could Karlson be so arrogant?

Couldn't he even take the trouble to maintain his palace?

She rounded a corner, saw vacant-eyed clerks leaning against walls as though their brains had been shut off.

Just like the troops on those Alliance ships, when I was pulled into a soldier's mind.

Kayla froze. The troops on those ships had been mindsalt addicts, empty to their cores. Was the capital of the Alliance filled with mindsalt addicts? A city full of shambling spooks, controlled by the groupmind? The fabulous city of Vardalia, a pest-hole filled with the walking dead?

Footsteps sounded behind her, startlingly loud. MacKenzie came jolting into view, followed by Iger, Martin Naseka, and Mepal Tarlinger.

"Get some people together," Kayla ordered. "Fan out over this building. I need to know if there's anybody functional running this place. If you can't find a medic for Evlin, find a mechdoc."

Iger's pocket com beeped and he keyed it, listened for a moment, murmured into it. "Katie, it's almost creepy. We've encountered no resistance whatsoever.

"Good. Get our wounded down and into medical facilities. Get Evlin down." *What's left of him.*

Minutes later two hefty men appeared, carrying Evlin in on a low-g stretcher. His eyes were open but empty. He gave no sign of recognition, responding not at all to her presence. Kayla felt another terrible pang. Then she remembered a memory. Not hers. Golias'. He had hurt people and he had grieved and then he had forgiven himself.

Remember his memories, she thought. *Learn from them.*

Evlin was carried past her and onward into the recesses of the Crystal Palace. Behind him streamed a line of War Minstrels. Those who were capable of moving under their own power walked. Others were supported by their fellows. Every one of them smiled as they saw Kayla. Some pumped their fists in victory. They called out to her, reached out to her, exultant despite their wounds.

"We did it, Katie!"

"We're here and they can't stop us."

"It's the beginning of a new age!"

"Let's take Karlson's castle to pieces and sell it for landfill."

"Free Trade for all!"

From somewhere Kayla summoned the energy to smile, to wave, to nod and say, "That's right," and "Get those burns dressed, comrade!"

She had to let those who had followed her know that she was pleased with them, that they mattered to her. But her mind was occupied elsewhere. She was wondering how she was going to find Salome, Rab, and Arsobades. Wondering, too, where Yates Keller and Pelleas Karlson were.

Parts of the palace were familiar to her. She had spent some time here years ago dodging police patrols. Kayla still remembered the way to Karlson's private quarters. Perhaps the prime minister was hiding there. She cocked an eyebrow at Iger and he followed her down a once-elegant corridor.

Thick reddish carpet underfoot gave off choking clouds of dust as they walked. Racks of glowglobes gave way to single fixtures of exquisite carved crystal, perhaps half of them still working.

They passed under an arch covered by crystal filigree and supported by pillars of black marble that still gave off faint opalescent glints, red-green-yellow, beneath a thick coating of grime. A niche stood empty that had once held, as Kayla remembered, a crystalline bust with laser-diode eyes.

There. A massive onyx door flanked by fluted amethyst columns. Carefully Kayla probed the rooms behind the portal. Empty, as she had suspected. There was no other functional mind nearby, save for Iger's.

The door opened at a touch. The floor was bare, of a polished green stone striated by veins of gold, dimly visible through the dust. Tarnished fixtures jutted from the purple marble walls. A row of wallseats were set under broad-paned windows carved from thick crystal. Outside, Vardalia could be glimpsed through cracks and chinks in the sooty panes.

A huge holoportrait of Pelleas Karlson dominated the far wall of the room. He peered out at her somberly from beneath jutting brows. Karlson's bald head glistened, and his mouth was curved in a slight smile. But his dark eyes weren't smiling, and they seemed to be following her and Iger as they moved through the room.

Karlson's private quarters were hardly lacking in rich appointments. But they were dark and silent, and every surface was covered with at least an inch of thick dust. There were no footprints on the floor, no sign that anyone had occupied these rooms in some time.

Several rooms led off from the main sitting area. One of them was a study filled with crumbling antique books. Just to the right of the library door was a mosaic wall panel: a depiction of the Cavinas System. The twin suns were depicted by a massive emerald and a diamond, side by side. A fire opal was giant Xenobe, trailed by her sapphire moon, St. Ilban. That topaz cabochon over there had to be Liage, and the ruby-flecked geode just beyond it was Styx.

Kayla couldn't resist reaching out to caress the model of her home world.

And something clicked. Machinery, long-unused, groaned and shuddered. Slowly a slab of marble paneling swung back to reveal a room in which metal winked under dust. Shelves were piled high with vid cubes. In the middle of the black stone floor was a table covered with laser gem-cutters, assay beakers, and jewelers' loupes. Kayla remembered now that Karlson had once been an amateur gemologist.

She touched a knob on the table and a vid cube came to life.

Pelleas Karlson's face appeared on screen, speaking. His eyes held a distracted look. "Evidence of a phenomenal mindstone, the likes of which can scarcely be imagined, has been brought to my attention. I've instructed several agents to begin immediate searches. I must have it. My theory of mindstone cutting and its effects will be put to the test with this so-called Mindstar. If I can have it cut precisely to my calculations, I should be able to utilize its powers through the groupmind."

Utilize the Mindstar? Control it through the groupmind? Kayla shuddered at the thought. Karlson's theory just might have worked.

"My notes follow."

Here the image stuttered and faded, and a moment later a message in glowing yellow hololetters appeared: CONTINUED ON CUBE EDI-347-B.

"Iger, we've got to have that cube."

He began searching the shelves that lined the walls. "Nothing," he said. "Just a jumble. Wait, here . . . I can find EDI-347-A and EDI-346-Z, but nothing after that."

"Maybe he took it with him."

"Or maybe somebody else did."

"Took something from Karlson?" Kayla said. "No way. He'd never have let something like that get out of his hands. Especially his prized theories about mindstones. He was a complete fanatic on the subject."

"Well, he's not here, and neither is that cube."

Kayla stared, mystified, at the dingy draperies and columns, the tarnished metal. "Why in the world would Karlson have abandoned his private apartment?" On the wall above her head the huge holoportrait of the prime minister stared down with what could have been a mocking expression on his face. "But it's obvious that he's not here and hasn't been in some time. And I get such confusing readings from my mind probe that I can hardly believe that he's even in this building."

"Let's get out of here," Iger said. "This is a creepy place. Let's try to find Salome, or Rab, or Arsobades."

"I've already probed for them. They're not here either. And neither is Yates Keller." But a memory of a vast room filled with people pushed its way into her consciousness. Kayla remembered another corridor, other rooms, other visions. "Let's try down this way."

She led Iger along a winding trail through the musty darkened halls of the palace, past faded portraits of former prime ministers and high government functionaries, long forgotten. The faded tapestries were a little less grand here, the rugs a bit thinner underfoot.

The doors, once splendid with jewels, had cracked nearly off of their hinges. Kayla gave them a light push and they fell away before her.

The chamber beyond was the dark shadow of a glorious memory: walls paneled in stained fuchsia silk embroidered with silvery flowers. The lighting was haphazard; two of the recessed lamps flickered on and off, on and off.

All around the wide table the cushioned chairs contained the still forms of the members of the groupmind, a group of empaths, mindstones glittering in their ears. Empaths they were, most of whom Kayla had once known. She saw familiar faces gone slack and helpless: big beefy Johannes Goodall, wasted now to near-skeletal thinness, and Miriam Crown, once kindly and gracious, now transformed into a haggard, dull-eyed witch. Neither she nor Johannes, nor any of the other empaths at the table, gave any sign that they were aware of Kayla's presence. They sat in their once-grand chamber, leaning forward. And at their very center, drooling, sat the vector of the groupmind, the medium through which all these minds had met and joined. Vacant-eyed, slack-jawed. Pelleas Karlson.

For a stunned moment Kayla said nothing. Iger's gasp was comment enough.

"That's him, isn't it?" Iger said, finally. "That's Pelleas Karlson."

Slowly Kayla nodded.

"What happened to him?"

"Looks like the effect of mindsalt addiction," she said. "A really heavy habit. Burned out most of his mind." She stared at the empty face and all hate for the man went out of her. How could she feel anything but pity for this empty shell? "He's been used as the link for the groupmind. I didn't think a non-empath could do that. But if Karlson has been the vector, who's been running the Alliance?"

She knew the answer to that before she had even finished speaking.

Keller.

Yates Keller had done this to Karlson. Had taken control of the government, the city, the Alliance. "It was goddamned Yates Keller."

"But I thought you said there was no trace of him here."

"No trace. But he was here. I can feel it. And he did this to Karlson. Hooked him on mindsalt, or at any rate helped him along with his addiction, gave him to the groupmind, and walked off with the vid cube containing Karlson's calculations on the Mindstar.

"And if we can find him, I think we'll also find Rab, Arsobades, and Salome." Kayla paused for one last, sickened glance at the stricken Pelleas Karlson. "Have somebody take him to a mechdoc and see if anything can be done for him." She paused. "And for all of them."

Iger stared at her. "But we nearly got killed fighting them. They would have killed us."

"I know that. But they didn't. And if what I suspect is true, they weren't responsible for their actions. Not ever. It's all Keller, and it's been him all along. We can spare some mercy for these others."

"And for Keller?"

"For him, nothing."

Iger nodded his approval. "And now?"

"We search Keller's rooms. Maybe we'll see something there that will tell us where to find him."

Keller's private suite was modestly appointed: A bed, a table, and a webseat were the only things in it. As Kayla touched the door frame, hidden machinery whirred to life.

In the middle of the room, a cloud of light coalesced, slowly forming itself into a holoimage of a dark-eyed, dark-haired man, good-looking in a slick way.

Keller.

"I knew you'd come in here," the holoimage said, and for a moment Kayla was tempted to put a laser bolt right through that smug face. "You're looking for me, Kayla, aren't you? If not, you should be."

The image blurred for a moment and quickly reformed to show perfect ebony features framed by swirling golden hair. Amber eyes stared defiantly.

"Salome!"

The image faded, replaced by the faces of Rab and Arsobades. Then they were gone and the picture blurred one more time and re-formed around Keller's grinning visage. "I'd like to suggest a meeting," he said. "Obviously, I've got something that I think you want. And you have something I want. I'm talking about the Mindstar, Kayla. If you'd like to see your friends again, come meet me on Styx. Alone."

She would kill him with her bare hands if she ever caught up with him.

"I'll be watching for you," the Keller-image said. "Come in a single shuttle. One passenger. Anything else will get blasted out of the sky. And if you try any tricks, I'll begin killing your friends, one by one.

"Meet me, Kayla. I still think we can do great things together. The Alliance can be ours. You weren't meant to be a rebel. Save your friends and yourself. Join me. I'm offering you much more than they can."

The image swirled back into mist and dissipated.

Kayla touched the door frame.

Keller's holoimage formed once again and began to speak, reciting the same speech as before.

"Let's get out of here," she said to Iger.

"Where?"

"Back to the *Antimony*. I want to think, and talk to Third Child."

Chapter Seventeen

"You're certain about this?"

Kayla sat beside the dalkoi in the captain's lounge and stared into her lavender eyes.

—*There can be no doubt.*

"But I don't understand it! How can something that powerful burn out?"

—*All mindstones by their very nature are inherently unstable. We've seen many of them decay before this. Most likely there was an inclusion, or a series of them, deep within it that provided enough of an obstacle to the stone's flow of power that the buildup of energies within the stone cracked it.*

"But it looks the same on the outside?"

—*The appearance is utterly unchanged, yes. Are you planning to have it cut and set?*

"Not quite. But I still may have some use for it." Kayla mused over the dead Mindstar. It sat quiet, its fires extinguished, within its casket. And since its death she had not heard a peep out of Golias, her mindrider. Had the end of the Mindstar meant his end as well? She probed herself cautiously, exploring herself in much the same way she might have probed for a sore tooth. There was no sign of the mindghost.

Iger loomed over them. "You're going, aren't you?"

"What choice do I have?"

"Damnit, Katie, it's a trap. I know it."

"You heard his terms! He's got Salome, Rab, and Arsobades. I've got to save them. I have no choice."

"Would they do the same for you?"

"I think so, yes. And it's my fault they're in this mess." She remembered Golias' ghostly mindvoice: "Guilt is a waste of time." She longed to tell him that occasionally it was a badge of honor.

"They might be dead already."

"I've thought of that. And if they are, he'll pay for it."

If you care about other people, you are lost.

No, Golias, she thought. *No, it's not like that at all. If you were here, I would tell you. The only way not to get lost is to care.* She smiled a tiny smile.

"What's so amusing?" Iger said.

"Nothing." Kayla turned to gaze fondly at him, and widened that gaze to take in Third Child and the rest of the War Minstrel crew in ops: lean, coppery-skinned Oscar Valdez who could plot courses in his sleep; heavy-muscled Mepal Tarlinger, still mourning Cristobal's loss; shy, diffident Martin Naseka of the blue-black hair, their engineering genius. She thought with affection of

MacKenzie, and even, gods-help-her, of Merrick. No doubt they were wrangling like mad as they tried to sort things out down on St. Ilban.

Only Elvin was missing. Kayla thought of the silver-haired dancer and vowed that he would be cared for. Cared for, and, if possible, rehabilitated. She owed him that.

And again her thoughts returned to Salome, Rab, and Arsobades. Her dearest friends. She would save them even if she had to nail Yates Keller to a cave wall and bash his head in with the defunct Mindstar. —*Here it is, Yates. You can have it.*

"Plot a course for Styx," she told Oscar. "And get a shuttle ready. I'm going back home for a visit."